The DarkLand Portal Series Book II

The Monk's Apprentice

Damien D. Kenworthy

SkyGoat Publishing House
www.skygoatpublishing.com

This paperback edition 2020

978-0-6489213-1-8

CONTENTS

ACKNOWLEDGMENTS

I have to dedicate this acknowledgement to my beautiful wife. She is an endless source of support and never ceases to amaze me with her talents and resourcefulness.

The final product of this saga would look nothing like it does if it wasn't for her.

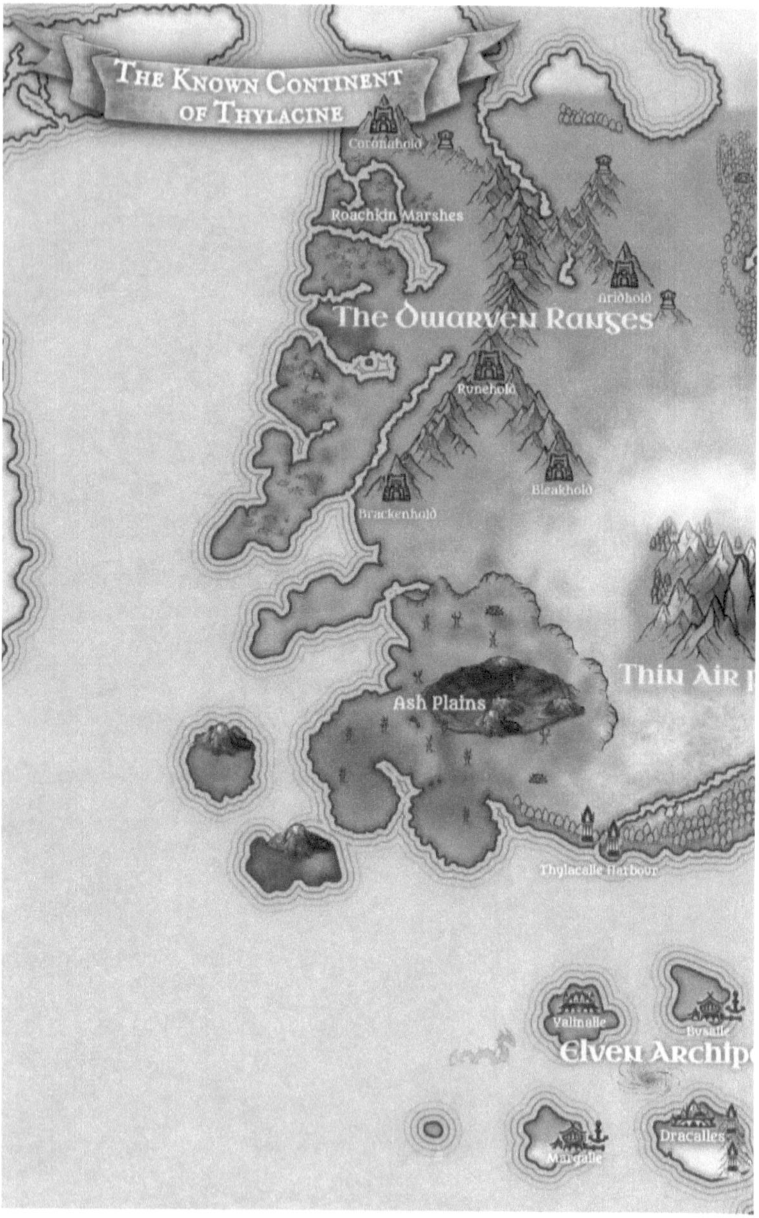

THE KNOWN CONTINENT
OF THYLACINE

Coronahold

Roachkin Marshes

Aridhold

The Dwarven Ranges

Runehold

Bleakhold

Brackenhold

Ash Plains

Thin Air

Thylacalle Harbour

Valtnalle

Bysalle

Elven Archipe

Margalle

Dracalles

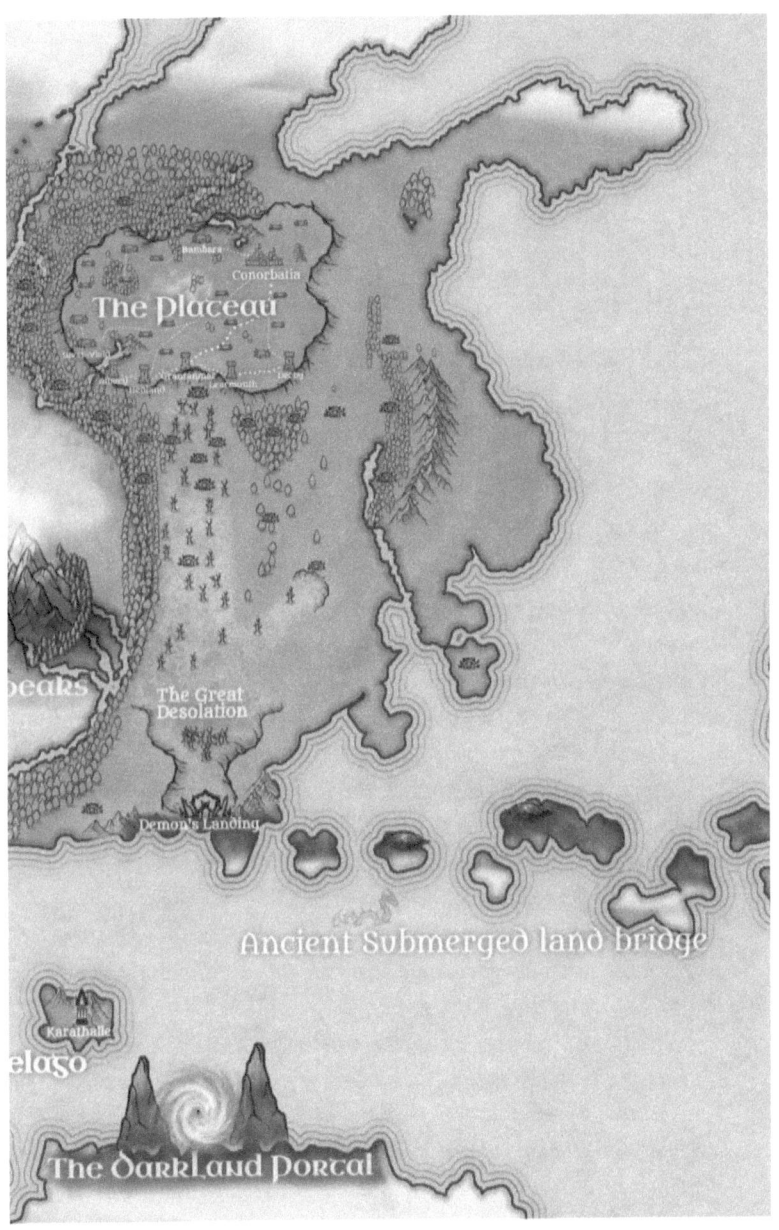

PROLOGUE

The Great Invasion of Evil is how we refer to the single most influential event in our world's history. In the year 1053 of the human calendar, the entire world shook with tremors for an entire week. The skies darkened and storms lashed the land, even in areas where the warmer months were traditionally expected to last.

It was the elves who later concluded that in this week, the six princes of hell had combined their powers to tear open a rift between our world and their world, The DarkLands. It is believed that after initially puncturing the fabric of this world, the princes exerted their powers to expand this rift, causing the violent storms and earthquakes that raked the continent. What remained after was a toxic portal near the southern pole, between two enormous mountains rising from the sea.

Nobody knows where the demon world exists out there. Only that after the portal was opened, an unnatural direct passage between our world and theirs connected us. There is one theory amongst the scholars of magic, that although the six constantly fight amongst themselves within their own realm, each prince is

4

constantly exerting part of their own strength to maintain this portal. The DarkLand Portal remains a violation of the laws of physics written by our planet itself. Because of this, it is believed that only together are the demon princes powerful enough to resist all the natural forces in this world to keep it open.

In the months after this terrible week, the world became a darker place. The lands to the south, closest to The DarkLand Portal, were abandoned by all who lived there, after the creatures inhabiting it became twisted and evil. All across the continent, savage scaleskin tribes began to appear in the jungles, slaughtering entire human settlements at a time. Colonies of roachkin also emerged beneath the mountains, ambushing dwarves in their tunnels and dwellings.

It didn't take the elves long to pack up and leave. At first it seemed like they had decided to leave all the world's troubles to the dwarves and humans, and even the poor halflings. However, many have since claimed that they had migrated towards an archipelago of islands near The DarkLand Portal in the south. It is vaguely understood that from here they have attempted to blockade the portal and the evil influence escaping from it into our world.

A lot of significant events happened in a short period of time after this, and not the least of them was the discovery by some few humans, that they could now perform magic. These abilities are now understood to be a direct result of The DarkLand Portal opening, and there are great risks to any man who uses magic, as it was never meant to be used for good purposes.

After a few decades of great losses, one man called Menzus gathered a migration of every remaining village, settlement, and displaced refugees that he could find. Menzus, who we now remember as Menzus the Great, led mankind up to The Plateau. It was here that we were able to unite and defeat the sparse tribes of scaleskins, who had also discovered the raised land mass that we now call home. Menzus then claimed complete lordship of The Plateau after reinforcing its borders, thus pioneering a nation and becoming the first human emperor of The Plateau that we live in today.

After the founding of The Plateau, mankind became both closer to one friendly race, and separated from another. Eventually the Dwarven Union became isolated from The Plateau, while the halflings joined our nation entirely to become a part of it. Initially residing in the far north, the little people were too small and unwarlike to survive their enemies. When they found that mankind had created a defendable empire, they joined it freely, providing agricultural prowess in exchange for the protection that our nation offered.

The dwarves on the other hand, lost many cities and settlements before drawing back to their largest strongholds in the mountains. To do this they were forced to close a lot of their underground networks and tunnels, which reduced our contact with them greatly. The last underground highway known to our people was destroyed in 1090, after the colonies of humans were finally forced to abandon all remaining satellite settlements beyond The Plateau.

Since that time, the other civilized nations of our world have only become more isolated, bringing us slowly towards the single diverse society that we know today. Here men, halflings and expatriate dwarves, now live alongside each other in the only country they have known.

- Professor Worley, lecturing first year students at Clouds College of Magic

1 SECOND YEAR

Aema took in her tranquil surroundings, feeling a mixture of calm and sadness. She had always liked this place. Last year it had been a favourite retreat for her and Jaeger. She had shown it to him after they had first met, and ever afterwards they would come here when they wanted to be alone together.

There was a sense of loneliness in this place without him. In the quiet spaces between studies and socializing, Aema could feel it. Life felt empty at times like these. She wondered if she might have been better off never meeting him at all.

Jaeger's departure seemed to have signaled the beginning of the end for everybody living in Conorbatia. Aema wondered if that was the real reason he had abandoned them. She had to continually remind herself that he had not fled from reality. He had simply chosen to face it by taking a different path. Right now, the path that Jaeger had chosen seemed like a pretty foolish one to her, but he definitely hadn't chosen it because it was easy.

Unfortunately, this didn't change the fact that what he had left behind was utter turmoil. The capital city was no longer filled with the single-minded desire for money that usually consumed it. That world of luxury was gone, and it had been replaced by an even sadder reality.

For the very first time, the self-serving population of Conorbatia had discovered that life had always been a game of survival. *That* was the real reality, a reality that had only ever been masked by a temporary illusion. And ever since Aema and her friends had visited that damned military base last year, the illusion had been ripped away.

There were almost no troops left in Conorbatia. The emperor had practically drained the city when the news arrived about the dwarven stronghold of Aridhold falling. He had left behind a thin skeleton of soldiers with his warden, and it didn't look like he would be bringing his soldiers back anytime soon. Since then, the private security business had become a booming industry overnight. Every wealthy business with spare cash was now investing heavily in paid mercenaries for protection.

Protection against what? it seemed a little obscure to say the least. It was mercenaries who had already unlawfully assaulted members of the public on a number of occasions now. The local taverns were the worst. Many young merrymakers had been beaten savagely for petty reasons, and there was no longer a strong enough presence of soldiers left to stop them. Donagarn, seemed to be benefiting the most from this new order.

It was Donagarn who had begun the movement of employing private security in the first place. He had already purchased a small army within a couple of days of Emperor Hildebrante's deployment south. Everybody saw this as a complete overkill at first, thinking that it was just another bid to flaunt his wealth. However, Donagarn now had more armed men under his command than the emperor's steward in Conorbatia. Fears were beginning to build that he had become dangerously powerful.

Aema now contemplated the whole conscription debate bitterly. Emperor Hildebrante had gone to great lengths to avoid this course of action, preserving that final freedom in a delicate balancing act. With hindsight however, Aema was now convinced that pressing all these mercenaries into service would have at least kept them out of Donagarn's reach.

She strolled along her quiet patch by the creek, as she pondered the thin security blanket that Cloud's College still offered. The College was probably the only place that still insisted on maintaining the sense of business-as-usual. Second year studies were now well under-way, and within the college grounds, mercenary presence was non-existent.

Kostian remained the insufferable prick that he had always been, but he knew his limitations within the campus. His incident with Jaeger on the night of the attack on Grantanmar had not gone down well with the professors at Clouds. Somehow a full account of Kostian's behavior during the field trip was widely known to the professors. Apparently, their supervisor Renold had not been as naïve as he had behaved around

The Plateau's late head battle-mage. Either way, whatever moves his father was making outside in the city, Kostian knew that he was tip-toeing on thin ice within the campus.

"Can I join you here?" a voice broke up the silence of Aema's musings. She hadn't heard any footsteps above the musical trickle of the creek.

"Sure" she replied politely.

"We didn't really talk, but I was in your group at Grantanmar," he began apprehensively.

"I can't remember all of that trip too well." Aema admitted. "You're Jates though, aren't you?" she replied as neutrally as she could.

Jates was slightly below average height, he stood maybe an inch shorter than Jaeger, and an inch taller than Aema. He had short, thick black hair that he combed to one side, and a warm smile that showed off a perfect set of white teeth against his pale face as he looked at her. He was one of Kostian's buddies and quite possibly Nasgro's least favourite person in the entire world.

"I am, and you're Aema," he grinned a little brutishly. "I'm sorry we didn't really talk on that trip. Kostian and Jaeger have a bit of history, so the excursion wasn't exactly pleasant, even before we were attacked." He seemed nervous behind his winning smile.

"I've never found anything to do with Kostian pleasant," Aema pointed out. She had never seen herself as a rude person, but there was something irritating about listening to someone point out the obvious, when she had no real idea why he should be speaking to her in the first place.

"I can't really argue with that," Jates conceded. "Not when I've seen your experience with him. Anyway, I'm sorry our friends haven't been on better terms too."

"Why would you apologise for that? I've never directly had a problem with you. Nasgro has, but I don't really know why you would feel the need to apologise to me about it." Aema wasn't stupid, she wasn't flattered either. Jaeger had been gone for a while now but his feelings towards Kostian and his friends really weren't any different to her own.

"Ah yes. Nasgro," Jates mused casually. "I think I will have to straighten things out between us one day. Maybe you could help me with that? I never meant to give the impression that I was trying to steal his ideas, but I know that's what he thinks of me."

"Is that what you wanted to talk about?" Aema asked. It was a pointless question because she knew it had nothing to do with why Jates was talking to her.

"Yeah, it kind of is," Jates took the lifeline without hesitating. "If you could pass it on, I would really like to put everything between him and me behind us."

"Sure," Aema nodded curtly, "I'll pass it on."

"Thanks so much," Jates said just a touch too dramatically. "I'll get out of your hair then." He took his leave a little bashfully and quickly walked away. Aema felt no better about herself over the exchange. She had never grown up with a desire to be rude to others, but there was almost no safe line to tread when it came to Kostian and his cronies. They were as much the enemy to her as the scaleskins.

Later that day Aema was back amongst friendly company. Her circle of friends had made a point of enrolling in mostly the same class timetables, giving them common classes and breaks. Jaeger's friends had also scheduled themselves into this timetable, allowing their larger group the excuse of getting together each day. She had Nasgro and Odette to thank for that.

As they left class, Aema watched Nasgro and Odette's shameless public displays of affection with patience. They had been inseparable since that infamous night in Grantanmar. What had started out as light antagonism the first time they had met, quickly turned into a year of petty bickering. Now it had bloomed into a slightly awkward romance that they seemed to have no problem with sharing in front of everybody. Aema laughed inwardly when she considered that they had actually been inseparable during the petty bickering phase too, and no less pleasant to be around.

"I had an interesting conversation about you today Nasgro," she decided to break them up with a little bait.

Nasgro broke away from Odette and flipped his head towards Aema, "Me?"

"Derrr me?" Odette mimicked affectionately. Aema almost lost Nasgro's attention immediately. This was going to be difficult.

"Yes, Jates came and found me. He wanted to talk about you." Everybody looked at Aema now. *That* had gotten their attention.

"That scumbag! what did he want? I hope you told him where to go?" Nasgro grumbled.

"I told him that I would pass his message on when he was done talking. I think he just wanted to talk to me to be honest."

"Why did he want to talk to you?" Nasgro looked even more puzzled, Odette laughed.

"Probably because he's into her dummy," she chided him.

"Okay," Nasgro was trying not to lose his bearings. "What message did he want you to pass on?"

"He said he wanted to clear up the misunderstanding about your spell and you thinking that he was trying to take credit," Aema explained. "His words, not mine," she added.

"Oh. I'm not sure I'd enjoy that chat, there was no misunderstanding. I explained to him my theory going into our first year, and the next thing I knew, he had put his hand up in a class I wasn't in to use it. He told professor Sharelle how he 'was a bit embarrassed to admit it, but he had come up with a spell theory that he was hoping to prove one day.' It was in his first Matter-in-Practice class."

"That's despicable!" Aema exclaimed.

"It's beyond despicable," Nasgro complained.

"What's worse than despicable?" Berran chimed in.

"Jates," Nasgro declared.

"And what word should we use to describe Jates, now that we know that he's worse than despicable?" Berran goaded.

Nasgro paused, contemplating Berran's query. "Deplorable."

"Debatable," Berran retorted.

"What's debatable!?" Nasgro looked outraged.

"Deplorable is worse than despicable."

"And?" Nasgro was getting worked up again.

"That's debatable" Berran said. Odette burst out laughing and Lisle slapped Berran's arm reproachfully "Stop it Berran."

"I'm just saying we need to get our words right if we're going to commit to this worse-than-despicable thing with Jates. After everything he's done to Nasgro I wouldn't want him getting off with a lighter title."

"I have to get my stuff for class," Aema interrupted. "Good talk guys."

"Debatable," Berran added.

"That's enough from you," Lisle poked Berran again. Aema chuckled as she walked away, at least their discussion about Jates had helped her take her mind off Jaeger.

2 THE MOBILISATION

Emperor Hildebrante thundered towards the enemy on his armoured warhorse, while Marrick did his best to remain as near to him as possible. Hildebrante had an entire bodyguard of knights, but Darroch had asked Marrick personally to ensure that no harm came to their emperor. The line of mounted soldiers spread far on either side of them, nearly five hundred strong, all in a single row of spears and lances. The scaleskins moving to besiege Sorrento had not been expecting this.

With a deafening clash, the line of cavalry struck the enemy; thousands of scaleskins carrying ladders and short weapons. Enemy shamans had already been singled out from the walls by the city's mages, while several battle-mages rode with the charge, focused solely on detecting more enemy magic users. As the emperor led the charge deeper and deeper into the crumbling enemy forces, the infantry of Sorrento followed up in their thousands.

Regiments upon regiments of spearmen raced

to ensure that the cavalry had left behind no surprises. They had lined up behind the short charge and fell upon the enemy only seconds after the shock cavalry. The pride of the infantry however, were the regiments of heavily armoured dwarf battle-axes. The weapons of the remaining enemies were almost useless against the thick metal plates and helmets of the dwarves, while the strength behind their battle-axes was phenomenal.

Marrick wheeled his warhorse left to break up the crowds of scaleskins that were starting to swarm in, as the mounted charge slowed and bogged down. He hacked to his right with his sword, quickly glancing up to see more knights begin this practiced manoeuvre. Once their initial charge slowed, they threw down their spears and lances, and began to peel off either left or right. This essentially created a weave of knights moving in and out of the front ranks, preventing the enemy foot soldiers from swarming them.

Hildebrante was in the middle of this melee, and refused to weave backwards deeper into the formation to protect himself. It was up to Marrick to keep an eye on him while his emperor played the war-hero. Every moment that the knights swirled around each other hacking at the scaleskins below them, was a moment closer to their infantry making their way deeper into the skirmish to allow a retreat. Marrick brained an enormous muck who had been seconds away from hacking Hildebrante's leg off at the knee. *Any second now would be great*, Marrick grumbled inwardly.

A loud roar went up at the back of the formation, and the first knights began to break free past the spearmen that had just made their way deeper into the fight. More and more knights broke free as the spearmen pushed their way forward skillfully. Still Hildebrante remained in the outer layer of knights where the fighting was fiercest.

"Emperor! Peel back, you're confusing the foot soldiers!" Marrick yelled as he pushed past Hildebrante, riding over the screaming scaleskins that the emperor had just stabbed.

Without looking up at Marrick the emperor finally responded, yanking the reigns of his barded charger and pulling left to nudge his way back through friendly lines. Marrick almost sighed with relief, hacking down one last scaleskin before making his own break for it. The armoured dwarves had now formed a solid wall and were pacing forward in unison with fierce rhythmic battle cries. Even the spearmen melted away to either side, allowing the moving fortification of dwarves to hold front and centre.

"We won't need a second charge," Hildebrante noted ruefully as Marrick caught up to him. Behind them the battle had become an utter rout, the enemy was being massacred.

"Then it has been a perfect battle," Marrick pointed out. "Second and third charges tend to get messy once your own foot soldiers have engaged the enemy."

"Of course," Hildebrante agreed. Marrick could see the emperor slowly shaking off his battle-lust.

They rode back through the southern gates of the city. Behind them, the sounds of their soldiers pursuing the broken enemy forces could still be heard. The infantry of Sorrento had now pushed the scaleskin horde back from the flat fields before their walls and onto the steep slopes descending from The Plateau.

Darroch stepped down from his command post overlooking the battle and joined the pair of them.

"We should probably head back out there and direct the clean-up now," Emperor Hildebrante suggested enthusiastically.

"It will probably be good for morale," Darroch winked. "Marrick, would you take over the vantage point for a little while for me?"

"I can do that," Marrick acquiesced.

"Thank you for your protection out there, Marrick," Hildebrante acknowledged graciously. "It is far easier for me to enjoy a battle knowing I had you by my side."

"Most welcome, Emperor. If you can't enjoy a little fighting, what can you enjoy?" Marrick noted facetiously. Hildebrante's eyes narrowed suspiciously at Marrick, before he turned and rode back beyond the city walls again with Darroch.

Emperor Hildebrante's arrival in Sorrento had been a huge morale boost for the frontline soldiers. Marrick watched, as both his commander and his Emperor paced out the battlefield together confidently. After their crushing victory before the gates, they were both now putting on a bit of a display for the population of Sorrento. Hildebrante had insisted on riding out to meet the scaleskin forces before they reached the city walls. It had been a decision that made Darroch visibly nervous, even after their battle-mages had confirmed no trace of enemy magic users.

Their attackers were not used to being met on the open battlefield. It hadn't happened for as long as any of them could remember. Between the Emperor's charge, and the vast array of forces supporting him under Darroch's command, the siege was overwhelmed and lifted before it could even begin. All the while, the entire battle had unfolded to the resounding cheers of Sorrento's population.

Some were experienced veterans manning the battlements, some were newly drafted servicemen in their first days of being processed and trained. No matter who was watching however, the sight of their Emperor leading his men to victory painted a glorious picture of serving on the southern front-line.

Even the halfling sharpshooters had cheered and hooted as they watched on from the city walls. Lord Alcorn had promised ten thousand halflings from The Plateau's northernmost province to serve on the frontline. The first thousand had arrived this week, and Darroch had immediately made sure they were positioned safely along the walls to witness their Emperor in all his glory.

Very well played indeed Darroch, Marrick chuckled to himself as he watched the pair casually assessing the battlefield together. The emperor pointed towards the bodies of scaleskins they had defeated, ordering men to pile them for burning, and conversing with wounded soldiers as they were helped back towards the safety of the city. Marrick knew that word of today's easy victory would spread like wildfire across the frontline fortresses. Darroch would make sure of it. Small victories like these would bring confidence to their soldiers in the difficult months to come.

Over the course of one summer, Hildebrante had mobilized his reserve forces to Aridhold and back.

He had mustered his men below the stronghold on its underground platforms, before breaking through the roachkin infesting the lower levels on his way to the surface. Emperor Hildebrante had met High King Fëadarliege of Runehold below the city that day. Together, their combined forces had broken the siege and emerged into Aridhold to find a very surprised king Borgisliege.

After proper introductions and expected celebrations, Hildebrante had swiftly returned to The Plateau with his forces, along with several heavily armoured battle-axe regiments. Each regiment was from one of the various kingdoms within the dwarven Union. It was then that the great mobilization had been prepared, and reserve garrisons from cities all over The Plateau were deployed south to Sorrento. The governors of each province had also led a mass recruiting push, and before summer was over, the ranks of each fortress along the southern frontline was swollen with reinforcements.

Emperor Hildebrante's approach had been clear; he intended to support his commander by providing Darroch with every able-bodied soldier he could get his hands on. Hildebrante intended to send a strong message to the enemies beyond his borders. The Plateau was no longer a nation of undermanned fortresses, and his people would match their numbers wherever there was a fortification to defend.

The number of soldiers along his southern front-line had doubled to fifty thousand men, and it was all due to Hildebrante's hard work. In addition to this, more halfling regiments were yet to arrive, along with the last remnants of recruiting from the most isolated northern towns of The Plateau. Dwarven architects and stonemasons had also joined the handful of infantry regiments from the mountain realm.

Commander Darroch now had everything he had asked for, and with it he had organized the south of The Plateau into a series of well trained and efficient fortresses. With his emperor now at the beginning of a frontline tour, Darroch had prepared for him with a series of shock attacks on their enemies across his fortresses. The demon-presence had mysteriously disappeared at this point, and suddenly it all seemed a little too easy. Marrick took in the new arrangements as he trotted out to join his commander and his Emperor.

"Can you think of any reason these demons would withdraw so suddenly?" Hildebrante asked Darroch. "I can't imagine it is to do us any favours, perhaps there is some way we can prepare for whatever they're up to."

"Whatever they're up to, they have given us more time to prepare than I had ever hoped for." Darroch replied. "I cannot think of anything for certain, but the best guess I have been able to make, is that there were not many demons this far north in the continent when Professor Worley killed one of them last year. Perhaps those few agents they have sent to trouble us decided they would wait until reinforcements could arrive."

"So instead of the individuals we have seen manipulating the scaleskins and roachkin, we can soon expect to be fighting an army of these demons?" Hildebrante tended to let his composed demeanor down whenever he was around Darroch. Marrick was glad that it was only himself nearby whenever the emperor turned to his commander for all the answers.

"I think it's entirely possible," Darroch informed his Emperor.

"From what the professors at Clouds and our master mages have told me, they are only confident that they can organize their teams to handle one of these creatures at a time. If an army of them did arrive, we could find ourselves losing our entire frontline very quickly." Hildebrante pressed.

"This is also entirely possible," Darroch conceded. "However, for now our defences are as well fortified and as organized as they have ever been. I don't know how many are mustering south of our borders, but what I do know is that the dwarves seem confident their runesmiths can develop weapons capable of targeting demons and resisting their spell casters. With a little more time and good fortune, we can evolve."

"Yes, our people can certainly evolve and rise to any challenge," the emperor agreed, he had gained the confidence he needed and looked the part of a statesman again.

The three of them passed back within the outer gate of Sorrento, as a thick black cloud of smoke rose behind them. With the few wounded men and dwarves in good care, and the bodies of their enemies burning outside, the fortress was now a picture of order once again.

"Emperor, how is Jaeger faring in his second year at the college now?" Marrick asked.

"My friend, I am very sad to inform you that he left," Hildebrante admitted. "Shortly after his graduation from first year, he approached me to tell me that he had other plans. He intended to travel as far south as he could via the underground highways of the dwarven union. Ultimately, he said it was his plan to journey alone to try to find the Thin Air Peaks."

"Wow! that is news," Marrick exclaimed. "What did you make of it?"

"I think it is a shame that he felt compelled to abandon his studies. The reports I received from Clouds College, were that he had worked very hard last year for his success."

"And his reasons?" Marrick probed.

"His reasons were very admirable. For a young man he witnessed a great deal last year, enough that he felt either driven or inspired to go seeking something greater to help us. I don't know which."

"That sounds familiar," Marrick observed, looking pointedly at Darroch. The commander laughed.

"Oh, the thought occurred to me too Marrick," Hildebrante laughed with them. "I was reluctant to give our fearless leader here dispensation for his quest last year. We missed your leadership when you left us Darroch, but I am happy to admit that you exceeded all expectations with your success."

"Perhaps you might find that Jaeger does too," Darroch suggested encouragingly.

"I hope so commander," Hildebrante agreed.

The three of them mounted their horses behind the safety of the city walls. It was nearly dinner time and they all felt that they had earned their food and rest today. Sorrento was looking impregnable, and the brief battle beyond the city's walls had achieved everything Emperor Hildebrante was hoping to achieve while touring his front-line. Tomorrow they would depart from The Plateau's southern headquarters, and begin the tour of every fortress along the southern border.

3 THE PEAK'S DESERT

Jaeger sighed to himself hopelessly. He had been trekking the harsh desert plains for two weeks now and felt exhausted. His beard had grown, it was long enough that he could now see it below his eyes on the edge of his vision as he walked. Behind the beard his lips were heavily cracked. Inhaling the dry desert air had left his throat hoarse and barely able to swallow.

As he walked, his mind was dominated by only two purposes; the mindless drive to keep moving, and the desire to find any source of water that might quench his thirst. He considered everything around him for its potential to provide water, but none of the vegetation gave even the slightest hint of holding moisture.

King Borgisliege had allowed him to take the underground wind-up carts to the southern-most stronghold in the mountain realm. From here, Jaeger was sent on his way with all the provisions and advice he could handle.

The best of both were the water skins (which

had run out two days ago) and the instruction only to travel at night. However, both of these had now taken him as far as they could and Jaeger was nearing the edge of his physical limitations. He often found that his thoughts drifted irrationally as his mind was starved of fluids. At times he staggered while walking in the cool night air.

He knew that morning wasn't far away and was now on the lookout for anything that could provide shade while he slept through the hottest part of the day. He hadn't come across a tree for days now and instead collected shrubs at the end of each night's march, packing them around his shelter to hide from the sun. Jaeger carefully assessed a tall bush for inhabitants, prodding at it with his sword.

Wearily, he draped his light but resilient sand-cloth from the top of the bush to the ground, creating a slanted low-lying roof to lie under. Once he had finished digging to the deeper cooler dirt a few layers beneath the sand, he slipped himself under the protection of his canopy and quickly drifted off into unconsciousness.

After what felt like it could have been either minutes or days, Jaeger woke suddenly. A shot of adrenaline ran through his veins that immediately dashed away any plans of drifting back to sleep. At a glance the sun was still high in the sky, which was unusual since he had become accustomed to sleeping through the hottest hours of the day. What disturbed him even more though, was how familiar this felt. There was a sense of unprovoked fear that he now knew only too well.

It had surfaced more than a year ago, in the

jungles with Darroch's troops. He had been right when he sensed something was wrong then. It had shadowed the journey to Grantanmar last year, where he and his friends had witnessed the city fall at the hands of the scaleskins and their demon. He had felt it when he and Faline had been chased before the raid on West-Yield, and for some reason he had also felt it before Faline had visited him in his dorm last year. Experience had taught Jaeger to trust these unexplained instincts.

He poked his head out warily from beneath his canopy. Its colours were interwoven very similarly to his dry surroundings, creating a good camouflage. On top of that was the light layer of fine sand that blew over everything in the desert winds. There was nothing out of the ordinary to see from his hiding spot, but the nagging sense of fear and dread was only getting stronger.

Afraid to breathe, Jaeger slowly crawled and then rose to his feet for a better view. He hugged against the wiry bush, hoping that standing next to it offered some sort of concealment. It didn't. He knew that he was only marginally less visible to them than they were to him.

Well within his sight, maybe only a couple of hundred yards away, he could see a handful of scaleskins following his trail. They weren't travelling very quickly but they had more spring in their step than Jaeger had felt for days now. There was no time for packing, and no chance of outlasting them in the heat of the day. If he ran, he died, either from being caught or from wasting the last of his strength under the relentless sun. He ran.

Jaeger only lingered long enough to snatch his

backpack from the ground and his sun-cloth from the bush. Then he was off. He could hear shouting behind him almost immediately. The first shouts had been surprised and alarmed, but they soon turned to cheers and harsh laughter.

He had not even covered half a mile when his running deteriorated into a slow jog, which really felt like glorified trudging. It looked like trudging too as he looked down at his feet rising and falling from the ground awkwardly. A brief glance over his shoulder showed Jaeger that he had barely extended the distance between himself and his enemies, who were already making up for his initial burst of speed.

As he turned forward deliriously, he realized he had stopped running altogether and was now staggering one foot in front of the other like an idiot. Again, he mustered up all the remaining strength that he had and tried to squeeze out one more sprint.

After maybe a minute, Jaeger had already forgotten why he was running and when he looked down, he realized that he was walking again. He looked back over his shoulder. The scaleskins were close enough to put a spear through him now and Jaeger turned forward once more to make one final attempt to run.

It was working, his legs were moving past each other faster now and there was little or no pain in the effort. Jaeger felt like he was floating, there was a rhythm to this that he could keep up for hours, maybe even days.

Looking up from his feet again, the whole world had turned a bright sandy colour, mixed with a glare that his eyes could not separate from the sun. Everything he saw was blurring into each other as hundreds of small black dots started swimming in front of his eyes.

As the last ebbs of energy perspired from his body, Jaeger felt his muscles turn to rubber, refusing to do what he told them. He briefly staggered against this resistance, before forgetting what it was that he was doing.

His mind kicked in again momentarily and Jaeger looked over his shoulder gasping. There were creatures behind him, moving quickly. As he looked forward again, he saw the fine desert sand rising up to meet him. He rolled onto his back as he fell, but not before collecting a face full of sand with the last remaining moisture in his body.

Scaleskins, he remembered as he watched the hunting party surround him. Stepping across his body, the largest of them leered down at him. A cruel looking scimitar dangled lazily from its right hand, confident that he no longer posed any risk. Jaeger grasped for the sword at his waist, but a swift kick sent it flying aside into the sand. His hand buzzed with numbness.

As the creature leant forward and grabbed Jaeger by the front of his shirt, he wondered why he still cared. Its breath smelt of blood and rot. Jaeger assumed that by this point he would no longer care if he lived or died, that exhaustion would make him wish it could just be over already. Unfortunately for him he did care, he just didn't have the strength to save himself.

The scimitar drifted down to his neck and slowly drew blood. Jaeger only lapsed for a fleeting moment to wonder how he still had any liquid left in his body, before snapping back to realize that this would be his death, and that these creatures were not planning on making it a brief experience.

The wet crunch was sickening. Jaeger was looking directly into their leader's eyes when a spear lodged itself straight through the creature's neck. The scimitar clattered across Jaeger's face and the scaleskin collapsed, partially trapping Jaeger beneath it.

With what little strength he had left, Jaeger struggled to slide out from under the scaleskin, reaching for his own weapon again. As he looked up from the sand, he saw spears appearing suddenly from everywhere, butchering the scaleskin hunting party that had been pursuing him.

His first glance at the new attackers was a single human. The man's skin was blacker than night and he was as thinly built as anybody Jaeger had seen. He held no weapon as he walked towards the body of the scaleskin that Jaeger had just removed himself from under, yanking the crude spear out from the creature's neck. The spear was no more than a sharpened shard of wood, but it had certainly done the job.

More men appeared from seemingly nowhere; the red sand, the tiny shrubs, it was hard to tell where they had concealed themselves, but there was about ten of them. The leader flickered his hand at Jaeger questioningly. With no idea what the gesture meant and no energy left, Jaeger slumped onto his back, closing his eyes.

4 THE FOOT OF THE PEAKS

Jaeger woke in the shade of a large white-limbed tree beside what could barely be called a lake. It was more like a large puddle in the desert that had refused to dry up. One of his rescuers was lifting his head up to a wooden bowl of water, trying to force Jaeger to drink from it. Jaeger raised himself further, desperate for the water now, forcing the bowl to his lips.

He gulped the small bowl down in moments and then feebly crawled towards the small billabong to refill. When he reached the water, he considered scooping it with the bowl but instead buried his face in the pool. A cackle of laughter erupted from the men around him, amused by this behaviour. Jaeger drank his fill and then sat back and acknowledged his rescuers.

"Thank you" he motioned to the one who had given him the bowl. "Thank you" he repeated, holding the bowl up in his left hand and pointing to it with his right. The nomad gave him a slight nod but didn't speak. Whatever he thought Jaeger was trying to say was good enough. Without another word he turned away, walking off with the entire group following him. Within moments, Jaeger realised that he was in danger of losing all of them. They seemed to disappear easily once they started moving.

Forcing himself up against exhaustion and dehydration, Jaeger pulled himself from the water to follow them, scooping one last bowl of water as he left. None of his belongings were with him except for his sword. It was the same one Karnsmith had made for him on his eighteenth birthday, his other sword he had left in Aridhold to be completed. He observed that the nomads (as he had decided to describe them) carried no belongings or supplies except for their spears.

Jaeger's first thought was that this must mean there were more pools and supplies nearby. But as he assessed the group, he also observed how they seemed to be far more suited to this environment than any other men he had seen before. Each nomad was tall, tall and thin but not in a way that left Jaeger doubting their athleticism.

The way they moved through the terrain was efficient and graceful. None of them moved within throwing distance of each other, and it appeared that they didn't need to look around to know that they were all still together. They seemed happy for Jaeger to follow them, but made no effort to see if he was falling behind.

Certainly not the type of people to coddle you, Jaeger contemplated as he tried to keep up. He barely had the energy to lift his head an hour ago, and was still slowly recovering from dehydration that had almost killed him. Keeping up wasn't easy. Still, Jaeger knew better than to feel sorry for himself. They *had* carried him to wherever that billabong was, and they seemed happy enough for him to keep following them now. He just couldn't figure out if he was tagging along with them, or if despite the pace they were setting, they were actually taking him somewhere.

He had heard of these humans before but had never seen them. Nobody had since the Great Invasion of Evil, although rumours of their existence still faintly circulated throughout The Plateau occasionally. Stories still existed of adventurers who had spent time with their tribes back in that earlier age. They had never traded with The Plateau however, *and why would they?* Jaeger wondered as he followed them. They appeared to live a lifestyle that had no need for stockpiled possessions.

By the end of the day, the hunters who had found Jaeger had led him back to the rest of their tribe. This included a handful of women and several small children that seemed highly capable of taking care of themselves. Tevin would have been proud. Once they met up, a small sit-down followed that involved the roasting of some large reptiles around a camp fire. Shortly after this, the entire small tribe moved off together, with Jaeger now following in silence.

None of them spoke to him, although the women pointed at him a lot and cackled amongst themselves intermittently. Now that the tribe was reunited, the men didn't move so quickly, although the small children seemed to be better at keeping up than Jaeger was. Nobody carried them, and often the smallest of them would trail the back of the group without so much as a glance back from the others. It was like nothing Jaeger had expected to find in his search for the

Thin Air Peaks.

As the days of silently following the tribe began to accumulate, Jaeger pondered the new lease on life that he seemed to have gained. Trekking under the powerful heat of the sun, the thought had occurred to him that he should probably be dead by now. He had walked further and harder than he had before he had been rescued, with barely a mouthful of food each day, and hardly any water. It was no more than any of the tribe members had either, although he was endlessly impressed at the resourcefulness they showed in finding water each day.

Despite all this, he seemed to have found the vigour and will to go on. He had easily adapted to walking for almost every waking minute of the day without breaks. Surely the lean diet and unburdened travel couldn't be the only reason for this change. The nomads wore almost no clothing other than some woven underwear. They carried nothing but their spears, and whatever prey they had caught for the day. At the end of each day, they made camp for the night and cooked what they caught. Their stamina was astonishing, but not quite as astonishing as the fact that Jaeger suddenly seemed to share this remarkable stamina now.

Everything everybody had told him about this journey being impossible should have been true. Jaeger was certain that they hadn't actually known why it was impossible, as none of them had seen this desert before. None of them knew for certain what laid beyond the endless plains of red sand and Spïrïntesa grass.

Here there were leagues upon leagues of soft

sand and dunes before the plants and animal life returned again. The only other living things in that desert were the scorpions that Jaeger consistently came across at night. They tasted horrible but the nomads seemed to like them.

When the enormous peaks came into view, the desert began to end. At this point they were still miles from the foothills. A sub-climate of rainfall around the peaks had created a green paradise here in the middle of the desert. Another quirky observation he made towards the end of the desert, was that all the rugged plants and shrubs ceased to have prickles on them.

They were the same vegetation he had seen for days now, but as he kept walking, he noticed more and more of them seemed strangely defenceless. Eventually his curiosity got the better of him, and he surrendered to his compulsion to approach one. He intended to discover the meaning behind this natural phenomenon.

As he moved nearer, Jaeger began to feel wary of the plant, skeptical that its mutation may in some way be a trap. But as he got closer his distrust left him, and the only desire left was to carefully examine it.

There was a strange aura about it that made him feel both dreamy and peaceful at the same time, and he reached out towards the leaves of a tall succulent to examine them. They were smooth and cool, evidence that this life form had thrived in the harshest environments. Here, it could provide a much-needed water source for any lone travelers that happened across it.

He thought how easy it would be to cut this plant for its water, it was so vulnerable that the thought occurred in his mind to exploit it, to take the final test that would put his cynicism to rest and prove that there was no trick behind the plant's design. He drew out his sword, fully intending to cleave the juicy branch away. He needed to drink anyway so it wasn't just senseless destruction.

However, as he lifted his hand, Jaeger found that he could not swing it down again. There was no force restraining him, just the same compulsion he felt when he had stopped walking to investigate the plant. Only this time it was compelling restraint. Something was telling Jaeger that if he followed through with this deed, he could never take it back and his moral conscience would forever be tarnished.

It was then that he realized why the plant had lowered its primary defence mechanism. It didn't need it. This land had somehow resisted the taint of evil, or more importantly it only attracted life-forms that shared the same desire for peace, coercing hostile life forms away. This wasn't achieved by magic or any other powerful forces, but by camouflage, flying under the radar and cajoling any evil creatures into ignoring its existence.

He didn't know how he knew this, he just felt it. He could sense that violating the plant's trust would be a serious crime, and that this plant was symbolically a welcome sign. Still staring at the plant, Jaeger paused. He noticed that all the nomads had frozen still, and were watching him.

Jaeger delicately removed his hand from the succulent and looked back at them. The same nomad who had helped him drink what seemed like a lifetime ago now, acknowledged Jaeger with another nod. A silent understanding passed between them briefly, and just like that the nomads turned and left, back from the direction they had been leading him for days. They had taken him to the foot of the Thin Air Peaks.

5 THE RISE OF SILO

Aema contemplated Jates' offer to join him later. She knew that from a practical point of view it was a stupid idea. Jaeger's instant confrontation with Kostian the day they met, had drawn a very clear line in the sand between her friends and his.

Jaeger had been right of course, Kostian was a bad egg. He had shown himself time and again to be the worst type of person and Aema had been left thoroughly appalled with his behavior during their field trip last year. Somehow in all of this she could barely remember Jates actually being with them at the time, although he said he had been.

To add to that, even if he had never been friends with Kostian, Jates was still not exactly the most popular person amongst her friends. Nasgro thoroughly loathed him after an attempt to plagiarise his work last year, and despite Jates' assurance that it was all a big misunderstanding, Aema was more inclined to believe Nasgro.

The only thing that seemed entirely genuine was his persistence. Aema had to admit that no matter what else was unclear about Jates, he was obviously very interested in her. And while the feeling wasn't exactly mutual, he was making a lot of effort, and it was nice to distract her mind occasionally from the dark thoughts of Jaeger never returning.

I still think I'll pass, she told herself. Practicalities aside, she just wasn't interested.

Instead, Aema asked if Dinara wanted to join her for some ingredient shopping in the city. She felt like trying some new recipes this week and knew that Lisle was probably enjoying some one-on-one time with Berran, while Odette and Nasgro *needed* more one-on-one time alone together!

"Have you noticed all these stores have SILO written on them lately?" Aema asked. She had now walked past a third store that she was certain used to belong to someone else.

"I have, I've heard they have been buying a lot of farms and businesses from other landowners lately," Dinara replied.

"Why now?" Aema queried. She knew Donagarn was Kostian's father, so it wasn't hard for her to decide that she didn't like it.

"Not sure," Dinara stopped to consider. "My guess would be that there is less standing in their way with the emperor and most of the army away in the south."

"Doesn't that worry you?" Aema asked.

"Yeah, I guess it does," Dinara shrugged. "Doesn't really affect me, but I'd rather he didn't.

Kostian and his family own enough already."

"I really don't like it," Aema commented. "Hey this is my favourite food place here!" she pointed to the store on their left.

"It's not your favourite place anymore," Dinara noted, pointing to the clear words *SILO* painted next to the store name. "Who does that anyway? Every other store just has a name, or says what they're selling. I don't know what the point is letting everyone know that you call your properties 'Silo' and that you own them."

Aema distinctly noticed the heavy scowl Dinara received for her comment from the two mercenaries standing at the entrance to the store. Dinara hadn't been looking.

They finagled around the store for different vegetables, herbs and ingredients. Aema had written a big list, and as usual the shop had everything.

"How much for all of these?" Aema asked Marin. The former owner was still working behind the counter.

"Let me add them up dear," Marin replied, shifting the items on the table apart as she wrote them down on a piece of paper. Aema watched patiently, wanting to talk without disrupting Marin's pricing.

"Marin, I hope you don't mind me asking something personal." Aema broke the silence as the last item was written down.

"Of course deary, what is it?"

"Why did you sell your business? I've noticed everybody has been selling recently." Aema noticed an immediately uncomfortable shift from Marin, as the security guards moved a little closer to the conversation.

"Oh, it's complicated. We were paid for our farm and I still earn a wage here in my old store" Marin started unconvincingly.

"Were you paid enough?" Aema pressed. Marin almost squirmed under the pressure of not speaking.

"Are you looking to buy something or just looking for trouble?" one of the security guards stepped in. Dinara hadn't noticed them and nearly jumped out of her skin. Marin looked terrified.

"Clearly I'm buying something, it's all sitting on the table waiting for me to pay for it," Aema retorted.

"Why haven't you paid for it?" the guard pressed, stepping into Aema's personal space. She immediately reached out to harness matter. "Don't do it young lady," the second guard warned her from behind. They both seemed familiar with the body language of mages when harnessing matter, and were both well within reach of her if she tried anything.

"It'll be eight crowns," Marin interrupted quickly. She pushed her piece of paper towards Aema imploringly.

"Just a moment, I can get it," Dinara added, reaching into her small coin purse. She handed her money across and helped Aema collect all her items into a pouch.

"What was that about!?" Dinara exclaimed once they had safely left the shop.

"Who? Them or me?" Aema asked incredulously.

"Them! That escalated from shopping to an arrest in a few moments. What the hell is wrong these guards?" Dinara shushed her voice as Aema grabbed her forearm. The entire street was filled with the same shops and security arrangements. Both girls felt like they were now tiptoeing in enemy territory.

"It's not an arrest," Aema whispered. "All of these guards are mercenaries, not soldiers. They're just hired thugs." She looked around as she spoke. It actually felt like they were being followed.

"Yes, well I have seen a lot more hired thugs than I have seen soldiers since we entered the city," Dinara noted.

Back within the campus they both immediately felt safe again. It was like walking through an invisible barrier where the constant mercenary presence on every street corner was not welcome, and even more importantly not tolerated. The master mages of the college were able to enforce clearer boundaries on campus, than the emperor's soldiers were able to enforce in their own city.

It was actually a terrifying thought the more that Aema considered this. She wasn't sure what she could do about it at this stage, but she knew something needed to be done. The first step at least, would have to be reporting the incident today to the college professors.

***

Worley listened patiently as professor Sharelle shared the latest round of updates coming out of the city. Donagarn had been throwing his money around like it was going out of fashion. The official word being spread by his inner circle, was that he was making the other prominent landowners in the region very rich, as well as offering them a seat on the council for Silo in exchange for their farms.

The unofficial word going around however,

involved stories of threats, abductions, beatings and extortion, in order to gain the signatures of farmers who Donagarn had previously been in competition with.

Details were emerging of a slow and methodical takeover of the city. There were now more private mercenaries employed than any other job going around in Conorbatia. The skeleton garrison of soldiers that had been left behind to police the city, were barely brave enough to even look at the large packs of mercenaries that now patrolled the streets openly. The mercenaries outnumbered the emperor's soldiers more than a dozen to one on every corner.

"Worley, there are constant calls from inside the city for us to intervene in this crisis," Sharelle informed the head professor. The Office of Student Administration had been closed for the day to allow the professors at Clouds College to hold a council. Free from interruption, Worley, Sharelle and the other heads of department now debated over what position the College should take.

"I understand Sharelle. I have also been informed that messengers are still regularly departing south to keep the emperor updated on the situation here. If he does not personally return or make any official declarations regarding Donagarn's activities, then it is not the place of the College to interfere with the governing of the city."

"How can he make any declaration with the thin military presence in the city? If he officially moved against Silo while they outnumber his men a hundred to one, he would be condemning his own soldiers to death." Sharelle insisted.

"We cannot declare war on a private landowner

because he has been intimidating and buying up his rivals. We do not police this city and we can't involve ourselves in private disputes without a declaration from the emperor," Worley asserted. "However righteous it would be, it is illegal, and we would be showing nearly as much disregard for the crown's authority as Donagarn."

"He's right," Harbold conceded begrudgingly. It was Sharelle and Harbold who had urgently requested the council, after more reports had come in from college students who had been threatened in the city markets. "What we do need to do then is make it clear to the emperor that if he needs our support to outlaw Silo, then he will have it."

"We can certainly do that much," Worley agreed. "I will write to Hildebrante today. I will inform him of what we have been observing, and I will make it clear that myself and the college are at his disposal if his soldiers need our support."

"Very good" Sharelle nodded, "and the incident today with our students? We may not be able to lawfully interfere with Donagarn's business takeovers, but we can certainly act if somebody threatens the safety of our students."

"We will continue to maintain our stance on college grounds. None of Silo's hired thugs will be permitted to step foot onto our campus. Beyond that, we can certainly make it clear that we will act if our students are harmed while they are abroad in the city."

"With all the abductions lately, I doubt we would know if they were harmed or not," Harbold disagreed. "It may be better to advise all students to avoid leaving the campus unless absolutely necessary."

"So be it." Worley announced. "Inform them all during tomorrow's lectures."

6 A FARMER'S TALE

Aema tried to look casual and comfortable walking the streets of Conorbatia again. It was difficult to know if she was managing it with her last visit still vividly clear in her mind. She had reported everything she had witnessed and experienced with Dinara to Clouds College Administration. Shortly afterwards, the message had been relayed to all students to exercise caution and restraint when they leave the campus, or simply avoid it altogether unless necessary.

Kostian had been one of the students to receive that memo, and although names had not been used, it wasn't difficult for Aema to imagine word getting back to Silo, and then her description being provided by the guards she had encountered that day. For all she knew, she could be public enemy number one as she returned to the streets of Conorbatia. *I'll call it 'Silo enemy number one' if that's the case* she thought defiantly. Donagarn's thugs may be watching every street corner, but they did not represent the public.

"Hello deary," Marin greeted as Aema stepped into her store. Marin looked incredibly uncomfortable to see that Aema had returned. Aema also observed guiltily that the kind old lady was doing a bad job of hiding a nasty black-eye beneath the hood she kept over her head.

"Good morning," Aema tried to greet her back casually. She noticed Marin visibly squirm behind her counter as the same mercenaries from the other day moved closer.

"You!" Marin's voice changed. "Listen young lady, you caused a great deal of offense asking me about my personal business the other day." The guards paused and waited where they were now.

"I'm very sorry" Aema apologized, "I was very much out of line." She quickly gathered a couple of pointless items and moved closer to the counter. "May I purchase these?" Aema asked loudly. She leant as far over the table as she discretely could when she placed them down. "Where can I find you at home?" she whispered.

Marin looked a little more unsettled, glancing past Aema for a moment before frowning back down at her. "You can't sorry, you're not welcome here anymore!" She leaned over the table to gather the food Aema had placed. "Number five Hocking Street, Northern District," she whispered, her hood completely concealing her face.

As she stood back from the table with the gathered items, she looked forward again at Aema sternly. "I'll put these away, just you leave."

Aema turned and left briskly, keeping her head down and ignoring the mercenaries who watched her leave.

"What's your name girl?" one of them asked menacingly.

"Aema," she replied meekly.

"Thought so," they laughed. "Aema the halfling-lover from Clouds College."

She kept walking briskly, hoping that they were satisfied with their clever threats. After walking some way without looking back, she began to relax a little. They weren't following her, but these people were clearly not mucking around. Whatever she was going to do next, she knew that she could not involve Dinara or any of her other friends in this again. She was glad that her family was far away on the borders of the halfling province, none of her friends had that reassurance.

Once Aema returned within the boundaries of the college she felt fully at ease again. She knew that she would have to venture out again soon, but for now she could relax for a little in safety. It would have to be after dark when she returned to find Marin at home. A lump of unforgivable guilt rose in her throat at the harm she had already brought upon the kindly woman.

She could still picture the black eye Marin had poorly concealed. That had happened because Aema had brazenly probed in front of Silo's security, and she felt especially bad that she had to come to her again for more information. Aema decided that whatever she could find out from Marin tonight, it would be the last time that she involved her moving forwards.

The sun had fully set when Aema stepped outside of the campus grounds and into the streets again. She had weighed up moving quietly in the deeper part of the night, but had decided that she could still remain relatively unseen in the early dark without being out alone suspiciously late. She had put together all of her darkest clothing and had a large grey scarf wrapped around her head and hair. Other than that, she tried to move quickly with her head down towards Conorbatia's Northern District.

After nearly an hour, she started looking at the dimly lit street signs. She wasn't overly familiar with the district and didn't know Hocking Street automatically.

"Oi you!" a voice called. "You look lost, what are you doing?"

"Oh hello, maybe a little. I'm on my way home to Hocking Street, and must have taken a wrong turn some time back while I was deep in thought." Aema would have preferred to complete her entire mission tonight without being seen, however the guards may help her find her way faster.

"Where were you coming from that you go lost?" the guard asked suspiciously. Aema realised that these guards were mercenaries not soldiers.

"From the Southern District, I don't come from that way often," she lied quickly, trying to avoid mentioning that she had come from the east. It was well known what sat past the eastern district in Conorbatia, and any local would think of Clouds College immediately.

"I didn't ask what direction you came from, I asked where you were coming from," the guard repeatedly sternly.

"I'm sorry sir, but that is none of your business. And rather rude." She added.

"I don't care if it's rude, and I'm making it my business." Both guards had already moved in on either side of Aema now. She was beginning to notice a trend in their intimidation techniques. "I'll ask you one last time, where have you come from and why are you sneaking through the streets of the Northern Districts?"

Aema paused, looking up at both of their faces. She tried to conceal the fact that she was discretely harnessing matter to defend herself. As the guard who was speaking moved in closer, she twisted her right palm at waist level in his direction. She could see where the quiet one was standing now at the same time.

"Hey! Over there!" a loud voice barked from further down the street. "What are you doing?" She heard the sound of feet running their way, and tried to look past loud-guard to see who was coming.

"None of your business, footman," loud-guard sneered, as two soldiers in the emperor's livery came into view. The soldiers ignored the response and walked closer now, skirting the group to get a closer view of who and what they were approaching. Aema noticed the soldier's shock when they both saw that she was standing between the two mercenaries. Both mercenaries were significantly bigger than she was.

"Is everything alright my lady?" The same soldier asked.

"I told you footman, it's none of your business."

"No!" Aema interrupted abruptly. "As a matter of fact, these two men appeared out of nowhere while I was walking home. They started asking me questions and wouldn't let me leave." The soldier's face went suddenly cold with anger. He wasn't a young man and Aema immediately recognised the look of a man who had daughters.

"Both of you take three steps backwards together, and drop to your knees." The emperor's men had gone from passive to deadly serious in a matter of moments.

"I won't be taking any steps for a footman, so why-"

"-Call me footman again and I'll put this spear through your face," the soldier interrupted. "Now, drop to your knees, you are both under arrest."

The quiet mercenary looked worried, and took a discrete step away from Aema before his loud friend spoke. "Arrest us and both the palace and city barracks will be surrounded by midnight. You footmen don't run this city anymore, Silo does."

Neither soldier hesitated for a moment. With trained precision, the first soldier punched his spear directly through the head of the loud mercenary. The second soldier thrust his spear towards the second mercenary. He kept the point just over a foot away to avoid having the weapon snatched at, but crouched low, ready to finish the thrust if necessary. A crude wooden club clattered to the ground as the quieter mercenary raised his arms in surrender.

"Get on your knees," the soldier repeated. Quiet-guard obliged him this time.

The two soldiers efficiently bound the mercenary's hands together at the wrists, while stripping the dead thug's trousers and wrapping them around his head to contain the blood that was pooling freely, before rolling him onto his back. Aema was then surprised to see the soldiers bound the dead man's forearms together extensively before she realised what they were doing. The prisoner was forced to help them lift his dead partner onto his feet. Draping the dead man's bound arms around the prisoner's neck, they hefted the body onto his back to carry.

"You will walk your loud-mouth friend's body all the way to the lockup quietly if you know what's good for you," the soldiers warned. Finally, the older one turned to Aema. "Now young lady, I must apologise for all of this, is there anything else we can do to help you?"

"Yes, I became lost and was trying to find Hocking Street before these two men approached me. Can you put me back in the right direction again?"

The soldiers both knew the district inside-out, and gave Aema extensive instructions explaining how to get there. She felt painfully aware that the second mercenary was listening, and hoped that no further investigating was done by Donagarn's people when the quiet one was released from the lockup. The black eye was bad enough, but she didn't think she could live with herself if they figured out this had anything to do with an innocent store-owner now.

It only took another ten minutes until Aema found herself counting the houses in Hocking Street to find number five. The lights were still on when she found it, which was a good thing. After staring up the front path to the doorstep hesitantly for a minute, she realised that there was no other way to approach this, than to walk up and knock on the door.

"Who's there?" came a man's voice from deep inside the home. He sounded tense.

"I'm here to talk to Marin if it isn't too late?"

Aema called back.

She could hear the footsteps coming closer beyond the door. "It's late, I'm sorry. Who is this?" the voice called again.

"My name is Aema," she replied as quietly as she could. She felt as though her name had become a dangerous word to speak freely in the city recently.

"What can I do for you Aema?" the man insisted. She heard no indication that he intended to unlock the door for her.

"I was in Marin's store today. I'm afraid I have caused a lot of trouble for her lately and just came to speak to her in private." The door handle twitched a little and Aema heard the sound of bolts unlocking before the door was opened. A medium sized man with a large beard and pronounced age lines on his forehead stood there with a hatchet in his right hand.

"Come in," he said quite sternly. Aema felt her guilt over Marin's treatment even more keenly in the presence of her husband.

"Hello deary," Marin greeted her as she passed Marin's husband into the kitchen. "I'm sorry for how I spoke to you today in my store. It was to avoid trouble you understand."

"Marin, I'm so sorry for the trouble I caused when I was there the other day. If I had any idea they would hurt you for it, I would never have said anything." Aema glanced uncomfortably at Marin's husband who stood silently now, watching his wife's visitor.

"It's quite alright deary, you weren't to know. This is my husband William," she introduced.

"Hi William, I'm Aema." William nodded

without smiling, although he received Aema's outstretched hand politely. He clearly wasn't warming to her and she didn't blame him.

"Now what can we do for you?" Marin asked. "I take it you're here to speak freely about what happened to my store? Have a seat. Would you like a cup of tea?"

"Yes please, if you are having one." Aema seated herself in their kitchen while Marin carried her kettle across to the fireplace. "So, what has happened here?" she asked.

The tension in the house had eased considerably once everybody was sitting down with a hot drink in their hands. William didn't volunteer too much to the conversation, but he had stopped frowning so deeply and allowed his wife to talk openly with Aema.

"So, nobody has been given any choice when they have sold their businesses to Silo?" Aema felt like she should have been taking notes like she did in her lectures.

"The choice we were given was to sell everything we own, or be driven out of business," Marin started. "When they offered to buy our store and the farms that supplied it, Donagarn himself came to invite us for a dinner on his estate. We have never been overly fond of him, but he assured us that he would spare no expense to accommodate our visit if we agreed to join him and listen to his proposal."

"And did he?" Aema asked.

"Spare no expense? Well yes actually. We arrived by a coach which he dispatched to our home to take us. And when we joined him for dinner, they put on a magnificent feast. It was impressed upon us that Donagarn hoped we could see how much he wanted our business."

"So, you were prepared to consider his offer?"

"We were prepared to listen. Neither William nor myself had any real desire to move on from running our business. The farms do well and we have always had good people working for us. He offered to pay us five times what we earn annually from the business, and then offered to pay us generous wages if we continued working there."

"I grew up on the borders of the halfling province," Aema mused. "When I was a little girl, I heard that he made a similar offer to their lord."

"Yes, we all remember that, Lord Barnaby was removed by his own people in disgrace when they found out. Although apparently Barnaby's signature was all Donagarn needed to demand compensation when Lord Alcorn replaced him and backed out of the deal. It was quite the scandal."

"He's not a popular man in our northern province." Aema agreed. "They are a cheerful and friendly people, but I haven't met a halfling that doesn't passionately hate Donagarn and Silo for that. How did he convince you to sell in the end?"

"Convinced?! I can think of other words," Marin scoffed. "We left that evening telling him that we would think about it. He told us not to think for too long because he was very busy and didn't want to have undue difficulty getting it done. At that point William told him that it was a flat no. Donagarn just smiled and thanked us for coming to dinner to hear him out. He even sent us back in the same coach that we were picked up in."

"I take it that wasn't the last you heard from him then?"

"No, it was not. Shortly after that night his mercenaries started to appear. They came into my store and told me that I needed to visit Donagarn again to tell him I'd reconsidered, and that I would have to ask first before I visited. Then they stayed, just outside my shop. All day they stood there telling customers to try visiting Silo's stores just down the street instead, and that we had been taking advantage of them. Well, William came down to the store the next day with a few farmhands to see them off. At first it seemed like they would leave, but then more and more of his guards started appearing from all over the street and it turned into a nasty brawl. A brawl that we lost."

"By the time it came to blows they outnumbered us two to one," William interrupted. "I paid those boys to work the farms with me, and I will never forgive myself for dragging them down to the store for that fight. If I had known, I would never have asked them."

"Some of them were very badly hurt deary," Marin explained. "William here took that very personally."

"And so, you ended up selling to them after that?" Aema summarised.

"Pretty much yes, we realised we didn't have any other option after that fight. We came back to Donagarn's estate just like they told us to, and ended up accepting a third of what he first offered us."

"A third!?" Aema exclaimed.

"Yes, he told us that we had lost his goodwill

after attacking his employees. William nearly lost his cool right there, but eventually we agreed as you can see. The rest was quite obvious when you came to visit."

"I'm so sorry Marin. Our Emperor has failed you to allow this to happen." It felt weird to say it out loud about a man most of the people looked up to.

"He has a lot to worry about. I don't think anybody could have anticipated this happening when Emperor Hildebrante rode south to war."

"I'm not so sure," Aema contemplated, thinking about Jaeger's frosty relationship with Kostian. "Has everybody been forced to sell to Donagarn then?"

"Most of the people who run businesses in the commerce district yes. There is one farmer, Justin. He saw what was happening very early and started hiring his own mercenaries to protect his business, not nearly enough though. I'm afraid that one is going to turn nasty very soon too."

"Justin? Where can I find him?" Aema asked.

"He owns cattle, and a lot. He owns half the street that comes off my store. There is a butcher, dairy stores, all next to each other at the start of the street. His guards protect the stores and the entrance to the street so that Donagarn can't block customers from reaching him."

"Thank you, Marin. I think if I speak to anybody from here without getting them into trouble, it will have to be him."

"I'm afraid so deary. If you are looking to do something about this Silo business, I'm sorry to say that he is the only one who will be able to help you. If I were you though, I would stay out of it and remain with the safety of your college. Some things only get worse when you interfere with them."

Aema made her way swiftly and uneventfully back to the college from Marin's house. They had both wished her well when she left. Even William had thawed out a little after his initial misgivings. He offered for Aema to stay overnight and leave in the morning, but Aema had assured them that she would be safer walking back at night. Conorbatia wasn't protected from Donagarn's thugs in daylight, so she would simply be better off not being seen. It was nearly midnight when she was finally back in her room and she had a lot to think about now. Tomorrow she would have to decide if she still wanted to do this alone.

7 THE INTERVENTION

Aema sat back on her bed. She had called an urgent private meeting in the morning and had just finished reporting her investigation findings to her friends.

"I think we need to help him," Nasgro declared.

"Whoa hold your horses guys!" Berran interrupted. "The professors have made it clear that Silo's hired thugs are not welcome here on campus. They also made it clear that everybody at Clouds College needs to avoid Conorbatia if they can."

"That was to make sure nobody here was caught in a situation they didn't understand. Like Dinara and me that day," Aema argued.

"No, it was exactly because of this! It was because the city is not safe anymore. Don't you realise that if *we* interfere in the city, *they* might interfere with the college? You will be putting every student here in danger."

"No Berran, cornering two second-year

students in a market store is completely different," Nasgro disagreed. "Even with every hired thug in the city, they wouldn't stand a chance if they tried to attack a college full of master mages."

"There is still an understanding between Silo and the college," Berran persisted. "If we go out there and get involved, we are dragging everyone into this, including any other students who leave the campus."

"Fair point," Lisle added quietly.

"Yes, it is" Nasgro conceded. "But consider this. That 'understanding,' doesn't benefit Clouds College one bit. It benefits Donagarn while he consolidates his power inside the city, while nobody intervenes. Once he has fully consolidated, Clouds College *will* feel the pressure at that point."

"This is ridiculous," Dinara complained. "Clouds. Silo. Emperor Hildebrante is responsible for protecting his people in that city. His soldiers should never have allowed this to happen."

"I actually said the same thing to Marin when she was telling me her story," Aema admitted.

Nasgro shook his head in disgust. "Okay so our Emperor let us down. It certainly wasn't for lack of caring. He has always had a nation to run and people to protect. Unfortunately, last year when he left the city to protect us from the monsters at our border, he left us alone with another. At some point we need to stop expecting our Emperor to make everything fair and nice, and do something ourselves. The thing I liked about Jaeger is that he always seemed to get that."

That seemed to settle it. Aema nearly gasped at the sudden and unexpected mention of her boyfriend, and everybody else seemed to have been given the same dose of reality hearing of his name.

"He's right," Ellis agreed. Dinara nodded, and Lisle looked at Berran.

"You're right," Berran also conceded. "I just needed to make sure that if we are going to do this, we all know what the implications could be."

Beneath his curly hair and gangly build, Nasgro was studying his friends like a falcon. Odette shifted closer into him with a look of adoration on her face. "So, what do we do now then?" she asked.

"We need to find Justin and speak to him," Aema replied.

They didn't waste much time. The next day every one of them freed up their afternoon to go out into the streets of Conorbatia together to visit Justin. Even without their robes, there was a distinctive appearance to the entire group that shouted 'student mages.' It made their little daytrip feel very conspicuous. Nasgro had surprised everyone by telling them that if they were accosted by mercenaries, he would be shooting fireballs first and asking questions later.

Aema had felt this sounded a little extreme until she remembered the way they had cornered her and Dinara in the market store. Silo's mercenaries had been advised on how to deal with mages if they could get close enough. With that in mind, it would not be good for anybody to let them close enough. It was also Nasgro's idea for the group of students to enter the streets of Conorbatia in two halves, making their way towards the markets on opposite sides of the street.

"What do you think we will be able to do once we speak to him?" Odette asked. She walked with

Nasgro and Aema. On the opposite side of the street, the other four members of the group tried to look casual as they moved together.

"I can't be certain yet," Aema replied. "Right now, I just want to start by asking him his story. The same way I did with Marin. I think we already know most of it, so I guess it will end with us offering to help him if he thinks we can."

"Help with this? A group of second year students at Clouds College?" Odette added skeptically.

"As far as I know, the only mage on either side so far is probably Kostian," Nasgro pointed out. "And don't forget that we have already seen frontline conflict in Grantanmar last year."

"Oh, I remember," Odette hugged Nasgro admiringly as they walked. Aema had some serious doubts that Odette was taking this whole situation quite as seriously as she needed to be.

At length, they all made their way to the main food sales district. Aema tried to keep her head down as they passed the private security loitering outside of the stores they walked past. She had felt like a wanted criminal whenever she entered the city lately, and this street had been where it all started.

"Hey Aema," one of the guards called as they passed Marin's store. Aema continued to keep her head down. Of all the places for her to end up in a fight, she didn't want it to happen anywhere near Marin this time.

Nasgro fell in alongside Aema with his head down as they walked. "Just remember, if any of them get too close and follow you, they are going to end up on fire," he assured her.

She smiled to herself remembering the soldiers

who had intervened two nights earlier. Donagarn didn't have control of the city yet, and she was not as alone as his thugs wanted her to think she was. At the end of the street, two clusters of guards stood apart from each other on opposite sides of the road. Both seemed to be quite intent on ignoring the other. Aema realised the men on both sides were probably well aware of the danger to their health that it could pose if things turned ugly.

The cluster of Silo mercenaries opposite Justin's street perked up as she and her friends moved to enter it. Evidently Justin's guards could allow safe entrance to his street, but they would not be able to walk his customers home once they left. They passed silently through Justin's security, who parted for them easily and then closed ranks behind the group once they were through. Whatever would be waiting for Aema and her friends when they were done here, for now she could breathe a sigh of relief that they were at least safe for a little while.

As they entered the first store in the street, they were greeted by an enormous slab of a man in the butcher's store. He wasn't exactly a picture of muscles, but it was clear that there was a mountain of strength hidden beneath his chubby outer layer. *Just the sort of man who could keep working under these conditions,* Aema observed.

"Good morning," he greeted, "what meats can I get you?"

"Ah, we are not looking for meat just yet," Aema responded tentatively. "We were hoping to speak to Justin."

The big man's demeanour shifted from amicable to hostile immediately. "He is next door. I will take you there myself," he added. Aema considered reassuring him that she meant no harm, before quickly realising that it would probably just make things worse.

"Thank you," she smiled as politely as possible.

As they were led outside, the big butcher nodded for some of the guards in the street to accompany him. Aema immediately lost the sense of relief she had felt earlier, as the tension and potential for violence returned. When they entered the store next door, the entrance behind them was completely blocked off by guards. The butcher who escorted them remained alongside Aema at the front.

"Justin here?" the butcher asked the lady at the counter. "This lot said they would like to speak to him."

"Robyn!" greeted a cheery voice, as its owner emerged from the back of the store. "Who wants to speak to me?" He wasn't what Aema had been expecting. Justin was a medium sized man, lightly built of lean muscle, with a head that was shaved all the way up to the tips of his ears. Above the ears a neat cap of light brown hair was combed neatly to one side. Whatever hardship this man was suffering while under siege from Silo, he wasn't letting it affect his demeanour.

"Students!?" he exclaimed. "From Clouds College too I assume. We don't see many of them on these streets anymore."

"Yes," Aema confirmed. "How could you tell?"

"Oh, just a lucky guess I suppose," he grinned with amusement. "What can I do for you?"

"We are here because of what Donagarn is doing to this city. I spoke to another store owner recently who told me about you."

"No other store owners left," Justin corrected Aema.

"Sorry she *was* a store owner. I visited her at her home to ask her what had happened to her farm and her business. She told me what Donagarn has been doing, and then she told me about you."

"She," Justin mused thoughtfully, pondering this clue for a few moments. "So, you are just up-to-speed with what has been happening outside of your college recently, and you want to speak to me about it now?"

"We want to do something to stop it, we wanted to see if there is something we can do to help."

"Don't know that anybody can do anything to stop it. Emperor is out of town and Donagarn's estate is locked up tighter than those frontline fortresses in the south. If you want to help, you can support me by buying from my stores."

"But don't you need this to stop?" Aema asked.

"Right now, I'm paying for more men than I can afford, what with the limited number of people who are brave enough to shop here. Best thing you can do for me is not be intimidated into staying away from my street."

"That doesn't sound like a sustainable plan, Justin," Nasgro interjected. "If Donagarn isn't stopped, then eventually he will run you out of business and get what he wants either way."

"Maybe all the other businesses that sold to him should have thought about that before they gave in," Justin said bitterly. "My farms have been with my family since the founding of The Plateau. I'm a fighter and I won't be letting Silo take my business that easily."

"Maybe you had more time to prepare because you weren't picked first," Aema countered. She could still remember Marin's tale and her black eye vividly. Justin didn't appear to appreciate this suggestion.

Nasgro jumped in before Justin could react. "We came here because we wanted to speak to somebody who is still fighting, because we want to fight with you."

"What can seven students from Clouds College do? Is the college ready to fight? Will your battle-mages join me if I confront Donagarn? Because if not, we don't stand a chance. The emperor's soldiers still patrol the streets, but they refuse to stay long in the markets because they're scared and outnumbered. The best I can do is guarantee that customers can safely walk into my stores."

"But they can't walk home safely once they leave your protection in this street. Your plan has a lot of holes in it," Aema pointed out.

"It's the best I can do," Justin shrugged. "The safe walk home is the emperor's responsibility, and his soldiers are cowards."

Again, Aema resented the judgement Justin was handing out. He was alone and was justifiably feeling very disillusioned, but she also remembered two soldiers who had killed a man to protect her just two nights earlier. Everybody was doing what they could.

"If all we can do for now is give you our patronage, then that is what we will do," she conceded.

The group spent a short while shopping half-heartedly through Justin's stores in the street. None of them particularly needed much, and Aema was anxiously aware of what was waiting for them all outside when they left. As they politely thanked Justin and paid for their purchases, he joined them as they walked to the entrance to his street. They lingered here for a short time while Justin made a casual display of chatting to them, before they had to part with the protection of his guards.

As soon as they passed back into the open market district, they could feel the watchful eyes of Silo closing in around them. They all walked together this time, aware that there was no disguising who they were or what they were doing here.

"Harness," Nasgro quietly instructed everybody around him. Aema could feel the swirling energy as it was drawn in to the little cluster of students. Dinara looked terrified and was struggling to focus. The rest of them did as they were told while they moved silently into the market streets. As they looked back, the large crowd who were blockading opposite Justin's street had spread out behind and were following them.

"We might as well do this here if they plan to follow us," Nasgro pointed out. He turned back and purposefully marched straight up to the crowd of at least thirty thugs. More were now accumulating along the street from the stores they were monitoring.

"I take it you plan to follow us," Nasgro announced loudly. The authority in his voice sounded nothing like the scrawny figure that was projecting it. "Don't." He released a flaming ball of purple fire into the road before the crowd. They froze and hesitated, as the crater at their feet smouldered with unnatural flames.

"You think you can do that to all of us?" one of the leaders threatened him.

"Actually, I do," he replied confidently. "If you don't leave this street right now, we will burn through every one of you, and then let Justin's people take care of whoever's left."

The thugs in front of him hesitated, they clearly wanted nothing to do with the fireball that was smouldering in front of them, but they still needed a little encouragement to abandon their posts.

"Let me put it this way for you," Nasgro explained. "You were quite comfortable to follow and intimidate a small group of students, just moments ago. You have been more than happy attacking people you completely outnumber, many of them defenceless women or elderly citizens in Conorbatia. I will have no hesitation killing all of you for that, and afterwards, any of you who survive will have to explain to your boss why you have now started a war with Clouds College and its mages. A war that Donagarn knows he can't win. Now, you all have a minute to clear this street before I start with this one here who opened his mouth first."

Nasgro held up both his hands for the crowd to see, the air above them shimmered and distorted with the barely contained energies he held within them.

"Come on lads," the same leader spoke again. "Let's find out how the boss feels about the college before we give this kid what he wants."

"Good idea," Nasgro gritted through clenched teeth.

The mercenaries throughout the street dispersed reluctantly, much to the cheers and amusement of Justin and his guards. Several of them still lingered inside stores a little further away, but for the most part the oppressed people in the commerce district could breathe a sigh of relief. Justin crossed the space from his usual territory to Nasgro and Aema. He sent his men up and down the streets in large groups to flush out any leftovers who might still want to eavesdrop.

"Not too shabby mate!" he whistled as he looked around. "I can't say I was familiar with what mages were capable of until I saw that with my own eyes. Especially from a group of undergraduates at the college."

"I'm glad you enjoyed the show," Nasgro smiled graciously. "Does this mean you have had a change of heart?"

"Honestly mate, I'm still not sure that this suddenly creates a simple solution to all of my problems, if any. I guess it would be handy to employ someone like you to help watch the street corner, but it still doesn't change much."

"And what about going after Donagarn and getting rid of him once and for all?" Nasgro suggested.

"For that, you would probably need more than a little fireball or two. He has a *lot* of men at his disposal across the city."

"So, what now then?" Aema asked.

"I'll have to think about it," Justin admitted. "I guess if I was going to take your plans seriously, I would need to know if I could get the support of the entire college. Your professors and battle-mages and what not."

"Clouds College doesn't have battle-mages, only master mages," Nasgro corrected. "We only become battle-mages if we deploy to the frontline to serve." Everybody stared at him. "Small detail in semantics I guess," he admitted eventually.

"Look mate, student mage, battle-mage, I don't care if you call them chicken-mage. If I am going to confront Silo on their home soil, I will have to do it with the full support of the college. Otherwise, the whole idea will end very badly."

It was only afternoon when they sought out professor Worley at the office of student administration. Worley was nowhere to be seen. However, professor Sharelle had offered to sit down and listen to them when they told the office that it was urgent.

"I'm not sure that I approve of what you have done today," she contemplated, after Aema had finished telling her story. "I'm not sure that I disapprove either, but you *have* acted on behalf of all of Clouds College today. Whether I like it or not, these incidents are subject to review by the college."

"We weren't acting on behalf of the college," Aema insisted. "We *are* here to speak on behalf of Justin though. He is asking that the college does act."

"Well, that is a grey area if I have ever heard one," Sharelle tisked. "Like I said, I'm not sure that I disapprove, but it is not up to me. As for Justin's request, this has already been discussed by the heads of departments. We are not able to interfere with the running of the city unless it is in support of the emperor."

"But the Emperor is not here to ask for your support!" Aema complained.

"Aema, the heads of department have had this same discussion. We have decided that it is still unlawful to act without instruction in a city that is run by the emperor."

"It's not run by the emperor anymore! That is exactly the point!"

"A poor choice of phrase by me then, but we still cannot," Sharelle insisted.

Nasgro had remained relatively silent while Aema had told their story. "Professor, has Clouds College reached out to the current steward in charge of the city to ask if he needs our support?" he queried.

"It may help you to know that our head professor Worley has been in constant contact with Emperor Hildebrante via dispatch from the palace."

"But has he offered the support of Clouds College to the acting steward of Conorbatia? If he needs to clear the streets of Silo's thugs, does he know you will help him?"

"I will have to ask professor Worley that specific question Nasgro," Sharelle replied curtly. "I will pass on all of the information you have given me today, as well as Justin's request."

"Thank you, professor," Aema acknowledged.

"You're welcome. Now, is there anything else you need me to hear before I start preparing for my evening tutorial classes?"

"No professor, I think we have said everything we needed to."

"Lovely, well thank you for reporting your activities to us immediately. We will have to process *everything* you have told us today before we decide our next step. In the meantime, may I suggest that none of you leave the campus grounds again until we tell you what that next step is."

"Yes professor, we will stay here and wait for your response," Aema promised.

8 ARIDHOLD

King Borgisliege chuckled as he received his latest brief from the underground hunting parties. Grokhammer's suggestion had started out as a loosely formed idea during a brainstorming session in Aridhold's war council.

Since then, both Borgis, his runemaster, and ground teams, had taken it very seriously. It had now been followed through from its earliest theoretical phase, through preparation and planning, to a series of successful executions below the city.

It all began on the advice from Hildebrante's professors from Clouds College. They claimed that during a recent field trip, they had discovered that demons were possessing enemy warlocks and shamans.

From here it had been deduced that defeating the possessed enemy spell-casters, would dispel the influence they held over enemy armies. It was Grokhammer who suggested that specific runic bolts may be suitable to assassinate the roachkin warlocks leading their armies in the depths of the mountains.

The suggestion had been received well by the war-council. They quickly began drawing plans and tactics to enable hunting parties to seek out enemy roachkin colonies, draw out the possessed warlocks from amongst them, and then carry out the assassinations without interference.

Aridhold's master runesmith had developed a simple yet effective warlock-killer quite quickly by runesmith standards. The runes were lethal to magic users, as well as designed to be immune to counter-spells and defensive magic.

The small rune was simple to engrave on crossbow bolts and suddenly the demand for hydrargyrum became a premium in Aridhold overnight. Bolts were now being mass produced across the dwarven union for the deadly weapons to be used on enemy magic users.

The dwarven mining units had then developed an impressive manoeuvre to take their enemy by surprise. Lifting their most experienced crossbow marks-dwarves high above their heads, they held up enormous shields as a platform to give them a sniper's view of the battle.

From there, enemy warlocks had been successfully assassinated on numerous occasions. Watching the surprise of the demon-possessed warlocks as their defensive spells failed to stop a runic crossbow bolt, was now said to be the pinnacle of experiences in Aridhold. The storytelling of these runic marksdwarves had immediately become the most in-demand entertainment at taverns across the city.

To add to this breakthrough, miners were

reporting immense success against the roachkin colonies in the moments after assassinating these demons. Their drills and maneuvers now included a surge attack after a successful assassination, capitalizing on the period of shock that overcame their enemies during the initial moments after.

Being released from whatever control the demons held over them, seemed to have quite a debilitating effect on the roachkin. For the first time in a long time, Borgis felt that the kings of the dwarven union were finally taking control of the deep dark spaces below and around their strongholds.

"Very good Geranpick," he commended his mining captain. "If the patrons tonight are anything like me, you won't have to buy yourself a beer all night."

"Aye, the lads have not lost their appetite for hearing about dead roaches," Geranpick agreed. "We all know it has been long enough since we could really sit back and enjoy a good success story against the pests."

"We have come a long way since they managed to invade my streets twice in one year," Borgis mused.

"We have. And we have a lot to thank the men's commander Darroch for now. He brought that boy into the city at the right time, and his mages have given us something to be hopeful for since we agreed to his plans to use the subways."

"A great man, as is *that boy* Jaeger," Borgis repeated a little menacingly. He wasn't partial to his young friend being referred to as a boy, but hoped he wouldn't need to hold it against his captain, who he was also quite fond of.

"That calls for my apologies my king,"

Geranpick observed respectfully, Borgis nodded with approval. "If that is all I will get myself down to those taverns before I can cause any more offense."

His captain departed promptly, while Borgis reflected that he really was a quality dwarf. These matters however, were always best nipped in the bud. He still had some work to do to repay Jaeger on the other hand.

The young man had arrived back in Aridhold sooner than Boris had been expecting him. He had been profusely grateful for the sword and the letter that had accompanied it, and had returned with the incomplete weapon asking if it could be engraved with powerful enough runes to slay demons.

Borgis had to admire the man's zeal. He had been so eager to kill demons, that he had left the college of magic early. He now intended to seek out the mythical monks of the Thin Air Peaks to help him. There was a touch of that Darroch about his unwavering confidence and ambition, Borgis pondered. Although perhaps not as calculating as the impressive commander. Borgis had done all that he could from there to prepare Jaeger for his journey. He hoped that he would return one day to collect his sword.

On that note, King Borgisliege rose from his throne. He had been enjoying the reports coming from the underground for weeks now, and had decided that it was time for him to witness the warlock assassinations first hand.

It was also long overdue for him to take part in the flushing of their colonies beneath Aridhold. He had not used his great-axe in anger for weeks now and could do with a break from running the city, for a day at least.

"We can expect to find something soon out this way," Grokhammer assured his king. They had been combing the lowest halls of the underground to its furthest point north of the city. There were no longer any traces of roachkin infestations anywhere close to Aridhold now, and the northern-most halls were the last ones to receive a thorough cleansing.

"You've done well to clear so much Grokhammer. From what I can tell this may have been my last opportunity to take part in any pest control."

"Aye you may be right. The miners have no longer been findings breaches once they clear an area now. The western and southern halls have been marked as fully eradicated."

"I've seen the reports," Borgis approved.

"Here we go," his general interrupted as a lone mining scout trudged back towards the hunting party.

"There is a small tunnel breaking into one of the halls up ahead," Skornpick informed his general. "It's new, only large enough for a dwarf to crouch through. The roaches would be down on hands and knees one by one if they came out through this one."

They gathered around the tunnel opening. The hunting party was only fifty dwarves strong, and mostly consisted of miners. Borgis had brought along his general and a handful of his bodyguard from his personal battle-axe regiment, but it had been impractical for his entire clan to join them.

At the back of the group, Koganmark hefted his crossbow loosely. The strings were drawn back and tense but the channel was empty. He patted the handful of runic bolts at his hip reassuringly as they peered into the darkness of the tunnel.

"I'll go through first," Skornpick volunteered. "When the tunnel opens out, you will know. When it is safe to follow after me, you will know." He nodded to his mining team as he drew on the enormous coil of braided line one of them was holding, and without any further discussion, he crouched down and disappeared into the tunnel.

Borgis watched with fascination as the reel continued to uncoil into the darkness. It stopped eventually, before three sharp tugs could be visibly seen. The reel carrier responded with three sharp tugs in acknowledgement and the reel then uncoiled a few more metres. Shortly afterwards, staggered handfuls of tugs came through.

"The tunnel opens out about a hundred yards from here." Grokhammer summarised. "Skornpick has not encountered any roachkin yet, so we can file through now and join him."

The party entered one by one, mostly miners to start with, until Borgisliege and Koganmark joined them. The last to follow behind these two important guests were Grokhammer and the king's bodyguard. As the last of them funneled out the other end, they looked around to see a cavernous expansion on the hole.

The walls and roof were unsupported and Borgis quickly assessed that the strong veins of rock and ore above his head would at least be adequate to avoid a cave-in. With some satisfaction, he noted that many roachkin must have been crushed to death over history using their primitive methods of burrowing so deep beneath the earth.

Skornpick lit the lanterns brighter and

Koganmark knocked a bolt into his crossbow. Evidently this was the part where hunting parties tended to find their enemies. The company spread out and formed lines. In front of them a mass of prone roachkin were assembling in the darkness, and the sound of scuttling could be heard coming deeper from beyond the cavern.

Skornpick retreated back to the army line. A crackle of static arced through the air from the roachkin colony, and the tunnel behind them collapsed in a pile of rock, dirt, and dark purple embers.

"Gotcha," Koganmark growled. "Up we go lads, we've found their demon."

Two miners dropped the shield to the ground and Koganmark stepped onto it. He held the butt of his crossbow to his shoulder as they raised him above their heads. A long moment went by as the marksdwarf sighted down the channel of his crossbow into the darkness. A sharp twang was heard as he pulled the trigger.

To everybody's surprise, in the centre of the roachkin colony a roach leapt high into the air, supported by the strength of those lifting from around it. The roach caught the bolt in its chest high off the ground, screeching in pain as its malformed little wings splayed about loosely and it collapsed back to the cavern floor. The colony then immediately charged with terrifying pace on all four limbs.

More crackles of static were heard through the cavern and this time Borgis saw the fireball fly overhead. The purple flames seemed to be wrapped in darkness and shadow simultaneously, while the warlock-demon's spell provided no illumination in the dark tunnels.

Fortunately, Borgis didn't need any light to know where it struck.

"Forward charge!" the king roared. His miners hesitated as he burst forward through their ranks with his bodyguard close behind him.

It wasn't a tactic that made much sense, but at the same time every dwarf in Aridhold knew their duty to the king. The company charged forward just in time to escape the ceiling fall down, this time just a little further from the collapsed tunnel. The demon was driving them further and further from their now-buried means of returning to the city.

Borgisliege crashed into the first cluster of roachkin alone. His great-axe whirled a low horizontal arc, shearing through several roachkin on all four limbs, as well as several others that were in the motion of leaping upright onto their back legs.

It was a good start as his bodyguard and Grokhammer fell upon the charging roachkin either side of him. Grokhammer splattered several that were not quick enough to rise in time, before the line of miners clashed with their foes along the width of the cavern.

Several miners went down, however many more roachkin went down with each one of them. Borgis had no idea how far back the colony spread, but the cavern did not seem to be a large one, and at the rate that his company was hacking through them, it seemed that the battle could be won.

Another crackle gave less warning as the ceiling directly above the battle crumbled. Rocks and dirt fell among both the dwarves and roachkin alike, before Borgis realised that their warlock was trying to kill all of them. It must have seemed like an easy trade-off.

"Forward again!" the king roared.

His bodyguard had not taken any casualties and his general was now furiously laying about with his enormous warhammer, paving a pathway ahead of his king. Grokhammer looked even more lethal than he did fifty years ago, and Borgis had to run with his great-axe whirling in both hands to keep up. They were near the opposite edge of the cavern now. Behind them, many miners had been crushed to death beneath the collapsing roof.

Grokhammer wound his weapon far back, but was lifted high into the air mid-swing. The warlock-demon held him there for a moment on the edge of an ebony staff that was now lodged into the general's stomach. A moment later the staff was hurtled down with terrible force. Grokhammer's body was dashed against the floor as if he had fallen from a tall building.

Borgis' bodyguard piled forward in front of their king as the demon-possessed warlock stood there, looking into his eyes with cold contempt. Black lightning leapt from its empty left hand killing two of his bodyguard instantly.

At the same time the creature lashed out again with its staff, sweeping left and right killing the others. Again, that cold contempt returned to the creature's eyes, it seemed to be observing Borgis from within the shadow that stood tall above the warlock's roachkin frame. It wanted him to attack first.

Borgis swung hard but sharp, restraining the reach of his swing to defend against any counterstrokes until he had sized up his enemy. The warlock-demon parried quickly, but not as quickly as he may have expected. A flurry of blows might have gotten past its guard, Borgis realised.

He swung hard and sharp, restraining his reach again, but this time to let fly with an even faster backswing. He was right, the creature was immensely powerful, but the king's runic axe was designed to be as light as a feather in his hands.

Borgis pressed hard now, unleashing a flurry of blows. He was finding gaps, but somehow wasn't connecting. The shape of the creature was difficult to distinguish. Among some of his heavier swings, the ebony staff cracked across his shoulders and chest.

Each blow that connected, felt like he had been hit by a wind-up cart. Borgis was certain that the last blow had broken his ribs. Stepping back Borgis rested on his axe. The warlock-demon didn't hesitate and lashed forward with the staff right for his head.

The king had been waiting for this and ducked the blow with a practiced right slip. Shifting all of his weight onto the crouched leg, he swung hard with a lightning-fast counter. The great-axe bit deep, halfway into the torso of the roachkin-portion of the shape in front of him. Borgis wasn't about to experiment if the demon's shadow could be targeted with his only window of opportunity. The warlock let out of shrill screech, while at the same time the demon-shadow engulfing it released a hollow howl of pain and frustration.

There were no roachkin left to scatter, as the warlock fell to the floor alone without its demon presence. The now-famous battle plan that Borgis had been so eager to take part in had gone terribly wrong.

He looked across the handful of miners that were still alive. Somewhere back towards the other end of the cavern, their secret weapon; Koganmark, lay buried beneath rubble, along with their plans, and their escape route. Beside the dead warlock, lay the broken mess of Borgis' general.

"That was impressive, I managed to see the whole thing," Grokhammer groaned weakly.

"You still live?" Borgis exclaimed, dropping to his knees. "You are one tough dwarf Grokhammer, can we help you to your feet? We need to mine our way back to that collapsed tunnel."

"No chance," Grokhammer rasped. "I won't live long, I just wanted to tell you that your little fight was impressive." The general slumped across the ground again, seemingly satisfied that his final words were good ones.

Borgis sat with Grokhammer for a short period. He knew that he didn't have the luxury of wasting much time. With the thin remains of what had earlier been a proud dwarf hunting regiment, they would not fare well if they came across any more roachkin colonies in these tunnels. Or even worse, another demon-warlock. Looking forward at the tunnel their enemies had come from, and then up at the collapsed roof, Borgis tried to calculate their best chance of survival.

"Do you think that roof will collapse further if we start digging back through this mess?" he asked his miners.

"There's no way to be certain," Skornpick replied looking up. "We don't delve like this. There appears to be a lot of igneous rock among the rubble which is encouraging, but I have no idea if it goes high enough to dig beneath without supports."

"Thanks, it's always important to know the risks before we make a decision. But I think we had better start digging."

"What if I scout ahead myself and first check where the other tunnel leads?" Skornpick offered.

"I'm no miner, but my guess is that it can only lead to more roachkin. These aren't our tunnels anymore Skornpick," Borgis sighed with grim acceptance.

"I agree, but if we're lucky they might open into our underground again before we find any more enemies."

"And if they don't, we will be in very big trouble. Also, I want these bodies returned to their families," Borgis added stubbornly. Skornpick shook his head.

"With all due respect my king, our first priority is to get you out of here alive. If I run into trouble ahead in these burrows, the lads here will know what to do to collapse the tunnels behind me. As for our dead, I'll come back here and personally lead a team to properly excavate the tunnel and bring them home if we survive and they haven't already been found."

"That's a lot of big if's," Borgis complained. "I've received a lot of reports from down here over the years. More often than not, when a dwarf who falls isn't returned from this place immediately, they usually only find his bones, cracked open for marrow."

"We all know the risks my king," Skornpick insisted resolutely. "Now with your permission I would like to scout ahead and see what I can find."

Borgis nodded grimly. He looked across at the

other four miners under Skornpick's leadership. They didn't hesitate to take their positions at the entrance to the roachkin tunnel. Picks raised; they watched as Skornpick passed between them and into the darkness. Two remained on either side of the tunnel, while two followed a short way after Skornpick, scratching professionally into the roof and walls to find the best location to collapse it if they needed to.

The minutes dragged out excruciatingly while they waited for Skornpick to either return or show some sign of trouble up ahead. Nobody lit flames in the darkness, however Borgisliege busied himself by moving from dwarf to dwarf along the cavern floor. They dragged the bodies that they could apart from the scene of the battle, and piled more roachkin beside the tunnel entrance. The stench of dead roaches was distinctive and unpleasant, but Borgisliege had grown to appreciate the foul odour.

He knew by feel when he came across the warlock. He wanted to light something to examine it, to see if there was anything that distinguished it as having been part-demon. He already knew the answer. Multiple reports from underground hunting missions showed no evidence that the possessed warlocks were physiologically any different from their kin, except for the ageing. All of them had been exceptionally aged and weathered.

It was difficult to determine whether these warlocks had been specifically picked due to their advanced age, or if they had aged as a result of the exposure to being possessed by their demon half. The feedback Borgis had received from The Plateau was that the professors believed it was likely the latter. They had observed that their mages had suffered similar degenerative effects when serving in the polluted catchment areas of DarkLand matter in their south.

At length, the miners at the tunnel entrance became alert. They held their ears to the walls and then tapped it with a pick in quick succession. "He has found a way out" one of them informed their king.

They waited in silence for only a brief period longer. Eventually Skornpick appeared silently at the entrance to the tunnel.

"There is another way back to the underground, but no lights. This is an active burrow so we need to be quick and silent. I can lead the way if you all just file behind me."

The miners immediately lined up in their pitch-black formation. Each placed a hand on the shoulder of the miner in front of them, the other hand at all times in contact with the tunnel walls. Borgisliege was placed second last while Skornpick led them, and with little more discussion they started moving. The stench of dead roaches lingered a long way into the tunnels, and Borgis did not shy away from the very real likelihood that the bodies of his people would be very quickly found by his enemies.

He decided that if they managed to escape, he would lead a small army back down to these tunnels immediately. He would arm several marksdwarves with runic bolts and they would target the enemy demon-warlocks from multiple angles on the battlefield. He would wipe out every last roach in these infested burrows before he left with the bodies of his brave kinsdwarves.

As he brooded in silence, he could hear faint scratching from the distant tunnels ahead. Every dwarf knew the way certain sounds could carry, and that there was really no guarantee that they were about to walk into more trouble. The sound however, was a strong reminder that they would need to move quickly and silently through this place. They all tried to keep their minds focused on what could be waiting up ahead.

The scratching occasionally sounded alarmingly close, while Skornpick gave no word to the dwarves behind him. After several minutes he stopped, holding the line.

"We are only minutes away from the tunnel that leads back into the underground" he whispered, lighting his lantern without warning. "We will encounter some roaches before we reach it."

Borgisliege stepped past Skornpick, giving him a look of clear warning not to argue. The tunnel was wide enough for him to swing his great-axe comfortably, and Borgis knew that with his weapons and armour alone, he was capable of far more than the five surviving miners combined. They had done their job leading him through these tunnels. He would do his job and take care of the killing.

More lanterns lit up behind him as the scratchy footsteps ahead picked up pace. "With me!" he roared.

Turning the corner together, they charged down the tunnel towards their exit. Ahead of them were nearly two dozen roachkin. Most were charging their way, while a handful ran in the opposite direction. There would be very little time after this melee before more of the colony found out where they were. The roachkin leapt upright as they came near the dwarf king, black sabres were drawn from their waists as they prepared to swarm the small group of survivors. Whatever they were expecting however, it was not what they were met with.

Borgis flung the great-axe directly forward like a spear, holding onto it as he leapt along with it. The runic blades sheared through the first roachkin he met, as he bowled through it and landed directly in the middle of their pack. He landed low, crouching for a fraction of a moment while surrounded on all sides. Sabres passed overhead as he crouched, before he leapt high, twirling with his great-axe in both hands as he left the ground.

A handful of roachkin fell dead before he landed, where he continued to spin. It was like a whirling blade of death had fallen into the centre of the small pack. Within moments he had blended them into a stinking pile of dismembered body parts. The miners had refused to fully stand back, picking off one or two roachkin, but the better part of a score of the creatures had died within moments to the blade of the dwarf king.

"We will reach our exit without further trouble if we move now," Skornpick advised.

They shuffled further down the tunnel quickly, leaving the lanterns lit. In a short time, they came to the small burrowed hole that Skornpick had found. He passed through first without discussion, tapping back to the team with his pick once he had reached the other side. Borgisliege knew the drill. As the king he would have to crawl through next, now that Skornpick had confirmed the underground was safe. He wasted no time and made his way through, emerging into the neat open space beyond.

As the last of the miners behind him followed, they all took in the welcome relief of their own halls. The expedition had been a disaster, but with typical dwarf determination they had salvaged what they could from the situation. The way up from here would be swift and easy to defend if the roachkin decided to use their narrow hole to follow them. Borgis knew that he would be returning here very soon.

9 THE WING OF THE PEAKS

Jaeger was only halfway up the first peak he had come to and was privately berating himself. The winds were icy cold and could gust powerfully from any direction at any moment. Somehow the nomad's preferred mode of travelling didn't seem so appropriate right now. Climbing without equipment, spare clothing, or provisions really wasn't an option at this altitude. The chill ripped right through him as he looked around for a suitable ledge or cave to rest.

With very little thought or decision making, Jaeger had immediately begun climbing the nearest peak he came to after the nomads had left him. It didn't seem plausible to stroll the foothills for days on end trying to pick which mountain was the most suitable to climb. To start with, he had no idea which one would have monks waiting for him at the top, it could be all or none or any.

Again, Worley's assertion that the monks could not be found against their will, seemed much more real to Jaeger. Without warning, the chill winds turned to icy sheets of rain, as he scanned his field of vision for a safe resting place. He had never enjoyed great heights and had been keeping to the least-sheer slopes he could find as he climbed. The incline he rested against now seemed dangerously precarious and slippery.

Jaeger looked down behind him, slowly turning until his back was pressed against the slope. At least he would slide rather than fall if he lost his footing. Unfortunately sliding would still end in a sheer drop eventually, and Jaeger's heart began to race as he looked back down the slope to this drop-off.

He tried to relax himself as he searched for his next move. Through the blinding sheets of rain, he thought he could see a large mountain goat. He watched as it casually scaled the sheerest section of cliff visible in the rain below him. *Alright for you I guess*, Jaeger thought jealously, as the goat continued to pick its way up the mountain.

The creature was fascinating to watch, it seemed naturally impervious to the stormy weather and quite at home on the edge of a fatal drop in this brutal environment. Jaeger contemplated that he would even prefer to be back out in the desert again over this.

The thought of the relentless heat seemed like a paradise to him right now. He relaxed a little as he contemplated; the goat, the mountains, the desert, and every other bad life decision that he had ever made. Readying himself to start climbing again, Jaeger's right foot slipped.

He pressed himself flush against the slope as a section of small rocks dislodged and bounced their way down the mountain below him. He was facing outwards with no confidence that he would find somewhere to place weight on his right foot again. He also didn't dare move to face the slope for a better grip. As he looked around for options, he noticed that the goat had stopped moving and was now frozen on full alert, staring out across the mountainside at him.

Another slight slip of the rocks beneath his left foot, and Jaeger pressed harder against the slope, using every inch of surface area on his back and legs to add traction. He felt like he was sitting at the top of the rocky waterfall slide back home in West-Yield, any slight movement would be enough to set him in motion.

"A little help buddy?" he called out accusingly to the goat, who was still frozen stiff watching him struggle.

It was too far away to hear, but Jaeger felt like directing his frustration at the beast. It was simply staring at him curiously while he tried to hold on for dear life. To his surprise, the goat casually leapt several large paces towards him, showing no doubt in its own footing along the sheer wet surface. Then without warning, it launched itself directly away from the cliff ledge, into the sheer drop that fell away from the mountainside. Jaeger gasped with shock at the sudden suicidal act and slipped again.

In the distance, the goat had suddenly sprung an enormous pair of wings, flapping powerfully as it harnessed the updraft and spiraled higher towards Jaeger. It wasn't a moment too soon, as Jaeger had begun to slide. Slowly at first, but he could feel he was starting to gain pace.

The skygoat wheeled away from the mountain then flapped again, gaining altitude rapidly. As it banked and turned on its right wing it was now level with Jaeger, gliding gracefully towards him.

"Please help," he breathed, this time seriously.

He was beginning to slide faster and faster, while his eyes remained glued to the skygoat as it soared closer. It was only a hundred yards away now, as he took in its immense size for the first time. For a goat with wings, the creature was proportionately the same size as a small horse.

The bottom of the slope was only a few yards below Jaeger, who was moving quickly now. He spun himself as he slid, facing the slope finally and desperately clawing at the rock-face to slow his momentum.

As he reached the drop-off, he heard the heavy beating of wings behind him. Enormous horns thumped into his back, pinning him to the slope and arresting his momentum. Jaeger heard the clattering sound of hooves on stone behind him, while the horns gently but firmly held him in place.

He twisted slowly, managing to place a stabilizing right hand on the horns and steadying himself to his feet again. Just another yard below him was the edge of the slope, and a sheer free-fall so far down that it was uncomfortable to think about.

"Thanks friend," Jaeger acknowledged the enormous hybrid gratefully as it neatly formed its wings back to its flanks. The skygoat's eyes appraised Jaeger thoughtfully, while he reached forward with his left hand to stroke its head.

"You saved my life you know?" Jaeger noted. "Of course you know," he smiled. "So where do we go now?" he continued to chatter away casually.

He didn't expect a response but hoped the

skygoat might at least understand his gratitude if he kept talking. To his surprise, the great beast folded its front legs, tilting its shoulders towards Jaeger. It appeared to be a clear invitation to climb onto its shoulders.

As Jaeger braced himself on the skygoat's back, he tried to pick the best place to hold onto. Reaching for the creature's horns at first, the skygoat flicked its head in protest. Jaeger searched its neck instead, finding that the thick coat provided something stable to grasp hold of. He was just settling himself into position when the skygoat charged its way to the edge of the ledge and then leapt.

The rush of freefalling for just a few moments was terrifying, before the skygoat's enormous wings snapped wide open and the free-fall turned into a controlled glide. This moment was unlike anything Jaeger had ever thought he would experience. It felt as though the entire world lay below them, as the skygoat soared effortlessly through the freezing clouds high above it all.

The lands far below them were stunningly green and mesmerizing to look down on. The sense of control while suspended in open air was possibly the most liberating sensation Jaeger had ever felt. No height could be dangerous to them, now that they navigated the skies as easily as Jaeger might swim in a lake back home.

They wheeled back towards the mountainside again, as the skygoat flapped its wings powerfully while seeking an updraft. Suddenly the sense of free-fall moments earlier was replaced by intense physical pressure, as they rapidly gained altitude. Jaeger braced every muscle in his body almost fearfully against the unnatural sensation, while they both soon surpassed the tallest point of their mountain.

"Thanks for saving me the trouble!" Jaeger called forward sportingly. "It would have taken me hours to reach that peak alone, just to find out there were no monks living there."

The skygoat didn't give any indication of responding as it continued to gain altitude. Eventually it began leveling out, soaring once again, this time towards a cluster of peaks beyond the first one. Jaeger's jaw would have dropped if he could handle the freezing cold air filling his lungs suddenly. Ahead of them the peaks were so tall that they made the mountain he had just been climbing look like a hill. It appeared that wherever his steed was taking him, it was somewhere up those mountains.

If Jaeger thought the cold winds and sheeting rain had been cold earlier, it was nothing compared to the freezing temperatures that they both now ascended through. Clutching to the thick woolly coat of the skygoat, Jaeger wondered if it realised that he would freeze up here. He was still only wearing the light clothing that he had run through the desert in, and could feel the freezing cold against his chest, legs and face.

"I think it's a little too cold for me up here buddy!" he called above the winds to the skygoat.

He received no indication that he had been heard or understood, and they continued to climb. Jaeger watched the mountain-sides intently, as the slopes continued to disappear below them. He wiggled his jaw as his ears pressurized, and began to feel lightheaded as he gasped for air.

He leaned further forward as he struggled to

satisfy his breathing, resting against the skygoat's back in a daze. The skygoat tilted forward and Jaeger realised that they had leveled out now above the top of a peak.

The mountaintop was as flat as a table and covered in snow. Jaeger could barely see for a hundred yards in any direction. But from what he could tell, the flat mountaintop had an enormous surface area, possibly the size of West-Yield. They hadn't landed yet and the skygoat continued to glide gracefully just metres above the white surface of the mountaintop.

To Jaeger's surprise, great trees were growing up here, their limbs stretched out in every direction while not a drop of snow appeared to have settled on their leaves. They were both now drifting amongst a forest of these unique bushy trees, when they finally landed. Jaeger's body shivered as he stepped down from the skygoat's back.

"Thank you again," he pronounced clearly to his rescuer. "I think I'm going to have to give you a name. I wouldn't be alive if you hadn't been there when I slipped on those pebbles."

The skygoat observed Jaeger thoughtfully while he spoke. He couldn't tell if it understood him but it seemed to enjoy listening. "Would Pebbles be okay?" The skygoat bleated affectionately and then started walking deeper into the forest.

"So, Pebbles then yeah?" Jaeger persisted as he followed. "I can't tell for sure if you've given me the nod for that name yet." The skygoat nudged Jaeger as they walked together and then to his dismay, nodded. Jaeger was so shocked that he stopped walking. Pebbles looked back at Jaeger's stunned expression and bleated at him to hurry up.

"Sorry Pebbles, I just didn't expect to get such a literal response from you."

They continued walking through the majestic trees along the top of the world, while Jaeger contemplated his own surprise in silence. He had no idea what they were doing, but after their little nodding incident, he had no doubt that Pebbles was taking him somewhere. He rested his arm warmly on Pebbles shoulder as they walked, tempted to inspect the enormously muscular furled wings that ran back along the mighty caprinae.

Over time, the trees became far denser, shielding the mountaintop from the natural forces of nature at the top of the world. A small path remained open through the centre of the dense forest, and Jaeger saw that it led to an enormous wave of rock with several cave openings perforating its surface. It was here that he laid eyes on the small community of monks who inhabited these caves.

"Hello there Jaeger," an old man looked up from some small succulents he had been tending. Jaeger waved wordlessly before looking across at Pebbles. His companion had stopped walking and looked back at him encouragingly. He had found them.

10 THE MONK'S APPRENTICE

Salmor was a kindly old man, whose self-assuredness regularly bordered on the verge of condescending. He was clearly one of the oldest people Jaeger had ever met, but he had a vitality that defied his age. He did not appear to have ever been a tall man, however he now stood a head shorter than Jaeger in his old age. His bald patch was clearly visible beneath the grey hair that was tied back in a short ponytail.

Once the surprised introductions were out of the way, Salmor had promptly returned to what he was doing while Jaeger asked questions. He had clearly been expecting Jaeger, but seemed casually disinterested in satisfying the questions Jaeger tried to put to him. After less than an hour, Jaeger had realised how frustrating this was going to become.

Every time a discussion ended, Jaeger got that unsatisfying sense that he would need to hold the entire conversation all over again to get anywhere. Hopefully he would get the straight answer he was searching for the next time he tried.

"So, you knew I was coming, and you also know why?" Jaeger persisted.

"I did of course, how else could I have known your name?" Salmor explained.

"But why I am here, you understand it was to seek help? Because there are demons attacking The Plateau?"

"Ah, The Plateau, are they still calling it that?" Salmor laughed.

"Yes. If they called it anything else it would be because the scaleskins and demons have wiped it off the face of the continent." The relief and gratitude of actually reaching his destination had now left Jaeger. Of all the things he had expected, trying to convince somebody that the genocide of a civilized race was a serious matter, had not been on his list.

"Perhaps," Salmor considered casually. "But it has always amused me the significance that mankind place on names."

"Amuses you?" Jaeger's voice had lowered without thinking.

"Yes, perhaps I have used the wrong word if you are taking offense," Salmor observed with sudden self-awareness.

"Its fine," Jaeger dismissed. "But you *are* part of mankind, you are still as much a man as you are a monk."

Salmor looked offended now. *Wounded*, Jaeger corrected himself, looking more closely at the hurt he saw in the monk's reaction. He decided to quickly move on. "Would I be right in guessing you have met Professor Worley, Salmor?" The monk's eyes lit up.

"Of course, I knew the young soul who called himself Worley very well. He was a man of incredible gifts. He only knew this place very briefly, but he assured me when he left that he would forever be grateful for the help and guidance I gave him."

"Incredibly gifted," Jaeger agreed, thinking back on the attack in Grantanmar. "He told me that I wouldn't make it here unless I was meant to come."

"That is true," Salmor confirmed.

"So, if I am here then I was meant make it," Jaeger continued.

"There is no other explanation for meeting our young caprinae in your moment of need is there?"

"I guess not," Jaeger agreed, looking fondly at Pebbles. The young skygoat had made himself comfortable when Salmor first greeted them, he now sat patiently beside Jaeger while they talked.

"It takes no guess," Salmor explained. "This noble young soul is only an adolescent among the caprinae of these peaks, but he was not playing around that mountain by chance. Whether he knew it or not, he was expecting you."

"Adolescent hey?" Jaeger teased. Pebbles only grunted and curled back into his comfortable patch of ground. "Salmor, I came here because of what is happening on The Plateau. I found you and all the other monks of these peaks, against all odds, in the hope of telling you that the world below these peaks needs you." Jaeger finally hoped that the point he was making would be acknowledged. He was struggling with the constant roundabout of conversation.

"You came here because of what is happening on The Plateau," Salmor repeated. "Does that not sound like you are here because you were meant to be here instead?"

"You think I need to leave The Plateau because of the problems it is having!?" Jaeger questioned incredulously. "I know we have just met Salmor, but that is not how my mind works. It goes against everything I know about myself, and my personality."

"I don't doubt it young soul, but stay a while. There is no rush. The urgency you feel is only the urgency you choose to place on yourself."

Jaeger thought of a dozen obvious responses to that comment but bit them back. He was not seeing eye-to-eye with this monk he had just met, but pointing that out wasn't exactly good manners. *When amongst dwarves, do as the dwarves would do* Jaeger reminded himself.

"Where should I stay here?" Jaeger conceded. "I need to warm myself up before I do anything else. The journey has nearly frozen me."

"You are only cold as long as you tell yourself you are cold," Salmor replied with his now-characteristic self-assuredness. "But let me show you our place among these peaks."

Again, Jaeger bit his tongue and followed the old monk into the caves.

"Coming Pebbles?" His mighty adolescent caprinae had drifted to sleep at some point.

The accommodation was a marvel to observe. Beyond the cavern entrances to the rock-wave atop the peak, the mountain was a honeycomb of rooms and hallways. They all appeared to be entirely naturally formed, and the rooms that the monks had made from this were ideally simplistic.

Jaeger passed rooms where the small solid beds appeared to have been shaped by the natural growth of small trees. These caves were barely large enough to house any other items, however when Jaeger was shown to a small uninhabited room, there was just enough space for Pebbles to curl up at the bottom of the small unique bed.

"How did you make these?" Jaeger asked, staring curiously at the corners of the bed.

"We did not make them," Salmor corrected. "We have a very special relationship with all the life that exists around these peaks. Because of this we are able to encourage the trees and plants to support our existence, by growing in ways that we ask them to."

"That was very beautifully explained," Jaeger noted encouragingly.

"It is simply the truth young soul," he was corrected again.

Salmor left Jaeger and Pebbles to take in his new home together. Jaeger figured that time was probably not a measure that was high on Salmor's agenda, and decided that he would have to make his own way back out of his cave when he was ready. He was keen to find and meet some of the other monks living here.

Jaeger had no idea what the time was when he woke. He felt both rested and reinvigorated, and was also a little surprised to note that he felt comfortably warmer in his cave-room with nothing but the fine woven blanket he had been given.

Pebbles was still snoring at the foot of Jaeger's small bed, and Jaeger wondered if this was what had eventually woken him. The room was perfectly dark, and Jaeger reached to harness matter in order to light a flame for light.

His attempt to harness and draw in DarkLand matter was remarkably difficult. Jaeger could sense the matter all around him, but as he drew it in it almost felt like he was doing it wrong. The only feeling he could compare it to, was inhaling water when he was supposed to be drinking it. It felt unnatural and uncomfortable, and after extensive tense focus, he was eventually able to perform the simple flame that had been a basic technique in matter-in-practice back at the college.

"Pebbles," he called gently to the large form still curled up at the foot of the bed. The SkyGoat opened one eye and looked up at Jaeger in the light of the flame. "Good sleep buddy?" Jaeger asked, ruffling his head. Pebbles leaned back and stretched. His wings spanned out to both walls of the room and his whole body arched and went rigid, holding the position for a few moments while looking at Jaeger.

"Good stretch!" Jaeger congratulated Pebbles, who was still staring at him without letting go of the pleasant ritual. "Would the mighty aves-caprinae like to join me for a little exploring today? Tonight? This morning? Outside." Jaeger concluded. "I have no idea what time it is."

Pebbles finished his stretch and stood up, furling his enormous wings back to his body. Jaeger held the flame as they left the room to the cavern hallways. The basic spell still felt uncomfortable as he held it, leading his way back out of the cave opening to the forest outside. Jaeger noted that he still had difficulty breathing and felt light-headed from just this light stroll. Perhaps that was part of what was affecting his matter harnessing.

"Good morning, Jaeger" Salmor greeted him as he strolled deeper into the forest, he was kneeling together with a robed halfling at the base of a tree. The tree appeared to have been felled by what must have been cyclonic winds outside overnight.

"Good morning, Salmor" Jaeger greeted, waving his hand politely to the halfling who nodded back respectfully.

"Jaeger, this young soul calls herself Delphine. Delphine and I are just sharing some final hours with our tree here." Jaeger looked down at the small mound they had shaped within the hole where the tree had been uprooted. He wasn't sure if they were mourning or practicing some serious ritual, so he kept his face neutral.

"Is this a funeral of some sort?" Jaeger asked.

"Of some sort yes," Delphine agreed. "We are harnessing the energy this tree had before it's time is over."

"Is that similar to harnessing matter?" Jaeger asked, suddenly interested. "I have noticed it is difficult to do up here."

"Of course you have," Salmor chided. "You and Worley both learned to harness DarkLand matter before you ever stopped to think about how toxic that is for the soul."

Jaeger couldn't argue with that, even at Clouds College it was widely explained that harnessing matter wasn't a healthy practice. His mind drifted back to Charnel's final moments last year before he had been overwhelmed by the demon-shaman. Salmor watched Jaeger patiently with a mild I-told-you-so expression on his face.

"But why does that make it hard to practice up here?" Jaeger asked.

Salmor nodded down at Delphine who was still kneeling by the small mound. Delphine got to her feet and walked across to the branches of the fallen tree. Without any real selectiveness, she plucked a small stem with some leaves attached to it, and took it back to the mound. Excavating the small hole in the centre of the mound, Delphine deposited the stem and buried it. She then leant back, kneeling before the little mound and closing her eyes.

Jaeger could feel the harnessing of matter as he normally would. He watched Delphine intently, as she knelt with her eyes closed and her hands on her knees. Normally Jaeger would hold his palms outwards to channel the matter into his body through them, Delphine slowly inhaled for a long time, and then finally began to exhale.

Within moments, a sprout emerged from the mound, growing towards the sky rapidly. Once it was nearly two feet tall, the sapling then expanded at the base, achieving years of growth and development without getting any taller.

By the time Delphine was done, Jaeger could not have linked his fingers around the base of the sapling if he used both hands. Delphine stood back and breathed in again contentedly.

"The trees up here are less likely to survive the powerful winds unless we encourage them to fill out before they grow tall." Delphine explained.

"And the matter you harnessed? It seemed different to what I am used to," Jaeger observed.

"We are not mages Jaeger, we are clerics," Salmor corrected him. "You will not see us hurling fireballs at each other and choking our souls with DarkLand matter like Worley was taught. The matter that reaches these peaks is purified, it has a lighter composition to DarkLand matter and does not naturally accumulate in the plains below. No, purified matter will elevate itself towards the atmosphere of this world before it settles."

"What purifies DarkLand matter?" Jaeger was intrigued.

"That would be the elves I believe, along with some very special species that they observed and learned this technique from."

"And this purified matter is harnessed differently?"

"Like I said, the composition of purified matter is different to DarkLand matter. It vibrates at an entirely different frequency and so doesn't like being forced into the body through the skin."

"How do you harness it instead?" Jaeger asked curiously.

"I thought you only came here to ask us to leave for The Plateau," Salmor pointed out with amusement.

"Nobody likes a gloater Salmor," Jaeger teased lightheartedly. Salmor's face almost went pale with surprise and hurt. For the second time, Jaeger realised that this self-assured holy-man was also quite sensitive to things that Jaeger didn't understand.

"Purified matter is harnessed into the lungs," Salmor explained almost meekly. "Close your eyes Jaeger, close your eyes and feel for it. When you sense the matter that is out there, forget everything you know about it and breathe in deeply."

Jaeger closed his eyes, searching intently for the sense of energy and activity that existed in the air around him. Once he had found patches of matter all around him, he breathed in.

"Think about the matter you have found as you breathe in, it will be drawn towards you if you tell it to."

Again, Jaeger focused and visualized what he had found. He was amazed at the results. Like a syphon; once the first traces of purified matter began to flow towards his lungs, it started to attract and pull more matter from further away. His lungs felt like the eye of a vortex, as a current of invigorating force and energy permeated his blood. He looked up at the small sapling that Delphine had created and then did something remarkable.

Looking past the sapling, Jaeger focused all of his new energy at the fallen tree behind it. He looked at the few roots it had, that were still partially connected to the ground, and then at the roots that had been ripped free.

Breathing out, he focused all of the power and energy he felt within him, channeling the exposed roots to reach back towards the ground. They immediately responded, knitting back towards the soil they had been pulled from, and once they reached it, they began delve deep.

Jaeger continued to force life into the tree's growth as the roots delved further into the mountain. He could feel them strike the solid rock of the peaks deep beneath the surface, and then breathed in again, encouraging the roots to contract.

Below him he heard Delphine gasp as the tense

roots began to pull the body of the fallen tree back upright. Jaeger continued to squeeze and squeeze as the roots contracted harder to pull the tree back into position. After another entire minute, the enormous tree stood tall again, pressed up protectively behind its child that Delphine had planted.

"I don't believe it," Delphine remarked. "I have never seen so much power in my lifetime."

"Jaeger here is used to manipulating matter very differently to us Delphine," Salmor pointed out. "What we just saw was the result of a mage harnessing our ways, while using his own techniques. Impressive though that was, we do not use our powers in such ways here."

Jaeger looked at the old monk resentfully, "And why not?"

"Because that tree's time had come," Salmor explained to Jaeger philosophically.

"Obviously not," Jaeger disagreed. Salmor looked both thoughtful and slightly hurt once again. He looked like he wasn't going to speak, before a look of calm came back to him.

"We all have our own path to take Jaeger" he added cryptically, and then left the scene of their work to walk deeper into the forest.

Delphine continued to admire their work, she stepped forward patting her small sapling affectionately, before looking up at its parent standing protectively above it.

"Beautiful," she admired, before leaving Jaeger and Pebbles to themselves in the clearing.

Jaeger didn't see Salmor for a week after the tree

incident. He did however meet many more of the monks living atop the peak. After numerous little discussions, he learned that there were several other tall peaks atop other mountains where a few monks were spread out. However, the majority of their community lived within the caves behind the wave-rock, on the same peak as Jaeger.

Deep within these caves were sherpa trails that led all the way to the foot of the mountain. Jaeger had been very lucky to meet Pebbles, as most monks had been required to find these trails and hike to the summit when searching for this place.

The community was predominantly human and halfling, however he was surprised to discover the occasional dwarf atop the peaks. Apparently, there was an elf living in solitude on one of the southern mountains of the Thin Air Peaks. All up, Jaeger estimated that there were probably five hundred monks inhabiting the region, living in perfect harmony with their environment. All blissfully ignorant to the problems of the world below.

Jaeger spent a lot of his time learning as much as he could about the monks' specific relationship with their environment, and the purified magic that existed high up in the peaks. He spent hours each day practicing the harnessing of purified matter, just how he had been shown by Delphine and Salmor. Predominantly, he practiced by copying their techniques of channeling this power into the plants and trees around him.

To begin with, Jaeger had decided that Pebbles really deserved his own bed since he had decided to stay in the caves with Jaeger. So, one day Jaeger discretely took a small branch from the tree he had revived, bringing it back to his room with Pebbles. He sized Pebbles up appraisingly, looking back and forth between the skygoat and the space at the foot of his bed. There was a bit more than a yard between the end of the bed and the wall of the cave, but much more width to that end of the room.

Eventually, with a rough idea of what he wanted in mind, Jaeger breathed in deeply. Closing his eyes he could sense the thick concentrations of purified matter throughout the room, this was easy. Sitting cross-legged on the floor in front of Pebbles' sleeping space, Jaeger held out the small branch and exhaled.

He could feel the living energy of the matter permeating the live graft. He could feel the stems and shoots exploding with rapid growth in all directions. Opening his eyes, he began to guide the shoots into a weave, watching the knitting of the live furniture curl at every corner that they reached. Jaeger continued to harness the purified matter and pour it into his design, and within a few minutes, the skeleton of an oval shaped floor cushion was evident.

"How does that look?" Jaeger glanced up at Pebbles who watched on with approval. "Give me one more minute to finish up, I don't think it can take your weight yet."

Pebbles snorted and stamped his hoof playfully. Jaeger turned back to the cushion and closed his eyes again. Breathing deeply, he drew in all the matter he could hold. He felt close to bursting point, but unlike DarkLand matter, this felt like Jaeger needed to go run a marathon in order to burn off all his excess energy.

Exhaling with the matter he was harnessing; Jaeger poured all this energy into the sofa. Again, growth exploded from every inch of living wood, the shoots became strong and thickened, even as new shoots wove around them, fortifying their placement.

As he opened his eyes, he looked at his handiwork again. The cushion was just over a yard wide and over two yards long, dipping slightly in the centre like nest. He looked up at Pebbles who was still watching on with approval.

"Give it a try," he encouraged.

Pebbles stepped forward onto his bed, the branches were strong and spongy under his hooves as he trod on them. After circling his own tail several times, which Jaeger now recognised as Pebbles' bedtime ritual, the skygoat settled into a position that finally suited him. Curled up into his new bed, Pebbles fit the design perfectly.

After completing his interior décor, Jaeger decided that he was overdue to speak to Salmor. He wasn't sure if there was a hierarchy in the peaks, but it was clear that Salmor was one of the most senior monks up here, and possibly their founder. With a little contemplation, Jaeger decided he would refrain from using that term to avoid being corrected, however he still needed to discuss other comments that had been made recently.

He found Salmor eventually at the far end of the forest. The old monk seemed to be expecting Jaeger, and wasn't doing anything in particular when he reached him. Salmor watched Jaeger as he approached, and after a brief silence Jaeger spoke.

"Salmor," Jaeger greeted. The monk inclined his head politely. "Last week you mentioned that the elves were responsible for this purified DarkLand matter. 'Them and some species that they studied' I believe you said. I was wondering if you could explain this further."

"I could explain a little yes," Salmor confirmed.

"Please do," Jaeger coaxed bluntly. Salmor sighed looking a little frustrated.

"What I understand, is that the elves long ago observed a natural aura that some of the creatures they ride have. A natural aura to resist DarkLand matter. There are unicorns, dragons, phoenix and many more on the islands they inhabit. Some of these creatures showed a powerful resistance to DarkLand matter when it first spilt into this world."

"What sort of resistance? Are they immune to magic?" Jaeger asked.

"Yes, if magic is what you choose to call it. You may not have noticed yet, but even the aves-caprinae of our peaks have a natural resilience to DarkLand matter. Your young friend who brought you here would not be so easily affected if you tried to use DarkLand matter around him."

"I'll keep that in mind," Jaeger added curiously, he wasn't sure if there was any appropriate way to test Salmor's theory. "Where does purified matter come into this?"

"Unicorns," Salmor explained. "You used the term 'immune to magic,' I said resistant. Most of these species are quite resistant to 'magic', but unicorns are completely immune. If those creatures were to have DarkLand matter thrown at them, most of it would bounce right off, and some of it would come back purified."

"And after the elves realised this, they learned

how to do it themselves?"

"In a sense. I understand that they have now mastered the ability to gravitate large concentrations of DarkLand matter for purification. Of this purified matter that is released back into the world, most of it slowly rises above the heavier components that make up the air we breathe until it settles. Small amounts circulate below us with storms and turbulence, but for the most part this altitude is the natural home for purified matter."

"I guess that makes some sense, it is a remarkable achievement. It is a shame that it doesn't sit lower, imagine if Clouds College had access to the same world that you do."

"That is still their choice Jaeger. When we go below, we can purify the DarkLand matter we feel around us. It is an unfortunate soul that feels compelled to embrace the DarkLand matter around them, like the mages at Clouds College do."

"You know how to purify DarkLand matter!" Jaeger exclaimed, ignoring the veiled contempt shown for his college. He could not believe this revelation had been kept from him.

"Of course, we all do."

"How?" Jaeger insisted.

"It has very little difference to how you harness purified matter. With years of practice, once you harness DarkLand matter in the same way you would harness purified matter, you will be purifying it on the way through."

"It's that easy?"

"I wouldn't call years of experience and familiarity with purified matter easy. If you are wondering why they don't teach it at your college, it is because they would all need to spend years up here with us first. And that is not a corruption we would welcome."

"Corruption? From allowing others to share this place too?" Jaeger was becoming tempted to engage Salmor in an argument regarding his exclusive philosophy.

"Yes, corruption I'm afraid. There are very few cultures that can coexist near these peaks. The nomadic peoples below are familiar with it, they can sense there is a need for preservation here and don't linger too close below. Do you remember anything in particular when you first reached these peaks?"

Jaeger remembered the nomads who had rescued him and brought him here. "Yes, the nomads left once we entered the lands below here."

"And do you remember anything else at that point?" Salmor pressed. Jaeger searched his memories. The trek had been a fairly pleasant blur. He remembered that here had been very little fanfare to acknowledge his parting ways with the nomadic people. Then he remembered.

"The cactus! When I first came here the cactus had no prickles. The cacti trusted me even though they didn't know me. I thought about using them for water, but I couldn't bring myself to do anything."

"Yes, they trust you, and as you can see their trust wasn't misplaced. As far as I know, no-one has given them reason to mistrust another living being. If all of the mages from your college were to visit this place, can you say that it would stay this way?"

Jaeger contemplated his classmates. He

contemplated Charnel. Charnel had been too deeply corrupted by exposure to DarkLand matter, the students at Clouds College weren't so far gone. He contemplated the rest of his year group. Kostian stood out the most, but Jaeger was certain that there were varying degrees of rotten, not just Kostian and then the rest.

"No, it wouldn't last."

"So, you can see why you are not the first person who has wished for us to return to our peoples, and join in their wars, and you can see that nothing is that simple. Understand Jaeger, we have been here for a very long time. I personally am ancient by the standards of humans. In the early days it was practice for a young monk to adopt a cactus plant growing wildly beyond the peaks.

"They would nurture and communicate with these cacti, sometimes verbally if they felt that helped. They would tell it that they were responsible for its wellbeing and that they would not allow anything bad to happen to it. And for this care, all that they asked in return was that the cactus trust them."

"So, after all the time and effort into making this place what it is, you don't want to lose it," Jaeger iterated.

"It could take a long time, months or years for some monks. But when it happened the reward was worth all the waiting and was equal to any joy that one can experience in their lifetime. When this feat was achieved, the young monks were considered to be a member of the community. The reward for this rank is the responsibility for the wellbeing of all other creatures. Even the evil scaleskins and roachkin you fight we hold no hatred for, just pity."

"I appreciate that you value what you have done here. But it is a bit rich to pity the evil that is trying to destroy what we have spent centuries building back home."

"Jaeger, you knew you needed to come here, you would not have made it if you did not. Why do I sense a constant impatience to leave now that you have found this life?" Salmor ignored the bulk of what Jaeger had said.

"I did not come here to join you. I came here to ask you to help preserve something just as significant if not more than what you have here. These peaks would not stay apart from the world for long once the demons are done destroying The Plateau."

"You may have thought you came to enlist us when you left your home, but I think you will find that you are here because you were meant to be here now." Salmor insisted.

"I *did* come to enlist you, if that's the word you are choosing. I *knew* I needed to come here because I *knew* that your policy of remaining separate to the world needed to change. I also know that I can't stay here indefinitely like everybody else. I came to try and convince your people to help the world that you live in, but there are people back home who I need to get back to. One person in particular," he added thinking about Aema.

"There is nothing more important than the path you have found yourself on Jaeger."

"Aema! Is more important than the path I have found myself on, especially if my time here has not helped to convince you to join us."

"I can only reiterate what I have said to you already Jaeger. Introspection and time will be the only way that you eventually come to terms with moving forward. Hopefully in the future you will be able to look back on this conversation and see how far you have come."

Jaeger knew the end of a productive conversation when he heard it. He had gained a lot today, but none of it was the enlightenment that Salmor seemed to allude to so zealously.

11 A MURMUR IN THE WOODS

Agon watched Tubby tip-toe ahead of him with an awed fascination. His partner-in-crime was a halfling, and his real name was Theodore which probably should have been shortened to Teddy. However, as Agon constantly reminded him, Tubby had already been shortened physically, so his name was allowed to be anything, and anything might as well be Tubby.

To describe Tubby as stealthy didn't do him any justice. Agon never ceased to be amazed, watching his friend drift forwards through the woods without making so much as an imprint of soft noise. Tubby was now moving at a slowed crouch, with his right hand reaching over his shoulder. He brushed the tallest arrow in his quiver lightly with the tip of his right index finger, while holding both his short-bow and spear low in front of him with his left.

Agon had seen him peg a goblin through the eye within half a second of the careless creature springing from its hiding spot. There had been times when Agon had struggled to even draw his sword before Tubby had shot and speared entire units from the tribes that they hunted. Goblin tribes north of The Plateau were few and far between.

They rarely caused anywhere near the trouble that their cousins on the Western and Southern borders were renowned for. But there were still some that ventured too close to the foothills, and they were still the enemy.

So it was, by assignment from Lord Alcorn, that integrated squads of human and halfling rangers be formed. Their job was to patrol beyond his borders for any threats, large or small. Together they tracked and hunted the enemy wherever they could be found.

Today the tracks they had found were halfway up the foothills to The Plateau, and far closer to their lands than they were used to. They had both just returned after months away at the north eastern tip of the province, and had come across the trail long after they had stopped expecting trouble. In the hundreds of miles of wild terrain they had returned from, they had only encountered 'contact' on a handful of occasions.

These contacts had been gradually occurring further and further away from The Plateau since Agon had taken up his post as a ranger ten years ago. It seemed that the goblin tribes had been getting the message up until now. He wasn't sure what might have changed, but they were following these tracks to find out.

"I was looking forward to being home and having my first shave in more than half a year by now. Why did you have to find these tracks in all the great wilderness we could have come home through?" Agon lamented.

Tubby grimaced at the noise Agon was making. Clearly he wanted his partner to take their current discovery a little more seriously.

"Would you rather we had missed them and left them undiscovered for maybe another six months?" he retorted. "Besides, I've heard that human women like a strong beard anyways, Aggro."

"Not Sherree, she would prefer if I couldn't even grow a beard like you, and I know better than to have my own preference on the matter," Agon sighed.

"Ahh, you should have never introduced her to me if you wanted her to love you so much," Tubby shook his head with feigned sympathy. "She will never be satisfied with you again knowing that there are more impressive men out there".

"Men!?" Agon laughed, "Tubby if you could pass as a man, then I coul-"

"SHHH!" Tubby interrupted, crouching sideways again and planting one foot in front of the other delicately.

"Reveal yourselves now or die!" A rough voice called from further down the trail. Both Tubby and Agon relaxed, it was no goblin they had come across.

"It's alright!" Agon called back. "We're not enemies. We are rangers."

"Then why did you not start by calling the password if you call yourselves rangers?" the dwarf growled, stepping into view from down the trail ahead of them.

"Password!? What bloody password?" Tubby laughed incredulously.

The dwarf did not seem to find his joke funny and scowled heavily as his company also came into view. One of them was a human, neatly presented and in military uniform.

"This is an outrage! What are these two doing in this area without permission? you have one job Barrett, one job! You swore to both our kings that you would control this spot, and we get two manky idiots wandering right up to our doorstep with jokes to greet us!"

"My deepest apologies," the soldier squirmed. "Every ranger coming through this area knows the rules. I have never met this pair before."

"And what rules would you be talking about? This area is very much our responsibility and more importantly I would like to know what *you* are doing here," Tubby demanded obstinately.

The noise that came from the head dwarf could only have been described as a snort of pure outrage. Tubby conducted himself without fear, something that Agon had found to have put them in a tight spot on more than one occasion. He quickly stepped in to prevent the dwarf from boiling over on the spot.

"I'm sorry but we have been posted in the far north for a very long time and have heard no word of your movements in our area. My name is Agon, and my outgoing little friend here is Theodore."

"You see, I knew there would be a reasonable explanation," Barrett tried to explain in earnest. "If they were posted north before our inductions, then there is nothing more that I could have done to prevent this."

"When a dwarf takes an oath, he doesn't include a list of excuses," the dwarf responded with disapproval.

Barrett did not appear to be having a good day, Agon could sympathise.

"Well friends, excuses or not, I'm sure that we can avoid trouble here," Agon interrupted cordially. "We would be happy to return to Lord Alcorn to confirm we are rangers and learn the right passwords."

"Not all the rangers are meant to know the passwords. Most of you are meant to simply stay away from this area," the dwarf replied obstinately.

"Well, it would appear that by unhappy chance, we are going to have to be part of the few who don't," Tubby explained belligerently. "What are you doing here that's so secret anyway? Anybody would think that such an angry group of dwarves this far north of The Plateau must be trying to hide their underway."

Within moments axes had been drawn all around Tubby, who had reacted just as quickly. Tubby was now pointing a drawn arrow at the dwarf who had been doing all the talking. Agon shook his head ruefully and drew his sword. He always knew that Tubby had a talent for provoking people, but he wasn't about to let a group of hostile dwarves kill him for it. The soldier Barrett had also drawn his weapon. This was going to get ugly.

"We are rangers on assignment from Lord Alcorn," Agon reminded them. "Whatever situation we find ourselves in, should be handled diplomatically. I have absolutely no desire to fight with you but I will."

"You will answer to your lord or our axes, one way or another," the dwarf grated, he seemed entirely unbothered by the arrow pointed at him.

"If you listen very carefully, you will realise that we have offered to answer to our lord several times now," Tubby baited.

"Infuriating as my companion here may be to you, he is right," Agon agreed. The dwarves were on their land and he was not going to side against his friend any longer for the sake of peace. "Lord or axes is entirely your decision now. Decide."

A long pause and standoff followed, the only one who appeared to want to be here less than Agon, was the soldier Barrett. At length, the dwarf lowered his axe and his company followed suit.

"Barrett, you will need to bind these prisoners and take them to their lord."

"We will go freely with you," Agon refused. "We are rangers of this province and until we discovered you here, we were protecting our own lands. I won't go so far as to accuse you of trespassing, because clearly arrangements have been made while we were on assignment, but we will not submit to binding in our own lands by foreigners. I assume that you and your company are not expatriate dwarves from The Plateau?"

"We are not," the dwarf replied curtly.

"Well then you are on our lands," Agon explained. "In my experience I would never doubt the word of a dwarf, so I believe you have every right to be here. Now let's go together back to Bambara, find Lord Alcorn, and get this mess sorted out."

Something seemed to soften just a fraction in the dwarf at this and he nodded his consent.

"You will lead the way then ranger."

The small party had barely covered a mile when Tubby became agitated. He froze with his fist in the air along the trail he led them through. Agon was familiar with the signal but the dwarves continued a few steps without pausing.

"What are you doing halfling?" the dwarf demanded.

"Quiet!" Tubby shushed. "Listen to that."

The dwarves looked outraged but took the alert seriously. Deeper into the woods, movement could be heard. Agon was more used to the trampling and bickering that accompanied scaleskins in the woods, however he could not deny that there were creatures out there.

"What's out there now?" the dwarf demanded.

Tubby looked back infuriated at the noise he was making then froze. A few moments passed as Agon realised that there was not a single sound coming from anywhere in the woods now. He turned back to Tubby who was now as rigid as his spear. Without a word of warning Tubby darted off the trail and into the woods.

"Hey! Get back here!" the dwarf shouted. Agon drew his weapon, fearful that their position had now clearly been given away.

The dwarves immediately drew weapons too, most of them fixed in Agon's direction. They stood silently in stand-off, Agon straining his ears to hear while looking back at the dwarves closely to watch for any sudden movements. Suddenly the sound of many feet running their way could be heard throughout the forest.

"Form up!" the dwarf bellowed.

Within moments, ten armoured dwarves had formed a flawless shield wall on three sides. Barrett crouched low behind them, unsure where he fit into their formation. Agon glanced back and then forwards again, he didn't feel particularly welcome in their scrum either. A moment later, the woods burst open with small scaleskin slags, all charging towards Agon and the shield wall behind him.

As Agon lowered his longsword, an arrow flashed from the bushes to the left, catching the goblin closest to him in the side of the head. This was all the encouragement Agon needed, he knew that wherever he found himself in this fight, Tubby's arrows would hit any targets that were about to harm him. He raised his longsword and swept his way deep into enemy ranks.

The scaleskins were cut down easily, but showed no fear of his swordsmanship. Agon had never seen them cut down so easily and still hold their ground. He spun around checking his flanks with a sweeping arc of his sword.

Two slags lay dead behind him with arrows in their eyes. The dwarves had absorbed the impact of the charge easily and now charged in to support him. Whatever their leader's feelings were towards Agon and Tubby, they were not leaving him to fight alone.

The scaleskins were dying all around him and still more poured out from the bushes. There were lots of them but they were not limitless. Between Agon and the dwarves, along with Tubby's mystery arrow lottery, the raiding party was quickly being brought under control. Only two dwarves had fallen.

Agon wheeled back again to keep his perimeter clear, when Tubby called for him to get down. He only had a split second to react, but years of hunting together had instilled absolute trust in each other's instructions.

A searing fireball singed across his head as Agon dropped. Behind him, both a dwarf and a slag were incinerated as they grappled. The dwarf had been holding the advantage until that moment. More fireballs came searing out from the tree-line and the dwarves immediately reformed behind their shields, the fire seemed capable of burning even through the steel.

With a few shouted orders from their leader, they charged towards the shaman that had stepped out from the trees. Those with ruined shields fell neatly back from their wall which closed in before them, while fireballs continued to rain forth from the shaman.

Agon dived and tumbled as some came his way, the shaman was the most terrifying scaleskin he had ever encountered. Above the skulls and staff, a dark shape shimmered and towered over the dwarves as they charged.

Half of them had fallen now. Shields or not, the spells were finding a way through. As Agon watched in horror, an arrow sprouted in the right side of the shaman's face. For a moment the creature paused, it should probably be dying or at the very least writhing in agony. But the shadow above it held the shaman firm.

As the four remaining dwarves crashed forwards, it swept its staff forward, knocking three dwarves back as if they had been ridden down by a bull. The fourth dwarf hacked at it with an axe that was effortlessly parried.

Agon charged. If there was going to be any chance of defeating this horrifying creature, it would have to be together. With another sweep of its staff the dwarf went flying, the three other dwarves picked themselves up gingerly, they had been hit horrifically hard but they were as tough as nails.

Another arrow appeared by the shaman's face,

this time stopping mid-flight and falling to the ground inches from its target. Without fail another arrow appeared where the first one had been stopped, it froze again mid-flight, but in that same moment an arrow sprouted from the shaman's knee.

Agon could have laughed as he cut down with his longsword. When Tubby had a picked out a target, there was no escaping. Agon felt like he had hacked the side of a tree as the shaman parried his stroke. Another arrow appeared in its neck as Agon's backstroke felt flesh. The scaleskin flesh was much harder than he was used to, it was like trying to chop through branches, but he had managed to break the creature's arm.

As the staff clattered to the dirt, another arrow appeared in the side of the shaman's head. It stared at him intensely for a moment. Agon wasn't sure he had ever seen a creature look so in pain.

He swung hard and fast for the neck. A charge of static raced back down his longsword shocking the weapon from his hands as the blade bit deep into its neck. They both fell, the shaman was dead and the shadow that enveloped it was gone. Agon felt like somebody had kicked him in the back of his spine.

"Nice work Aggro!" Tubby called from the trees. "Looks like you got to deliver the killing blow after I did all the hard work again."

He stumped across the long grass somehow silently as usual, looking across to the three remaining dwarves as they picked themselves up off the ground. They were a little worse-for-wear but they were alive.

"You can thank me later when we get back to Bambara," Tubby shrugged, and continued past them to the shaman's corpse. "He was tough. Nothing special about him to look at now he's dead though."

12 THE SOUTHERN FRONT

Emperor Hildebrante was near the end of his tour of the Southern Front. He was sure the visit had given a false sense of hope to his men, which was all that Darroch had said he needed from his Emperor. The series of battles they had won across the frontline fortresses had been seen by every soldier and mage in the south. They now knew that their Emperor was not a man to take a backwards step, not against the scaleskins or their demon allies.

Hildebrante however, had cautiously noted that the demon-backed forces appeared to have disappeared from the moment he had arrived. He was now months into his campaign at one of the last fortresses left to visit, and they were still yet to be sighted. As they trotted back across the lawns of Learmonth, there was only Derby in the far east to visit. From here Hildebrante would take the roads north back to Conorbatia.

"You have done remarkable things with our situation Darroch. I don't know if I have ever said this to you before, but you were also right not to challenge Charnel's self-appointed authority last year when I deployed you here."

"The state of our defences was too far gone for me to justify wasting time and resources on an internal conflict," Darroch agreed. "Any strong-arming between me and the head battle-mage of the south would have been a disaster. Besides, Grantanmar was a lost cause anyway. Sorrento is a far more suitable headquarters for our operations."

"Sorrento is a fine headquarters Darroch. The soldiers you have trained are now competent and disciplined. It is the perfect base to reflect the pride of our armed forces." Hildebrante congratulated.

"High praise Emperor, thank you," Darroch winked.

Emperor Hildebrante chuckled slightly and then turned his attention to Marrick. "How is your halfling project going Marrick?"

"Very good sir, all ten thousand have arrived in Sorrento now, and their training to assimilate into our wall formations was flawless before we left. I have been informed that the new recruits are fitting in just as well as the old ones."

"They played their role well when we fought in Sorrento" Hildebrante agreed. "How is their deployment going?"

"We left five hundred behind to train the new arrivals when we took the first thousand west with us to Albury. A thousand more have arrived behind us at every fortress you have toured so far Emperor. And I believe another thousand will arrive here within the week after we leave. They will be spread across every fortress in the south within the month. A thousand at each major base, with the remaining numbers deployed to minor watchtowers in between."

"More fine work Marrick, thank you. He will end up having your job one day," the emperor commented turning to Darroch.

"I don't doubt it," Marrick's close friend agreed.

Marrick smiled but shook his head disapprovingly. "There can only be one man in that position gentlemen, so let's hope you're not talking about a date anytime too soon," he pointed out.

The trio dismounted and led their horses to be stabled. Their work in this fortress was done and their last dinner in Learmonth was calling from inside the barracks. Tomorrow they would be back on the roads again to the east towards Derby, and then the emperor's tour would be over.

The idea of returning to Conorbatia at the end of all this, seemed incredibly bland to Marrick. Fortunately, that burden was Hildebrante's to bear, Marrick surmised rather smugly. The emperor would just have to make do, running his nation again from the rear once he returned to his palace.

Marrick woke early in the morning for breakfast, remembering his distaste for food after a night of drinking. Why did he always seem to remember too late, he could have sworn he had learned his lesson from the morning before that, and he was certain he had pointed this observation out to himself sometime earlier in the week before that time too. He sighed with acceptance; *some men were brought into this world to suffer* he conceded philosophically.

Commander Darroch and Emperor Hildebrante were sitting with their troops, pleasantly enjoying their bacon, eggs and toast when Marrick entered. The sight of their food was enough to make Marrick realise that this wasn't for him, however the coffees beside their plates smelled amazing. He would start his day with one of those at least.

His two superiors watched him with amusement as he joined them with a hot mug. Neither of them had lingered as long as he had with the soldiers last night, drinking after dinner. It was yet another lesson he had promised himself to learn earlier in the week, before remembering his revelation that it was his lot in life to suffer.

"Good coffee?" Darroch asked.

"Great coffee thanks," Marrick confirmed sharply.

"Great coffee in Learmonth," Emperor Hildebrante agreed. "I must remember to compliment the man who makes the coffees here before we leave."

"Don't forget the eggs," Darroch added.

"And the eggs," Hildebrante agreed.

"And the bacon," Darroch reminded him.

"Can't forget the bacon," Hildebrante noted.

"Gentlemen, I'm sure you will remember to compliment them on the toast here too," Marrick jumped in before they could have the satisfaction.

"Why yes, the toast as well now that you mention it Marrick," Darroch agreed. "But how did you know? You haven't had any yet?"

"Must be the smell," Hildebrante offered.

"Fresh toast does have a distinctively nice smell to it in the morning," Darroch noted with feigned realization.

"Alright, that'll do you two. What time would you like to be on the roads this morning?" Marrick asked.

"We are just finishing up our breakfast now," Darroch replied. "So, without rushing you, we will be happy to wait until you've enjoyed the famous breakfast in Learmonth also before we are ready to go."

"No need my friend, I have enjoyed it on other mornings this week and will not delay you by having it again this morning." Marrick responded, rising from the table with his mug of coffee in hand.

"Well, if you're ready then we can be off at once," Hildebrante concluded.

"Don't add that last part from Marrick when you compliment the cook Emperor. You might hurt his feelings."

"Good point commander, compliments from the emperor and the commander only." Hildebrante agreed.

"Pass on a compliment for the coffee from the lieutenant," Marrick reminded him as they both rose from the table too.

Within an hour, the jovial pair were back on the roads with Marrick at the head of the small army escorting them. The southern countryside was quite pleasant now that they had cleared The Plateau's central catchment of DarkLand matter, which was now behind them to the west. Learmonth had been strategically placed just east of The Great Desolation to escape the worst effects that Grantanmar had suffered.

Having passed the demolished ruins of the

former headquarters weeks ago, Marrick realised the valuable barrier that the southern slopes of The Plateau provided for the people living further north. The choking decay that came from DarkLand matter was clearly evident to the south.

From atop their walls, soldiers could see the barren waste that was The Great Desolation, stretching south from The Plateau all the way to the southern pole below the continent.

It appeared that while the central fortresses on The Plateau . bordered with this unwholesome phenomenon; the natural slopes of the land somehow protected it. The currents of DarkLand matter dispersed in every direction, as the foothills of The Plateau rose up to meet The Great Desolation.

While fortresses like Grantanmar had been toxically affected in their location, it remained far worse at the base of The Plateau's foothills. Darroch had gone to great lengths with his battle-mages to keep the majority of his new fortifications on either side of this central catchment area since Grantanmar.

Now as they traveled further clear of these lands to the east, the countryside again became green and vibrant. The great southern highway sat just behind the frontline walls of The Plateau, passing watchtowers regularly as they marched.

Despite this, lands and livestock from nearby towns on their left roamed freely and close to the walls protecting their nation. Marrick was going to comment that they were lucky the enemy was drawn to the major fortresses rather than the watchtowers in between, before closing his mouth and keeping that thought to himself.

"Enjoying the morning ride?" Darroch asked.

"Actually, I was thank you," Marrick responded tartly. "I was just appreciating the countryside clear of The Great Desolation."

"Yes, it is always visibly noticeable whenever you put a bit of distance between the unfortunate fortifications that have to sit above that area. We will never make the same mistake of leaving men to fester in that place for too long," Darroch noted gravely.

"Well, we know now," Marrick pointed out positively, his morning had improved significantly from where it had started.

"A good lesson learned, even if it had to be learned the hard way," Darroch mused.

"Wasn't learned the easy way," Marrick agreed.

Emperor Hildebrante appeared happy to sit and listen in silence astride his warhorse.

As the morning wore on, a rider from ahead of the convoy appeared in the distance. He was riding hard back west in their direction from Derby where they were headed. *Clearly a messenger*, Marrick observed as he came closer into view.

The emperor's bodyguard routinely positioned themselves forward, restricting access to Emperor Hildebrante until the rider could be verified. The man stopped short and held a small scroll of paper high for them all to see.

"State your business sir!" Darroch called out professionally.

The messenger dismounted from his horse and approached the assembled bodyguard of Emperor Hildebrante purposefully. When he stopped in front of them, he gave no indication that he intended to hand the sealed parchment to anybody but Hildebrante directly.

"Emperor, I have an urgent letter for you. It's from the head of Cloud's College, professor Worley.

13 THE ADVENTURES OF PEBBLES

Jaeger meditated on the edge of the mountaintop patiently. He had been enjoying the newfound access to purified matter for a few weeks now, and although he had not completely shaken the nagging desire to return home, he had accepted that he at least had a little time to learn what he could before he left. He had even refrained from debating the world below with Salmor for over a week now.

The old monk had taken this as evidence that he had been right. He behaved as though Jaeger had now realised that he should wash his hands of The Plateau and remain in the peaks. Jaeger had been clear to point out that this would never be the case, but that didn't stop Salmor from his ongoing assumptions.

Salmor had even set aside some time with Jaeger to expand on the applications of purified matter. The possibilities were quite broad. Similar to promoting growth and development in trees, the practice of harnessing pure matter also had great powers in healing.

DAMIEN D. KENWORTHY

Salmor's one caveat, had been to make it explicitly clear that the monks did not use this gift to heal themselves. Somehow, he described this as a pathway to vanity, or 'a refusal to accept one's necessary suffering' as he put it.

Personally, Jaeger felt that he had seen enough suffering in the world, but reluctantly acknowledged that he understood. He tried to use his time in private meditation to contemplate Salmor's philosophy, as well as his teachings. Jaeger knew very clearly that they did not see eye-to-eye, but also challenged himself to keep an open mind. It was only fair if he was prepared to accept the monk's time and tutelage.

Somewhere out in the misty skies, Pebbles was wheeling and plummeting in playful flight. Jaeger had seen the skygoat on numerous occasions enjoying somersaults in the powerful updrafts that ran along the sides of the cliffs. It was a pleasant sight to see when he came within view. Since he had rescued Jaeger, they had developed a very special bond. Pebbles had rarely left Jaeger's side since then.

As his thoughts drifted back to his companion, Jaeger heard a distant bleat echoing across the skies. He looked down to see Pebbles flapping towards him powerfully up out of the clouds below. When Pebbles drew level with the ledge, Jaeger realised that he was flying a little erratically. Pebbles appeared to have some injury that he was overcompensating for as he beat at the air violently. Jaeger jumped up and ran over as his companion landed heavily.

The left wing was visibly broken along the smaller bones towards its tips, and Pebbles had a large gash down the left side of his torso. It was a wonder

138

how the skygoat had managed to ascend in flight at all. The pain must have been unbearable.

"Ouch mate, how did you do that?" Jaeger sympathized, trying to hold the wing away from Pebbles' body to assess the deep cut in his side. Pebbles retracted the wing sharply at first and then delicately extended it again. Jaeger tried not to hold it too forcefully.

"Give me just a moment buddy," Jaeger said soothingly, and began to draw in the abundant purified matter all around him.

He poured all of the force it carried into the wing, just above the break where it was healthy. Jaeger then tracked outwards towards the injury. He could feel the shape of the break as his exertion traced over it in his mind, pulling the wing painfully just as the healing melded the bone to avoid any deformities.

Pebbles bleated once and yanked back with his wing, before realising that it was perfectly strong and healthy again. Jaeger continued to grasp the end of the wing, finishing his searching exertion right through to the skygoat's feathered tips.

"Sorry Pebbles, how's that now?" he asked.

Pebbles tested both wings together powerfully. Jaeger stepped back by reflex, his heel treading dangerously close to the edge of the cliff. He had become far more complacent with heights since he had been flying with Pebbles.

It wasn't that he had become used to heights, it was just the simple logic that as long as he had one of the mighty aves-caprinae nearby, he was unlikely to fall to his death. Take away Pebbles and he didn't doubt that his phobia would be as bad as it ever was.

Pebbles appeared to be satisfied with his friend's handiwork. "Just keep the wings out for another minute and we'll get this sorted too," Jaeger said, pointing to his side.

With a few more deep breaths harnessing matter, he exerted again, knitting the flesh back together neatly. It was far simpler than the broken bone, however Jaeger had no idea how to replace the thick wooly coat above the pale white hide he had sealed together. He considered for a moment the similarity between tree growth and sprouting fur, before deciding that it was unnecessary for now. Pebbles would just have to grow his coat back naturally.

"All better," he patted Pebbles when he was done.

Pebbles snorted and wiggled again with excitement. Jaeger patted him but Pebbles continued to prance and feint at Jaeger playfully. Clearly his little injury had interrupted Pebbles' playtime before he was finished, and he still had excess energy to burn.

Jaeger surprised Pebbles by reacting with lightning-fast reflexes, snatching at the skygoat's horns when they butted within reach. Pebbles yanked backwards with excitement. He had finally managed to get his friend to take the bait. After a quick wrestle, Jaeger let go and Pebbles continued to niggle him playfully.

Eventually the skygoat began to get impatient and dropped onto his front knees. "What now?" Jaeger queried.

Pebbles flicked his head and inclined it the same way that he had when he first rescued Jaeger. With no reason not to join him, Jaeger leapt onto his companion's back. Pebbles leapt up powerfully and charged the edge of the peak. Jaeger could feel the ground rumble beneath them as they thundered towards the open skies.

With a mighty leap, Pebbles carried them both over and then down. Jaeger felt his stomach lurch with terrifying acceleration, before Pebbles finally snapped open his wingspan, steadying their descent into a powerful glide.

The updraft closest to the cliff-side helped them to gain altitude rapidly and Jaeger could feel his ears blocking. He had adjusted fairly quickly to the altitudes since arriving, but often felt the need to harness the purified matter in the peaks to help with his breathing. The effect this had was both invigorating and necessary. His lungs felt like they had been infused with efficiency and the thinly available oxygen in the skies now seemed drawn to him.

Pebbles appeared to be navigating the various peaks with clear purpose. He was cutting a deliberate line between several mountains to the south east, while Jaeger simply held on and enjoyed the ride. None of the other mountains had the thick forest that protected the flat tabletop above the mountain where the monks lived. There were simply sporadic trees and vines here and there, clinging tenaciously to the crevices they had managed to impregnate.

In short time, Jaeger could see a taller summit than any other in the ranges. Pebbles was making his way towards it. He was trying to make out some shapes on a distinctive ledge in the distance, when suddenly a powerful displacement of air swooped in from above.

Almost losing his grip for a moment, Jaeger regained his hold on Pebbles to see an enormous skygoat now doubling back on their left. He watched it intensely, as it glided down in a graceful arc below them. Pebbles' wings beat excitedly as the skygoat appeared beside them again on their right this time.

Suddenly, as if this giant had been the opening of the dam gates, skygoats appeared all around them in the skies, frolicking and swooping each other and Pebbles. Jaeger was quick to notice that all of them were larger than Pebbles, though none as large as the first one that had appeared. As they came closer and closer to the ledge he had seen earlier, Jaeger could clearly make out several more skygoats hugging to the wall of the cliffs. They were ignoring the game in the skies, instead grazing on the wild plants that grew along their ledge.

"Settle buddy!" Jaeger reminded Pebbles, who was beginning to become dangerously boisterous with his passenger. The young skygoat only flapped harder and appeared intent on ramming the side of the mountain. Jaeger looked over his shoulder and realised that two skygoats were now pursuing them. They were only metres behind and none of the trio showed any signs of slowing.

"Pebbles!" Jaeger shouted only seconds from death.

At the last moment, Pebbles spread his wings into a momentary glide, banking hard to the right and landing up against the cliffside with his feet. Jaeger felt the powerful muscles in Pebbles' rump bunch up and then flex, as he cannoned them back into the open skies sharply. The two skygoats chasing them both landed the exact same maneuver, even closer now than before.

One of them managed to ram Pebbles in the rear, causing him to bleat and pull up, using his wings this time to break speed.

This seemed to be the game, as the successful skygoat immediately dipped further below and ahead, before entering a plummeting dive. Pebbles took a moment or two to recover his momentum, before dragging Jaeger down for the dive with him. Jaeger's newfound confidence with heights was now shattered. Whatever faith he had put in Pebbles acting as a safety net from being hurt was gone. The young caprinae was playful to the point of insane.

If Jaeger was not immediately reminded of his own constant adventures with Grum, he would have been furious. Instead, he was just terrified. To think this was how Mendel saw all of the games that he used to play, was an enlightening experience.

After a short while realising that there was almost no point stressing, Jaeger tried to embrace the unique terror of being hurtled upwards, down, and towards mountains of immovable rock. The game may have only lasted for an hour, but by the time Pebbles seemed satisfied, Jaeger was just as exhausted as his mount.

Several skygoats appeared to be funneling from the various points in the sky towards the enormous sheer mountain they had been playing around. Heavy snow piles balanced precariously above sheer cave mouths that appeared all over the southern face of the mountain.

Jaeger saw skygoats above and below him as they disappeared into the mountain through several of these caverns. Pebbles picked out one directly ahead of them. Like the click of a lock, the cold roar of the mountain winds disappeared, replaced by the echo of hooves and bleating within the deep hollow cave they entered.

Inside, Pebbles continued to slowly glide deeper and deeper down the open tunnel. The super-summit was a honeycomb just like the one the monks were living on. There was a distinctive livestock smell in here and Jaeger counted that from the small sample he had seen playing, there must be hundreds of skygoats all making their nests within this giant among mountains.

"Is this the only mountain where skygoats live?" Jaeger asked. Pebbles didn't seem to indicate yes or no, but slowly broke speed before landing.

"Is this where you lived before you found me?" Again, Pebbles didn't worry himself with Jaeger's conversation. The light was significantly darker this far into the labyrinth of caves within the mountain.

The roof began to taper in lower, as Jaeger created a dull glow of light using the purified matter inside easily. He dismounted and walked alongside Pebbles, down the narrowing tunnel. Several other skygoats were walking further into the tunnel ahead of them, while Jaeger could occasionally hear the *clip clop* of hooves behind them too.

Eventually the tunnel began to open out into a particularly pungent cavern. Jaeger had spent his life growing up on a farm, but within the confines of a room that had probably never been cleaned, the evidence of long-term habitation was distinctly clear to the nostrils.

"Tell me you can smell that too?" Jaeger implored his companion. Pebbles snorted with amusement and nudged Jaeger playfully. The cavern opened up sharply, revealing an enormous natural chamber possibly as large as the emperor's throne room.

Jaeger increased the intensity of his glowing light, pushing the shadows away from every corner of the room. He could see over a dozen skygoats curled up peacefully towards the back of the room, while a steady influx continued to enter and settle into little nooks to lie down.

They were all visiting an enormous and ancient looking skygoat in the centre of the group, before finding their own space. Each new arrival approached the peaceful creature, nuzzling it affectionately and then settling down nearby.

Pebbles led Jaeger through the small gap they were all leaving to reach the majestic caprinae. When they reached it, Pebbles left Jaeger's side to nuzzle. He stepped forward and nudged the old creature gently with his horns, before licking its cheeks affectionately and dropping onto his front knees to curl heads with it, in what could only be described as a hug.

Jaeger realised that the ancient creature was a female, and that she appeared to be dying. She moved slowly in response to all of Pebbles gestures, acknowledging the love he was trying to show with peaceful acceptance. Jaeger remained a few steps back, aghast at the incredibly intimate experience he had been welcomed into.

Without thinking, he began harnessing purified matter to explore the ailment that was troubling the old girl. Pebbles sensed the action immediately, turning back towards Jaeger and shaking his horns with a sharp bleat.

Jaeger immediately refrained from any further action, releasing the invigorating power within him gently. As Pebbles stood back from her, he looked at Jaeger approvingly. Jaeger stepped forward slowly and then knelt down beside the dying caprinae. He realised that he had absolutely no idea how long skygoats lived for, Pebbles seemed so young that he had never bothered to think about it. Reaching out he stroked her lightly on her forehead. She seemed to respond well to the gesture, nudging towards Jaeger's hand approvingly.

He wasn't sure how long he sat with the ancient creature, but by the time he stood up again, he felt reassured that she would be just fine now and he had made his peace with her. It was a strange thought to have, knowing that he had only just arrived here and met the dying skygoat, but looking around the room Jaeger realised that was why they were all here.

Jaeger had known for a long time that Pebbles understood him, but it also seemed like the skygoats had their own way of communicating their thoughts and emotions to each other. For Jaeger that emotion was reassurance, and he had received it directly from the old skygoat in the centre of the room after patting her. He followed Pebbles to his own little space in the room and sat down with him quietly. Pebbles circled several times and then curled himself up on the floor beside Jaeger.

Jaeger wasn't sure how long they stayed down here, but over time, more and more skygoats continued to proceed into the chamber. They all first filed in towards the old matriarch to acknowledge her and be acknowledged, before finding their own little space to curl up in the room. At some stage he had drifted into sleep, resting against Pebbles. When he woke, he realised that the life was gone from the old skygoat in the centre of the room.

Pebbles was still asleep and snoring slightly as Jaeger looked around. He created the faintest glow, and with his eyes adjusted to the darkness he watched as several of the skygoats roused themselves quietly. One by one they all led themselves out of the room. There was no real urgency to rush Pebbles, so Jaeger leaned back into his snoring friend, patiently drifting off into his own thoughts of everyone back home.

His mind was immediately drawn to the townspeople who had died in the raid on West-Yield. He forced himself to remember the companions who had been killed in the jungles while journeying towards Aridhold. He had never properly processed all of them or what they must have meant to their families and loved ones. Jaeger had been living his life from one adventure to the next for quite a long time now, and had finally stopped to realise how much he missed home.

He wanted to see his family to remind himself they were okay. Deep down something told him that they were. He wanted to get back to Conorbatia as soon as he possibly could to see Aema, something deep down told him that she might not be so okay. It had been a growing concern he felt after leaving.

He felt Pebbles stir suddenly and rouse himself from sleep. Pebbles looked around the room, reorienting himself. He seemed to gather quite quickly that the old skygoat he had come here for had passed away now. Without any communication, Pebbles slowly picked himself up, leading Jaeger out from the chamber and back into the open world again.

The flight back to the other mountain was more subdued and less exciting. Jaeger wouldn't have described it as a sad ride, but neither he nor Pebbles felt that it was particularly necessary to communicate or be playful. Jaeger remained in his own thoughts for most of the time they spent gliding through the powerful winds of the peaks. He had realised something that he was quite sure he had noticed before and was hoping to find Salmor to discuss it when they returned.

He found the old monk not far from the entrance to the wave rock-face. Salmor was patiently busy in his own little world, but drew himself out of it when he saw Jaeger approaching.

"Good evening, Jaeger," he greeted.

"Good evening Salmor."

"You have had an eventful day I can see" the old monk noted observantly.

"We both have yes, Pebbles took me to his own peak among these mountains to share something with me" Jaeger explained.

"Ah yes, the skygoats have their own private habitat among the Thin Air Peaks and our young friend here showed you today. I was taken to this mountain a long time ago when I first arrived in the peaks, it is a very spiritual place."

"Yes, it definitely had that feel about it," Jaeger agreed. "I was actually hoping I would find you when I was leaving. I was reminded of something that I have been observing for a long time now."

"Yes, and you have found me," Salmor added.

"I have," Jaeger agreed, there was a brief pause in conversation as Jaeger realised Salmor had contributed all that he intended to. "Well, it has to do with what lots of people call a gut feeling. Except that I seem to have it for a lot of different things."

"You are talking about foresight Jaeger. It is something unique to the monks that are drawn to this place."

"So, you are saying that we all have the ability to see the future?" Jaeger queried.

"I am saying that nobody, not even you, would find this place without that foresight of knowing that you needed to come here," Salmor clarified.

"And this foresight? It seems like it can apply to a lot more than just feeling the compulsion to seek out the Thin Air Peaks. It has seemed like I could tell when something is wrong, even when there is nothing nearby that I could possibly be reading into. It sometimes feels like I have been in danger when I have been."

"That would be consistent with the foresight," Salmor confirmed.

"How many ways is it possible? Would it be possible to know that enemies are nearby? Or even that I am about to have a sword swung at my head?" Jaeger could remember many occasions when he first began fighting. He had remembered clearly after some battles that he had known every time he needed to raise his sword, or duck, to avoid being struck.

"A rather crude example that I have no experience with, but yes. The foresight that monks are all innately connected to, is the knowledge that this place high up in these mountains is where we were always meant to be. It most definitely holds a connection to the wellbeing and safety of loved ones or anything you care about. I understand the stories from your country about blind mystics that can look into mirrors and see the futures of others walking inside of them. But the foresight is much closer to what you have been picking up on all these years, it is your 'gut feeling' that has consistently been proven to be right."

"What if my gut feeling was telling me that I need to return home to The Plateau urgently?" Jaeger asked.

"Does it?"

"It sometimes seems that way." Jaeger added a little defensively.

"You no doubt have foresight Jaeger, but it is important to let it guide you, not try to manipulate it. Like I said, we are not mystics who can conjure up visions on demand. We feel what we feel when it comes to us, and you can trust that feeling when it does."

"Thank you, Salmor. That was an excellent explanation and advice," Jaeger said genuinely.

"Don't act so surprised," the old monk added with a hint of good humour.

Jaeger laughed and left Salmor to go back to what he was doing. It was now dark and both Pebbles and Jaeger had had a very big day. They made their way back through the thick forest to the tall wave of rock towards their room. Pebbles was still quite subdued from their visit to the mountain of the skygoats and the ancient skygoat they had stayed with in her last hours. By the time they found their beds the two were completely exhausted.

"Thanks for taking me to your mountain today," Jaeger called out pleasantly once he had climbed into his bed.

Pebbles bleated pleasantly back at Jaeger,

circling his tail several times in his own bed and prodding it with his hooves in his usual bedtime ritual. Eventually after twirling around over and over again until getting it just right, Pebbles curled down and settled in a comfortable position.

"Good night" Jaeger leaned back after he was done watching in amusement. Pebbles yawned in response and then closed his eyes. Moments later they were both fast asleep.

14 SILO'S REACH

Things had settled a little following the confrontation with Silo in front of Justin's street. Aema hadn't actually had the chance to seek out Justin again, but heard that his resistance was still hanging in there in the city. Messages had also been passing back and forth freely between the college and the stewardship of Conorbatia. Aema had not been invited to hear these discussions, but she had at least been told that the steward and the soldiers in the city had the full support of Clouds College.

Beyond that, professor Sharelle had assured her that she should simply be grateful that college management had agreed not to sanction her and her friends. The trouble they had caused had called for even stricter limitations on students within the college leaving. All students had been advised to treat the environment beyond the campus as hostile, and somehow the obvious exception to the rule; Kostian, had not been formally addressed by the professors.

What had been left to fill this large void in time and freedom was a very unpleasant feeling. Aema continued to spend more and more time alone down by the creek in her own private retreat. Here she had begun to suffer from a persistent sense of melancholy and loneliness. There was something profoundly unsatisfying to spending time with her friends, when the only thing she wanted was to have Jaeger here with her by the creek. She reviewed this thought and corrected herself slightly, there was no knowing how alone she might feel if she didn't at least have her friends. The problem was that they were still no suitable substitute for what was missing.

To make matters worse, Jates was clearly aware of her favourite little retreat now. He had become a little more comfortable recently with the fact that he was seeking her out there to show his interest. This did not completely justify the constant interruption, but Aema had recently found that these little disruptions were drawing her out of her melancholy ever so slightly. Eventually, Aema had made up her mind that she would seek out her friends' advice again on this topic to get their thoughts.

Nasgro and Odette walked ahead of their small group as they left the lecture theatre for Alternate Applications of Magic. Everybody seemed happy to move off in their own directions, giving Aema the best opportunity she would get to speak quietly alone with Lisle. Jates had promised to get off her case for good if she just came out with him for one drink. And despite all of her instincts, Aema hoped that it might help to go somewhere without thinking about how much she missed Jaeger.

"Lisle," Aema called as everybody was breaking in their own directions. Lisle and Berran turned back towards her. "I kind of need to chat and get your advice on something," Aema began tentatively. Berran looked confused, Lisle didn't.

"Go on," Lisle encouraged with a slight smirk.

"I have been seriously considering going for that drink with Jates," Aema explained. Berran scoffed, his eyes looked like they were going to pop out of his head.

"Did I miss some joke you girls have had going?" he asked incredulously.

"Quiet you," Lisle shushed him. "You have missed out on the fact that it hasn't been easy for Aema this year not having Jaeger here."

"Oh, sorry Aema" Berran apologized.

"It's fine, and you are right. Going on a date with somebody I don't like is probably not the smartest way to deal with things either."

"Not just somebody you don't like," Berran started again. "Jates! I think terrorizing Silo the way you have been all year, has probably been a much healthier method of processing your loss," he continued to joke.

"Berran, enough!" Lisle scolded, Aema had never heard her use her voice above a soft murmur before. "It doesn't matter who it is, Aema has a right to start thinking about herself as open to meeting someone new."

"I'm not saying that she would be doing anything wrong, but we're not exactly in mourning. Jaeger might still come back soon." Aema felt the same heart-wrenching hope that she had been experiencing all year when Berran said this. She didn't speak but Berran seemed to somehow realise as he watched her react.

"I think we all hope that he does Berran, but I don't think this is healthy. Aema if you want to go on a date with Jates, I support you."

"Yeah, me too," Berran added contritely.

"Thanks guys, I haven't even made up my mind though. I just wanted to have this chat before I do. He wants me to meet him at The Pilgrim's Oasis this evening."

"Well, if you do decide to go you have my full support Aema," Lisle reiterated. "But only on one condition."

Aema felt immediate regret as Jates offered her a seat in the dead centre of his friends. Kostian and Faline were now sitting right beside her. Lisle had been surprisingly supportive of Aema getting out, for what unfortunately could only be called a date. Both her and Berran however, had insisted that Berran came along discretely. At first as a chaperone, but after a little discussion about the etiquette of the whole situation, they agreed it would be better if he just came in with Aema. Berran had found his own little corner and now settled down quite happily by himself with a beer.

The Pilgrim's Oasis wasn't as busy as usual. Aema noted that along with Kostian, Faline, and the rest of Jates' friendship circle, there was also a number of Donagarn's private security hovering nearby. The sense of dread and awkwardness was even worse when Aema recognized that one of the mercenaries was the same one that had tried to intimidate her and Dinara recently in Conorbatia's shopping district.

"Can I get you something to drink?" Jates offered.

"Oh, I'll just start with water for now," Aema responded, trying her best to look comfortable.

"That doesn't sound very sociable," Kostian observed, as Jates went to the bar. Aema felt a sudden impulse to get up and leave.

"Don't be cheeky Kostian," Faline luckily intervened. The two of them had become an item at some point before the start of second year. Aema didn't even know where to start processing that one, she knew that Faline and Jaeger had grown up together in West-Yield and had been quite close at one point in time.

"I'm just saying, Jates here has brought her to a tavern with us but she doesn't want to have a drink," Kostian continued.

"Perhaps you should buy all your dad's mercenaries a drink then Kostian. You brought all of them to the tavern too," Aema retorted. She was now comfortable with one quick argument and an excuse to get up and leave.

"They're working, you came here to socialize. Supposedly." Kostian added.

"*They*, are not even allowed on campus grounds," Aema said sharply.

"Who says they're not?" Kostian argued. "There have never been any laws until now to say that the only people allowed on campus are students and staff."

"But there are now. Worley made it perfectly clear at the start of this year that your father's private security was not welcome on campus grounds, Kostian.

You have deliberately broken those rules by bringing them here." Aema saw the hired thugs get up from their seats and move closer at this last comment, she decided that after the next response from Kostian she would leave.

"Don't you think that is just a little bit authoritarian Aema?" Faline joined in. "You're supporting a rule that singles out one person bringing visitors to Cloud's College while everybody else can."

"No, it doesn't!" Aema could feel herself losing control of her temper. "Kostian can bring you here any time he wants. The rule is to stop him from bringing his hired thugs onto college grounds to intimidate students the way they have been terrorizing everybody in the city."

"I think you need to educate yourself a little more before you make statements like that Aema," Faline said in her most patronizing tone. "Donagarn has guaranteed employment for almost everybody in Conorbatia now in one way or another. At the same time, he is ensuring public order in the city after Emperor Hildebrante took nearly every soldier we had and sent them south."

"Public order!?" Aema nearly screamed. "Those mercenaries have taken advantage of the lack of soldiers, to bully farmers into selling their livelihoods and intimidate citizens on every street corner. Emperor Hildebrante would have been better off conscripting every last one of them if he had known this is what would happen when he left Conorbatia." The entire table had stood up and Kostian's mercenaries were now moving around the group behind Aema. Kostian had gotten out of his seat too, and now stood smirking behind Faline with his hand on her shoulder.

"Again Aema, that is a really ignorant thing to say. Do you know what a slippery slope it is to live in an empire that can forcibly conscript citizens or mercenaries into the military against their will? At least Donagarn employs and trains mercenaries of their free will, he has already promised to step in and donate assistance to the military if needed."

"Donate if needed!? It's needed Faline. You didn't see the frontline last year. Kostian did. Your boyfriend spent the entire trip sucking up to the mad battle-mage and torturing scaleskins with him. Whatever bubble you're living in, every man who could fight has already been needed for a long time now"

"Mad battle-mage? So now you insult war heroes too?" Faline scoffed contemptuously. "I think that says everything I need to know about arguing with you, Aema."

"Charnel was a cruel pig, both him and Kostian were as bad as the scaleskins during that trip. Jaeger nearly thrashed your boyfriend for what he di-"

The fist came out of nowhere as Kostian stepped forward and struck Aema so hard she blacked out. The next thing she saw was Berran tangled in a sea of arms and bodies as Kostian's friends restrained him.

"If Jaeger were here, he'd kill you," Berran roared as he struggled. At the second mention of Jaeger's name Kostian snapped again, striking Berran repeatedly while he was restrained.

This was all the invitation Donagarn's mercenaries needed. After vacating their discrete corner when the argument had begun, they now piled in from all angles, dragging Berran to the ground. The privatised arrest was a scene that had almost become normalized in Conorbatia, but no student had ever witnessed it on Clouds' soil before. The entire tavern went silent, as Berran had his hands and ankles tied and was crudely dragged outside away from sight. Several more mercenaries then blocked the entrance to the tavern so that nobody could follow them or witness what they were doing to Berran.

Kostian had relaxed how, he calmly watched as Berran disappeared outside while Aema slowly collected herself to her feet. "He will have to stand trial for assault," Kostian remarked passively with a smirk, watching the terror in Aema's eyes as she tried to get away from The Pilgrim's Oasis as quickly as she could.

15 THE WRATH OF CLOUDS

Lisle couldn't get to her door quick enough to stop the banging. When she opened it, she saw Aema, eyes red from crying and a nasty bruise on her mouth.

"Aema! What happened?" Lisle nearly started crying too.

"Berran, they bashed Berran and took him!" Aema cried. "We need to stop them now, they said he was going to be punished."

"Punished for what? Aema what happened to your face?" Lisle tried to gain some footing of what they were talking about.

"KOSTIAN!" Aema cried. "He hit me when I was arguing with his stupid girlfriend, Faline. How could Jaeger have ever liked her? How could he leave me?" She bawled. She was on the verge of hysterics.

Lisle stepped forward and hugged Aema. She knew this had been a long time coming and felt some degree of anger towards Jaeger now. She felt nothing short of fury towards Kostian. She hugged and soothed

Aema for a few minutes while the sobbing hysterics ran its course.

"You're going to need to explain everything that happened to me from the beginning," Lisle told her.

Lisle had immediately gathered Berran's friends, as well as Dinara and Odette once Aema had finished her story. They were all gathered in Ellis' room discussing urgently what they were going to do.

"We will need to speak to the professor about this immediately," Nasgro pondered. "Donagarn's mercenaries have clearly known to stay off campus grounds until now. The College has stayed out of Donagarn's business in the city, but Worley will have to step in if they are abducting students from the campus."

"And if Worley takes too long?" Lisle demanded.

"Then we pay Kostian and Donagarn a visit tonight," Nasgro assured her. "We can give Worley an ultimatum, either he steps in and gets Berran back immediately, or we do it ourselves."

"Nasgro!" Odette gasped. "You could get expelled if you speak to the professor like that!"

"I don't care. Our friend has been bashed and abducted because of Kostian and his father's mercenaries. Kostian will be expelled for this, not me," Nasgro assured her confidently.

They decided not to waste any more time, and Nasgro led the group urgently to the professor's home on campus. Thankfully, Worley took no convincing that Cloud's College needed to act fast while one of their students was being detained by Donagarn's thugs. Worley wasted no time gathering the other professors and outlining what they were about to do.

Within the hour, the head professor of Clouds College was leading a small regiment of mages from the campus grounds and into the city. Worley had explained his plans with ruthless efficiency. He had no intention of deviating to the palace first to discuss their situation with the steward. Instead, he cut a clear path through Conorbatia Square, beyond the palace, and on to Donagarn's heavily guarded estate. Clouds College had been provoked into war.

"You can't come in here," Donagarn's estate guards informed Worley nervously.

The head professor of Cloud's College was trailed by no less than twenty other master mages along with Aema, Nasgro, Ellis, Odette, Dinara and Lisle. Aema and Lisle looked like they were waiting for any opening they could get to jump past professor Worley and tear out the guard's throat.

"Open the gate, son," Worley ordered the guard clearly. "Whatever he's paying you, it's not worth your life." The professor wasn't mucking around, and Aema felt just satisfied enough to let Worley continue running things.

The guard told two of his peers to run ahead and send word to Donagarn about what was happening. He then turned back towards the less-than-impressed mages, opening the gates to the estate. The procession marched in past the guards and deeper along the exquisite cobbled roads towards the mansion. They were quickly beyond the view of the emperor's palace, which stood out clearly opposite Donagarn's estate across the city square.

When they reached the end of the long road into the estate, they found Donagarn standing there with a small detachment of nearly twenty guards. Kostian and Faline were also with him, as more security trickled in from all over the private grounds, clearly responding to a distress call that had been put out.

"What can I do for you professor?" Donagarn almost purred as he greeted Worley.

"Your son brought mercenaries into my college this evening. They left with one of my students, against his will."

"The safety of my son has become one of my highest priorities recently. Without the Emperor's strong military presence, this city has become very dangerous professor."

Worley didn't bat an eye. "I'm not here for your political charade Donagarn, you will return my student immediately if you value your wellbeing." Worley then turned his gaze to Kostian who was standing behind his father with his girlfriend. "Your son will remain here with you from now on. You are expelled from Cloud's College boy." Faline gasped with outrage. Kostian was a picture of devastation, looking at his father almost for confirmation.

"I will do nothing for any man who comes onto my estate and threatens me," Donagarn replied confidently. "Remove yourself from my lands, we are done talking."

"Berran," Worley insisted. "Now!"

Donagarn inclined his head towards his head of security. Two guards immediately stepped forward to arrest Worley. A shock passed into both of them as they laid hands on the professor and they fell to the ground dead. Worley's eyes remained fixed on Donagarn the whole time.

"Alright men, just relax," Donagarn placated the rest of his security detail. There were now more than a hundred mercenaries outside his mansion, many of them had arrived behind the professor and now surrounded the mages.

"You want your student, right?" Donagarn reasoned with Worley. The professor gave no word or movement and continued to stare at Donagarn. With another nod to his head of security, two mercenaries dragged Berran out from inside the mansion. He had been beaten viciously.

"You assaulted him," Worley noted quietly.

"I can't undo any harm that may have come to him when he attacked my son professor. You have come onto my property for him and threatened me, and I have given you what you asked for. There is very little more to discuss."

Worley seemed to consider the angle Donagarn had taken before nodding acceptance. "Any man associated with Silo who steps foot on my grounds again will be arrested Donagarn, along with you. Do you understand me?"

"I do. If my son is no longer welcome on your campus then I see no reason for me to worry about his protection there anymore." Kostian remained silent, a tear rolled down his expressionless face.

Berran joined Lisle and his friends who wrapped around him. Worley turned his procession away to leave.

"You can't just expel one of the students at Clouds College without giving him a chance to defend himself!" Faline burst out as they walked away. "This is a complete abuse of power!"

Worley looked like he could have been amused if he wasn't so furious, and briefly scoffed to himself before turning to Kostian. "Did you punch another student tonight at the College Tavern?"

Kostian looked bewildered put on the spot, "Yes," he admitted "but Jaeger punched me last year on a field trip and never had any case to answer for. From what I remember he was thoroughly praised during the graduation ceremony and was never asked to even explain himself."

"He never punched you," Aema gritted through clenched teeth. Worley raised a placating hand to Aema and looked back to Kostian.

"You are expelled from Cloud's College for assaulting this girl this evening and bringing your father's thugs onto my campus to kidnap students. If you or your father have any problem with this you are welcome to discuss it with me back at the College, where you will be immediately arrested for trespassing." Without another word, Worley led his small army of mages back down the long carriageway off the Silo estate.

Donagarn watched silently as the mages made their way beyond his gates, back towards their campus with their precious student. He then looked sideways at his sniffling son.

"Oh, stop your crying Kostian, that college will belong to me by the end of the year."

As he turned and left the front of his mansion, he paused for a moment as he passed his head of security. "The silencing begins tonight."

16 THE MAGE AND THE MONK

Jaeger tried to spend as much time as possible among the other monks now. Since his visit with Pebbles to the surrounding peaks, he had realised that he had gained a great deal from his journey, but would probably not be here much longer. He had however committed much more to his regular routine of meditation, harnessing and becoming familiar with purified matter, while using it to interact with and sculpt the life that existed above the peaks.

He was also making a much greater effort to get to know all of the monks that lived up here. The powers they possessed were phenomenal. Even without the training that Jaeger had received at Clouds College, the monks could harness immense amounts of purified matter for healing and growth. Jaeger sensed that they also possessed powerful auras that could protect them if they ever did have to defend themselves against hostile magic users.

It felt like an incredible waste having all this

ability tucked away at the roof of the continent. Just looking around him at the entrance to the wave rockface outside their living quarters, Jaeger saw the potential to protect entire armies standing around him, and right now all of that potential was basically being used for gardening.

These monks could hold a frontline without casualties. Short of being decapitated, soldiers could fight alongside each other without ever dying. Battle-mages could support their armies while protected by the defensive auras of the monks beside them. Their healing and their ability to ward off DarkLand matter alone, could turn the tide of countless battles.

Jaeger considered all of these possibilities as he walked with Delphine. They were visiting the special location where they had both created life from the fallen tree months earlier. He wondered how devious he would feel to try to discuss leaving the peaks and helping The Plateau with her. For some reason he had contained all his discussions about assisting The Plateau to Salmor.

He wasn't quite sure that Salmor made collective decisions for the monks, it wasn't really how things worked here. But at the very least he knew that it would be disrespectful to go behind his back. No matter how he turned it over in his head, he would be undermining the old monk and the entire way of life of the monks if he asked them all individually. By having multiple conversations, he would essentially be poaching them into military service.

"He's growing nicely don't you think?" Delphine asked.

"Is it a he?" Jaeger asked, looking at what had

once been a tiny sapling not so long ago.

"I think so," she smiled. "And your tree is a she. His mother," she added.

Jaeger considered the two trees thoughtfully, Delphine and himself had encouraged them to entwine with each other symbiotically. Delphine's smaller graft now reached up towards its parent, wrapping arms around the two most powerful branches above it, while more encircled the older tree's trunk in an affectionate embrace. Jaeger's tree now reciprocated with several new branches reaching down to the younger tree, supporting him at several points.

"A nice thought," Jaeger mused. "A lot of those branches grew without our direction," he noted, pointing to the several hugs and points of contact.

"They are sentient Jaeger. Can you not feel the bond she has formed with her son?"

"I can see it," Jaeger replied.

"No feel it," she laughed, placing a hand on the sapling's trunk.

"I'm not certain so I'm going to say I can't," Jaeger admitted.

"That's okay, you have only been here for a few months, the relationship we have with everything in the peaks grows over time."

"I'm not sure that I will have that time," Jaeger began, wondering if now was the time to have a more direct conversation with Delphine. Just as he paused on this thought, Salmor appeared down the path from the far end of the woods.

"Ah, your own special little grove," Salmor acknowledged the trees he had witnessed both Delphine and Jaeger plant.

"Good morning," Delphine smiled.

"Morning Salmor," Jaeger inclined his head, Pebbles' roused himself from his nap at the foot of the trees.

"I see our young soul here is pleased to have given you a glimpse into the natural habitat of the aves-caprinae," Salmor smiled at Pebbles appreciatively. "They lead a remarkable life with us up here in the peaks."

"It certainly was a treat to see them all," Jaeger agreed.

"Well said young soul. You are beginning to settle in this place Jaeger. The trees, the caprinae, they are all very happy to have you here."

Jaeger considered the genuine compliment for a few moments before he could bring himself to say anything. Salmor showed no signs of his normally contradictory nature and was trying very hard to acknowledge Jaeger's progress. Unfortunately, it didn't change reality, Jaeger realised.

"I was actually just thinking this morning that I should start planning to return home soon," he admitted.

"But why?" Delphine blurted suddenly.

"Jaeger here is still very much attached to his home, and the troubles of his people," Salmor explained. Delphine looked confused.

"The Plateau is in danger, Delphine," Jaeger explained. "You know I was a student at Clouds College back there?"

"A first-year mage," Salmor added.

"Yes, like I said, a student. But I grew up on The Plateau's western borders, and also have seen the southern frontline as a student at the college. Things are bad back home. Our people. Humans, halflings, the dwarves across the jungles, we are all in danger of being wiped off the face of this continent."

"We are?" Delphine looked distraught, Jaeger realised that for all the conversations he had been having with Salmor, the rest of the monks in the peaks were completely in the dark about their homelands."

"Every life has to work through its own struggles," Salmor reassured her. "Even these very special two trees here."

"Every life on this continent will have to contend with demons soon," Jaeger corrected him. "Eventually even in these peaks. Do you think that when they are done exterminating everything below, that they will tolerate all the purification of their evil matter up here?"

"This is terrible!" Delphine continued to become more distressed.

"Nobody said that life was meant to be a clean and easy path from beginning to end," Salmor insisted stubbornly.

"I don't disagree with you Sal, but I can't stay up here indefinitely where things are easiest."

"It sounds like you are yet to realise that staying in these peaks is actually the hardest option for you," Salmor pointed out philosophically.

"Okay," Jaeger relaxed. He didn't want to become harsh with the old monk, and he didn't want to distress Delphine any more than he already had. "I think I'll meditate on that thought."

Pebbles trotted across to Jaeger and the two of them left to venture deeper into the forest. Jaeger felt a war of frustration and contemplation as he navigated his way through the thick cluster of trees. The peaks were meant to be a place of peace and harmony.

He saw this peace in all of the monks he spent time with, but for some reason he rarely felt any himself. He felt constantly frustrated by Salmor, while everybody else seemed to be able to live in the moment and get along.

There was a time in Conorbatia where he didn't feel like he fitted in with the masses of people all urgently trying to serve their own selfish needs. He had even wondered if he belonged at Clouds College at first when he had clashed with Kostian.

He was reminded of what Worley had to say about the attitudes of students when they first met. Ironically it was here, in a place where everybody was good natured and accepting, that Jaeger felt like he was the most out-of-place.

Perhaps he was being a little hard on himself. He enjoyed the time that he spent with everybody, getting to know them and listening intently to the broad variety of monks who had come here. But even then, Jaeger realised that he seemed to be the only one interested in their lives before the Thin Air Peaks.

He was intrigued by where they had lived, and what they had done before they felt the compulsion to begin the pilgrimage to a place they knew nothing about. It wasn't exactly disharmony that was his problem, he just knew that he thought differently to the monks that called this place home.

Pebbles nudged Jaeger playfully as he drifted too deeply into these thoughts. Pebbles and Jaeger had pushed deep in no general direction into the forest.

Above them, the canopy of the trees was thick and very little light could pierce it. Pebbles seemed to have the right idea, it was a great time to go for a little flight around the peaks. They just needed to find a break in the trees above them now to get free of the forest.

Eventually they reached the very edge of the peaks and the forest at the same time. The direction they had been walking blanketed the mountaintop with trees, right up to the cliff's edge. Looking out at the peaks beyond, Jaeger took in the beauty of the altitude they were at. There were always more peaks out there.

He wondered if anybody had made a point of mapping them or even just counting them. Cartography didn't appear to be a profession that mattered to the monks up here. Jaeger decided that if he ever had decided to stay, that this would have been his purpose.

With a run-up and a powerful leap, Pebbles carried them both into the freezing winds beyond the forest. They both traveled further south than they had before, passing peak after peak until they were eventually clear of the last of the Thin Air Peaks. The lands below were still rich and green like they had been at the northern plains below the feet of the mountains. Eventually Jaeger nudged Pebbles to drift left, moving east across the landscape below.

They must have been flying for hours when the gradually shifting terrain suddenly disappeared into lifelessness. They had drifted east from the peaks until they had eventually reached the great southern desolation.

This enormous longitudinal stretch of land was a catchment for DarkLand matter. The desolation spanned all the way from the DarkLand Portal at the pole in the south, to the foothills of The Plateau where the razed fortress of Grantanmar used to be.

Seeing the desolation so far away from home shocked Jaeger. He knew that it existed from his studies at school and Clouds College, but it was very different to see it continue on in such a distant part of the continent.

The magnitude of the damage that The DarkLand Portal had caused to his continent, was on a scale that he could barely comprehend. Entire races of evil creatures attacked his people because of it, and the portion of land that had been irreparably destroyed by exposure to DarkLand matter was enormous.

Disgusted, Jaeger nudged Pebbles to turn back. He had seen enough and wanted to return to the purified bubble above the continent again. He knew that he wouldn't stay there forever like the monks, he simply wanted to enjoy the counterpoint to this waste of everything for a little longer.

It was nearly night time when the two of them finally circled the wave rock-face where they were living. Back in their room Jaeger watched Pebbles fondly as the skygoat circled his own bed several times before finally settling down and curling up.

The next morning Jaeger woke up less conflicted. His time in the Thin Air Peaks had benefitted his skills beyond his greatest expectations, but amongst the monks he knew that he was not one of them. Salmor's self-assured refusal to leave the peaks now frustrated Jaeger, and just like he had felt an overwhelming determination to find the peaks months earlier, he now felt the same overwhelming determination to return home.

The Plateau had been struggling terribly when he left. His parents had been distraught when he had visited them and told them where he was going next, and he also missed Aema. The entire time he had been with the monks, Jaeger had felt a sense of urgency and impatience to see her again. Deep down he felt like anything more than a week or two had been too long to leave her.

His journey had now extended beyond half a year since he had said goodbye to her in Conorbatia. Good or bad, whatever was going to happen to The Plateau, Jaeger knew that he needed to be with Aema for it. He needed to leave.

He found Salmor meditating silently on the furthest edge of an enormous rock-shard that protruded from the peak like a long platform above the sky. The view was like nothing to be seen anywhere else, although Salmor's favourite seat looked dangerously precarious; sitting cross-legged at the rock's edge. The winds were icy cold, but Salmor looked perfectly comfortable stripped to the waist, looking out at what one could easily be convinced was the edge of the world.

"You've come to tell me you're leaving," the monk told Jaeger without turning to see who was behind him.

"The time is more than overdue," Jaeger replied.

"Eventually here, you will realise that there is no such thing Jaeger, we find this place because we are meant to stay."

"I don't think we were ever meant to stay here permanently Sal. Maybe the first monk who discovered this place was meant to spend his lifetime here, maybe he was meant to show others what he had learned. But like it or not, everybody here used to be a part of this world, and if the world falls apart below you, then eventually it will find you here too."

"If that is how it is meant to end, then that may be what happens." Salmor considered philosophically.

"So, you would welcome the end of the world just because it doesn't conflict with your beliefs?" Jaeger asked incredulously.

"We will, and you will too once you have had time to adjust and truly understand why you are here." Something about Salmor's self-assuredness was beginning to grate Jaeger.

He could never have used the word *smug*, Salmor had always been too good natured to be guilty of that word, but *deluded* had started to creep into Jaeger's head. He suddenly felt incapable of hearing another word of the monk's teachings or philosophy.

"Listen to me," Jaeger annunciated clearly. "I'm going to leave. I'm going to take the skills and powers I have learned here and do some *real* good for this world with them. More good than everybody here combined has ever done. This lifestyle of 'enlightenment' you all live is selfish. More selfish than anything I have ever seen back home.

While you hide in these peaks serving your own desire to enjoy peace and tranquility, you leave everybody below you to war and suffering." Jaeger was finally starting to get Salmor's attention, but he wasn't finished.

"There are noble men Salmor, soldiers, who will not know a day of peace in their adult lives. Those men will die for the peace of others in this world. Those men would never in a million years trade their sacrifice for this life of avoidance that you live.

"*That* is enlightenment to me, to sacrifice everything you have to give, to allow others to have the peace that you enjoy so much up here. Meanwhile you remain aloof to it all, selfishly hoarding your powers for your own personal gain."

There was a look of hurt on Salmor's face that nearly broke Jaeger's heart to see. The saintly old man had a sense of vulnerability about him that Jaeger had seen before, but had never fully understood until this moment.

"I didn't realise that is what you saw when you look at me every day, Jaeger," he said eventually.

"It's not," Jaeger tried to apologise. "I just think you have got it wrong. I don't believe you were meant to stay here forever when you found this place."

"I'm sorry Jaeger, I can see that I haven't listened to you if you have felt this frustrated with me. I have not considered what you have said, I have only corrected you whenever you suggested we leave this place."

"You're a very good man, Salmor."

"Good but selfish," Salmor laughed.

"Perhaps not deliberately," Jaeger offered. "I have to leave Salmor, urgently."

"I know Jaeger. That much I *can* see."

Jaeger prepared himself and Pebbles efficiently after his farewells with Sal and the other monks he had lived with. He had grown fond of all of them, but it was time to leave. The journey home was going to be long and indirect.

Jaeger knew that before he could see Aema, he would need to first visit Aridhold where he hoped his sword would be ready with some very special runes engraved. From there, West-Yield would be the perfect stop-off along the way back to Conorbatia.

The prospect of having his companion Pebbles wherever he went, suddenly made regular visits back to his family in West-Yield far more practical, Jaeger chuckled to himself. *That's if I am even welcome back at Cloud's College*, he realised, *or if there is even anything left of The Plateau*, Jaeger considered sickeningly.

It didn't seem possible with what he had learned about his ability to sense the future, although there was no guarantee that Jaeger's urgent desire to return home wasn't exactly that. It didn't feel like there was any more time to lose.

"Ready to see the world buddy?" he asked Pebbles.

The young skygoat bleated enthusiastically and motioned to Jaeger to hurry up, flicking his head towards his back.

"I'll take that as a yes then," Jaeger patted Pebbles, and leapt onto his back.

"Let's go mate," he patted the great beast again vigorously.

He was amazed at how much Pebbles had grown in the recent months. He had become larger than many of the other caprinae in the peaks while Jaeger had been there, and was the size of a large warhorse now. His enormous shoulders rumbled beneath Jaeger's hands, as Pebbles commenced his run-up before leaping into the sky.

17 THE NIGHT OF SILENCING

The sound of broken windows pierced the empty streets throughout the night. Donagarn's mercenaries had informed the entire city that a curfew was in effect, and the eerily quiet city was now punctuated by the same sounds of vandalism over and over again. Neighbours watched fearfully out of darkened windows at the screams and shouting, as entire families were dragged from their homes.

It was hard for the citizens of Conorbatia to tell what the victims had done to cross Silo. Some of them were simply farmers or store owners who had already sold their livelihoods to Donagarn. Most though were parents and relatives of students at Clouds College. The College was not a small institution, but Donagarn was determined that every student there would have a family member detained, to ensure that their precious mages and professors never undermined his progress again.

He didn't need everyone on his list alive. Donagarn's security detail had been making notes for him about those who had been heard speaking out against Silo. As long as they weren't needed as ransom for the college, he had elected to have them eliminated instead. One way or another he would be putting a stop to the disruptive voices in and around Conorbatia. Tonight had been a long time in the planning.

Julia scaled the side wall above her bedroom window easily like she had done hundreds of times before. The chimney was her favourite seat in the whole world, looking out above the city at night as more and more lights were extinguished in Conorbatia. She remembered this time to put the plank of wood that she kept on the roof down before she sat. She had been told off more times than she cared to remember for blackening the seat of her pants on the chimney.

Her older brother, Nasgro, was somewhere out to the east living at the magical college. He had promised her she would be able to study there too when she was old enough. She remembered the day late last year, when he had told her that he knew how to perform the matter perception test himself. She had felt the force of his test almost immediately, and he promised her that she would be a powerful mage one day. In the meantime, she would have to settle for the title of the greatest spy in the city. Or maybe assassin was a better description for her unique set of skills.

Out in the night she heard a window break, it was a long way away but she could swear she had heard windows breaking earlier too. There must have been a lot of torches in the streets a few blocks away, she could see the glow standing out against the darkness in the rest of the city. Gradually, she began to hear more windows breaking, closer to home now and more clearly. The light of torches in the streets could be seen in several locations, some of them were moving closer to her own street.

Julia contemplated climbing back down to her bedroom and going to sleep before she got in trouble. She was not supposed to be on the roof and her parents had said they were running out of patience having to tell her. At the same time the torches and breaking windows seemed like a big deal, what good was being the greatest spy in the city if you didn't report your discoveries. Maybe she could climb back into her room and then tell her parents that she had heard the windows breaking from her bed? She could tell them it was because of her superhuman hearing instead of admitting she had been sitting on the chimney again.

"Mum, dad! There are torches in the streets all around the city! They are breaking windows!" she shook her parents awake.

"What? Who is in the street darling?" her mother asked.

"I don't know, but there are windows breaking all over the city, they're everywhere."

"Go to the basement," her father leapt out of bed. "Move, now!" he urged.

"But don't you want to know how I heard them?" Julia insisted.

"We know how you heard them," her father replied. "You were on the roof on that bloody chimney again." He grabbed her hand and started to pull her from the room.

"No, I have superhuman hearing," Julia

explained, but nobody was listening to her. Her parents both looked very concerned. Whatever information she had found, she knew she had spied something very important this time.

Her father picked her up and handed her to her mother. He then raced back to Julia's room which had the best view of the street outside, while her mother carried her down towards the basement. There was something exciting but terrifying about this at the same time. Seeing her parents respond the way they had meant that Julia had done something very helpful. It also made her feel like she wasn't sure she wanted to play this game anymore.

They had waited quietly in the cellar for an hour now. Julia was uncomfortable and felt like whatever they were waiting for was becoming very unpleasant.

"Quiet please, darling," her mother urged. "Listen Julia, I have another mission for you."

"Yes?"

"If the men with torches come here, I want you to hide between the barrels no matter what. Even if your father and I have to leave with them. Then once we are gone, you have to go to the college without a single person seeing you and tell your brother what is going on."

"I can do this tonight? Or do I have to wait until it's daytime again?" Julia checked.

"You can do this mission at night darling, but you have to make sure you get to Clouds College without anybody in the city seeing you," her mother insisted.

"That's easy," Julia laughed.

At that moment, the windows upstairs were broken and the door was kicked open. Julia's father picked up a knife, as voices could be heard moving loudly through the house. Julia slipped in between the barrels silently. The cellar door opened loudly and the voices could be heard clearly now.

"They're down here," one called, and she heard steps coming down into the cellar. A sharp cry was cutoff quickly and Julia saw her father step back into view with blood on his knife. "Kill him!" another voice called from the top of the stairs and several feet could be heard racing into the cellar.

For the rest of her life, Julia struggled to remember what she had heard next. But when the cellar was empty again and her parents were gone, she did remember that her mother had given her a mission of great importance. She needed to reach her brother.

18 THE ARID KING

King Borgisliege brooded over the losses he had allowed his people to suffer. They had continued to make progress flushing out breaches in the underway below his city, but the price of progress had risen again. Ever since he had joined the campaign and lost his general, the roachkin had evolved to manage the tactics of his marksdwarves. The only silver lining to that disaster was retrieving the bodies of every last dwarf who had died in the cavern where he had fought.

As he listened to reports from his mining captains, his mind could clearly visualize the roachkin that had leapt into the path between his marksdwarf and the demon-warlock he had killed. His enemies had fought ferociously but mindlessly while the creature lived, literally prepared to intercept a deadly bolt for their leaders. Battle-plans and assassination maneuvers had needed tweaking after that. Some days the reports came back, describing easy success in cleansing the tunnels. Other days reports would return of a new measure the enemy was taking to protect its leaders.

"This is a game of turn-for-turn strategy," Borgis concluded. "We will need to constantly evolve to stay in control of this situation."

"It truly is my king. We appear to have been one step ahead for the last few weeks at least," Kirranpick agreed.

"Yes, but we need to stay two steps ahead. We have increased the number of marksdwarves that accompany our mining teams recently, yes?"

"Correct."

"After initially raising more than one simultaneously, we managed for a period of time without the enemy intercepting our runic bolts from multiple angles at the same time."

"Yes, until they started watching for them," Kirranpick confirmed again.

"So, we need to anticipate what they will do next to curb our latest tactics. Any time that we allow a single roach to escape, we know that their warlocks are likely to find out what we did next that worked. Then they will come up with a fitting response, and as always, we go back and forth again. We may be winning this game of tactics more often, but it is a war of attrition nonetheless. We can't win any war of attrition with roaches."

"So, we will plan to stay at least two steps ahead of them from now on," his new general Berninghammer concluded.

"At least two," Borgis decreed. "And long-term I want our underway permanently sealed from further intrusion. Runemaster?"

"You and High King Fëadarliege," runemaster

Federsmith replied sagely. "His runesmith's have been working at this all year. With your leave, I will visit Runehold to discuss their progress now that I have completed Jaeger's runesword."

"As long as you take the bodyguards I provide to protect you, you are above needing my leave to travel wherever you like runemaster."

"I can do that," the runemaster conceded. "I will prepare to leave by the end of this week then."

By happy coincidence, an unexpected visitor arrived before the week was finished. Late one evening, Borgis was informed in his dining hall that Jaeger had returned and was waiting outside the rarely-used external gates of Aridhold.

"Why was he left to wait?" Borgisliege demanded.

"The guards said he looked different to the young man who departed Aridhold late last year"

"Of course he looks different! If he has arrived at the southern entrance then he has been living in the Thin Air Peaks this whole time!" Borgis complained. "Any man who turns up at the gates to Aridhold claiming to be Jaeger son of Tevin, is going to be Jaeger son of Tevin. And if he's not, I would still happily meet with him to kill him myself."

"As you say king," the messenger nodded, departing immediately.

"And ask for runemaster Federsmith to bring Jaeger's sword to me if he is not busy." The king added.

Borgisliege quickly finished the last of his meal and poured himself another dark ale to take with him before leaving for his throne room. Runemaster

Federsmith arrived in the throne room just before Jaeger, carrying his completed sword with him. The runic blade was sheathed, but even at a glance Borgisliege could tell that his runemaster was holding one of his finest creations.

"It took a while longer installing the runes into an already forged blade, but they are potent," the runemaster assured him. "The runes are derivative from the ones on our demon-killer bolts, although far more complex."

"This sword will prove to be incredibly formidable against demons." Borgis observed, turning the weapon in his hands without removing it from its sheath.

"It is a kingly gift Borgis."

"Then it will be a fitting gift. I continue remain in your debt runemaster." Borgis bowed sincerely.

"A good king isn't doing his job if he is not in debt to his runemaster," Federsmith laughed. "That or his job is too easy!"

"Well then I hope to one day be out of your debt," Borgis laughed with him.

At the end of the hall, the great doors to his throne room opened. Both the king and his runemaster looked up to see a lightly clothed man with a bushy beard enter. Alongside Jaeger, walked one of the enormous legendary aves-caprinae. The pair walked the length of the throne room confidently, Jaeger's hand held reassuringly on his beast's shoulders as they approached.

"Jaeger!" Borgis called to him, descending the steps from his throne to greet the young man. "They told me that they held you at our gates because you looked different. I thought it was an inexcusable mistake until now!" the king laughed.

"Completely understandable," Jaeger laughed with him. "I have not held a razor or many other luxuries since I last saw you. I'm looking forward to using one again."

"Are you sure? For a man your beard is quite impressive. Just needs a little treatment and maintenance, but it certainly has potential." Borgis noted appraisingly.

"I'm sure," Jaeger confirmed observing the dwarf king's own long beard. Several golden coils marked various stages of colour, as the beard descended to the king's belt. "I doubt it could ever rival a dwarf's and it's not quite me."

"Well, we can provide the razor and many other luxuries you have missed while you're here then. Will you be staying long?"

Jaeger appeared to consider the offer more seriously than seemed necessary. Borgisliege observed that the young man had changed in many more ways that his appearance while he had been away.

"I will stay for a day, possibly two if you can forgive my hastiness. It would be hard to explain but there is some urgency to me returning to The Plateau, my home town in particular."

"Stay as long or as briefly as you like if you are pressed for time Jaeger. We will have more opportunities to catch up again. In the meantime, I have something for you. Although, I was just discussing with runemaster Federsmith that I am already in his debt, so perhaps it would be fitting for him to present this to you."

189

Federsmith scoffed at the suggestion but didn't argue. Stepping forward wordlessly, the runemaster held the sheathed weapon up to Jaeger. The young man's eyes lit up with excitement.

"You have completed the runes on my sword" Jaeger murmured, lifting the weapon reverently from runemaster Federsmith's hands.

"Quite recently actually" Borgis confirmed. "The runemaster here was just discussing leaving for his next assignment this week."

"Finished this one only a few weeks ago" Federsmith agreed. "I'll be off to Runehold shortly now."

"What assignment do you have there if you don't mind me asking?" Jaeger asked.

"We are going to seal the tunnels and underground to permanently prevent future intrusion by the roachkin. With the right application of runic wards, even their demons shouldn't be able to break through into any new sections without paying with their lives. High King Fëadarliege has had his runesmiths working on it for a lot longer than me. So, I figured I would visit to get up to speed on their progress, rather than start from scratch."

"That makes sense" Jaeger agreed, he had stopped looking at the weapon politely to listen.

"Take a look at the blade Jaeger, that's what we're here to show you" Federsmith insisted.

Jaeger finally drew the sword as he was instructed. The indentation that had been left in the blade when it was initially forged was now filled. One large sentence of runes had been engraved along the length of the new metal that had been added to it, with many smaller runes almost too minute to read, interspersed between them. The entire blade held a slightly radiant quality to it that Jaeger could swear was either a burnt sienna red, or turquoise blue, depending on each time he glanced back down at it.

"The blade is magnificent. I can never thank either of you enough for this."

"A small token of my gratitude, Jaeger," Borgis said without the slightest trace of exaggeration.

"Thank you again." Jaeger knew better than to argue about Borgis' concept of his debt to Jaeger.

"Now, you interrupted dinner when I found out you had arrived. Would you care to join us there for a drink or two and a bite to eat?"

"I won't say no to either," Jaeger laughed, shaking the king's hand and leaving the throne room with both Borgisliege and Federsmith.

Jaeger looked at himself appraisingly in the mirror. Despite the several small cuts he had incurred, his face looked fresh and lively after the extensive shave. It felt rather 'fresh' too as he washed it again. The sensation of his dirty beard was now gone, replaced with a raw stinging that might have been normal if he had removed half of his skin with it. He had also enjoyed the long cleansing bath and new clothes that had been provided. Months of conditioning his body against the harsh elements high up in the peaks, had made him used to them. He had almost forgotten what it felt like to have a clean reset. It was a simple pleasure that he hadn't realised he missed.

His dinner the evening before had also been a welcome change. Months of simple vegetables for his diet, gave Jaeger an appreciation for every mouthful he had eaten. The famous dwarf beer had only enhanced the flavours, although he had not needed much before he became laughably drunk. Even Borgisliege had seemed to have put aside all of his worries while the pair of them caught up.

Jaeger contemplated all of this pleasantly. He was nearly ready to tell himself that he might stay here for a week and try to enjoy a little peace and luxury for once. No sooner had the thought entered his head, than a massive shock ran through his body, sinking itself into his gut debilitatingly. He couldn't remember feeling this guilty. After trying to pinpoint what was making him feel so bad for a few moments, he realised what it was. This was no underlying memory or guilt. This was the urgency that had driven him to leave the Thin Air Peaks. Only it had now escalated to an entirely new level.

19 SHRINKING ISLANDS

"What's the matter?" The colonel of Hedland watched his battle-mages intently as they withdrew behind the battlements suddenly.

"It's their shaman's sir. We were warned about this, they're far too powerful to just be ordinary scaleskin spell casters," Headland's master battle-mage, Seamus, explained the situation between labored breaths. The resistance he felt when he was casting had nearly forced the DarkLand matter he was harnessing back down his throat. If it hadn't been for the combined efforts of the team of battle-mages supporting him, he would have died before colonel Glenning ever had a chance to understand the danger they were in.

"Demons then?" Glenning asked.

"I'd say so. Send a rider for all the off-duty mages in the city, together we may be able to take him," Seamus gritted with determination. Beyond the walls, the roar of thousands of scaleskins charging up the slope was getting louder.

"Soldier! Rouse the off-duty mages to the city gate immediately. Bugler! Sound out the call for all the reserve troops in this city to join us on the walls. Archers!" Glenning called assertively.

He had seen Darroch his commander drill the city extensively for this scenario, most of it had been under the watchful eye of their Emperor at the time. Darroch had given him the confidence not to panic, and Glenning felt a degree of personal pride at stake, now that he was left to carry out his orders without his Emperor or commander supervising. His soldiers also responded professionally to the orders. As long as a firm hand and level heads prevailed, this was what they had all been preparing themselves for.

"I also want a messenger ready to ride to Sorrento," Glenning added. "Once Seamus confirms what's out there, commander Darroch must be informed of a demon sighting."

***

Darroch watched silently as again the wave of attackers were massacred. They were charging across what was now referred to as 'the killing fields' beyond the city walls of Sorrento. The few that made it past the killing fields, were picked off by the short-bows of halfling sharpshooters before they could reach the walls. Not a single ladder had made it to the base of the wall in weeks now and Darroch patiently pondered the mindless attacks that he had come to expect again. He wasn't fooled. He knew that it was just a waiting game until the organized demon-led forces returned once more.

Until then, whatever game the enemy was

playing was at least good for morale, and had given him time to organize his forces across the frontline. The Plateau was better prepared than it had ever been before. There were more soldiers manning the southern forts than any other time in history, and after the emperor's tour of the region, they were now more confident and better trained too. The temporary withdrawal of the demons from his borders had allowed Darroch to prepare his people as well as he could hope to be, for what was inevitably going to come next. A messenger rode out across the grounds of Sorrento to find Darroch.

"Any word yet from Learmonth? Have they managed to push back the siege?"

"No word yet sir. The relief contingent of battle-mages will have arrived there earlier today though sir, so we should receive an update very soon. I have letters here from both Hedland and Derby sir. They both arrived at the same time today."

Darroch descended the battlements briskly and took both letters from his messenger. He studied the first one silently. It was from Colonel Glenning in Hedland, the second one from Colonel Hurn. He read the last part of Colonel Hurn's letter twice, it was less categorical and Darroch needed to draw his own conclusions.

Four mages were killed instantly while performing routine spells against our attackers. When called in from off-duty, our battle-mages determined that their death was the result of 'very powerful enemy magic-users'.

Colonel Hurn had always prided himself on relaying facts rather than conjecture, Darroch mused.

"Is everything alright sir?"

Darroch looked up at his rider, the word *yes* wasn't exactly appropriate, and *no* certainly was out of the question. "The demons have returned."

***

Tevin, Mendel and Bellan had gathered all their livestock within the safety of their pens, with the help of a farmhand Bellan's age named William. All of West-Yield had gone quiet and for some reason everybody was battening down their houses and staying inside as if in preparation for a storm. There was no movement in the air and in the distance to the west they could all see clouds stretching across the horizon as dark as night. But it wasn't the weather that they were worried about, the weather seemed to have just come along for the ride.

William had gone home now, leaving Tevin and his family alone sitting quietly in their kitchen. "What was that blasted Jaeger thinking?" Tevin complained to himself in front of Mendel and Bellan. "He should be here with his family looking after them, not running off into the desert to die on some pointless errand that nobody else even cares about. I did everything I could for that boy and now he's probably dead."

The words ended in utter silence, both inside and outside the house. Mendel glared at the table, trying not to direct her anger and her obvious response at Tevin. He hadn't been the same since Jaeger briefly passed through West-Yield at the start of the year. Their son had been ranting on about some special mission he had given himself to reach the fabled Thin Air Peaks beyond the desert.

Tevin's spear was resting against the kitchen wall, along with his chainmail armour and helm. The whole town was on high alert and everybody was similarly prepared. Nobody knew why, but nobody disagreed when Thelonius gave the order. It seemed inevitable in this ominous dead silence. Bellan thought about commenting that even the sound of birds and other creatures outside was gone, but realized she didn't really feel like speaking. Instead, she sat and waited with her parents in the kitchen. It could have been hours or it could have been minutes, but eventually the silence was broken. The town bells began tolling.

***

Colonel Hurn again called for a volley as he led the small force of mounted soldiers back in behind the safety of the gates. Every man looked at the colonel with a profound look of respect as he trotted back from his desperate charge beyond their walls. They knew what was out there. After the sudden loss of several experienced battle-mages earlier in the day, every magic user in the city had been called onto duty.

It had been an incredible effort, but they had managed to overwhelm the demon-shaman standing brazenly before them in the killing fields. Several more mages had lost their lives during their combined efforts, but Harbold had assured them that what they had achieved was very rare. He had fallen short of saying it was worth it. The soldiers on the walls had witnessed a display that few men on The Plateau had ever seen before.

Lightning, fireballs, and clouds of static black-and-purple energy, had filled the skies between the battle-mages on the walls and the demon-shaman before them. Walls had cracked where a dozen battle-mages stood, some of their peers lay dead at their feet. It had seemed likely that they would all die until Harbold had unleashed. He had thrown everything he had at the demon while somehow burrowing the ground beneath it. It was only during a momentary lapse when the demon slipped into this hole, that Harbold was able to manage a direct hit of lightning.

Colonel Hurn had managed to send out another message intended for commander Darroch in Sorrento, after Harbold and the battle-mages had finished the demon off. He had not had the opportunity to send any more when another of the demon-shamans had appeared. He looked up to the battlements, the professor looked exhausted and so did the handful of surviving mages slumped beside him.

"Did that help at all?" Hurn called up to the professor.

"It was nice to sit down for a few moments, but we need more time!" Harbold called back. He stood again and peered out into the fields beyond the walls. "That volley isn't troubling them, their shamans are catching them easily and the demon-shaman is pulling down more walls! If you can just do something to distract or kill their normal shamans, we will try to wrestle with the demon again!"

Harbold looked exhausted just shouting to project his voice from the walls. Hurn could not imagine how the old master-mage was going to go any more rounds with the enemy's second demon. He looked around at the mounted knights beside him, there were about fifty left. They had just managed to ride down an entire cluster of shamans, maybe twenty, but they had lost two-thirds of their regiment before they even reached them. More than a hundred good men and their horses were dead beyond those walls.

"Open the gates!" the colonel roared. "Cavalry!"

***

Tevin took up position atop the wagons blocking the western town entrance. He now watched the defenders populate their designated places in the newly-built guard towers and walls that funneled towards him. The army that had emerged from the woods moved slowly. They held a perfect front line, with rows upon rows of formations marching behind this front, in unison across the fields before West-Yield.

As the frontline came almost within range of the town, men nocked arrows and held, patiently measuring the scaleskin's advance. Just before the army came within reach it stopped. Every scaleskin, from slags to mucks, remained perfectly still as a ghastly shaman pushed its way forward. Tevin had never seen or heard of anything like it.

He struggled to distinguish the shape he was looking at, unsure but assessing that the shaman was possibly of similar height to what he was. There was a haze that obscured it, and it appeared to cast a shadow that stood taller than any other creature on the fields by double. As the shaman stepped in front of its forces, an arrow arced gracefully into the sky towards it. Nashaw owned the largest longbow in West-Yield and had measured his target perfectly.

The arrow clattered away harmlessly against an invisible shield, just a metre short of the shaman's head. It now raised its hands menacingly. What happened next was beyond Tevin's wildest imagination. The newly built walls funneling into the town buckled and crumbled under some invisible weight. Screams were heard from the men concealed along the walkways above them, as they were crushed where they had been crouching. The guard towers on either side of the town entrance exploded in a ruin of purple fire and black smoke.

Nashaw was one the men blasted clear of the wreckage, his body seared and lifeless. Tevin had to tell himself that the town sheriff had died instantly. All around the drilled formations of West-Yield, buildings were crumbled and burning. The townspeople held their line, unsure whether to move or even consider escaping. The still, silent ranks of scaleskins now erupted with a roar and charged.

As the enemy covered the last few yards to the town rapidly, Tevin reminded himself that he still stood between the dreaded shaman's force and his family. There were no wolf riders this time, but the weight of the frontline charge crushed the defenders in front of the wagons. Tevin stabbed frantically down from his position above them, unable to look left or right to see if his neighbours were holding their line across the town entrance from on top of their wagons. It didn't matter, the towns defenses and organization had been obliterated when that shaman had raised its arms.

As the tide of scaleskins began the wash around the defenders, the wagons began to look like shrinking islands among a sea of enemies. The screams of his townspeople could be heard all around him, and Tevin began to think desperately about his family. Could somebody still reach them and tell them to try to escape? If they left now from the town's eastern entrance, would they be able outrun this army with fast horses? He wanted his family and everyone he cared for as far away from this doomed place as possible.

He stabbed and stabbed below him feeling completely hopeless, when suddenly the enemies in front of him parted. The shaman walked confidently forward through its army again, watching as its forces fell silent and parted wherever it approached. A brief moment of silent reprieve fell over the battlefield as Tevin looked up at the vile creature. The shaman was still obscure to look at, but he could see the shadow that stood above it far more clearly now.

Tevin could almost feel it sneer at him, just as a sound louder than a thunderclap erupted from the back of the forces attacking West-Yield. The shaman-creature turned back in alarm as a handful of scaleskins were flung so fast and so hard that they hurtled through the air into the ranks before them.

20 RETURN TO WEST-YIELD

Jaeger had urged Pebbles harder and faster through the night, constantly healing the fatigue and sore muscles in the mighty aves-caprinae as it thundered through the sky towards The Plateau from Aridhold. He had never felt this much fear for his family in his entire lifetime, not even when he and Faline were being hunted before the town entrance all those years ago.

The impatience that had caused him to leave the Thin Air Peaks had turned to urgency now. He had ridden through the night and deep into the morning, high above the scaleskin jungles below. He began to feel like every moment now counted, as he and Pebbles neared the edge of the jungles. In the distance ahead he saw mountains of smoke rising and his stomach sank.

"Faster please Pebbles!" he urged.

The scene below looked devastating but not over. Jaeger saw that the horde of scaleskins had somehow destroyed West-Yield's walls and towers and had just reached the town's defenders. With a howl of rage, he clenched all the matter he could into himself. The air was thick with DarkLand matter and he raced to filter and purify it how Salmor had taught him, unbothered that not everything he drew in was pure in his urgency.

With one last gasp, he clenched more energy than he had ever poured into his body, before lunging down from the sky with Pebbles. As the Skygoat dropped its horns and hurtled into the rear ranks of the scaleskins, Jaeger released every ounce of power he had been holding with a roar. The effect was devastating.

Handfuls of scaleskins erupted into the air with an explosion louder than a thunderclap. Pebbles' horns now carried enough power to level a building, punching into their enemies with Jaeger's supernatural powers infusing them with brute force. Pebbles continued to hurtle through the ranks of scaleskins as he now thundered across the firm fields, churning the turf beneath his hooves.

Almost halfway deep into the army they both stopped. All around them the scaleskins rallied, they were completely fearless of Jaeger and his skygoat despite the devastation they had both caused. Among the front ranks, an enormous muck chieftain ran howling back towards them. Jaeger leapt from his mount's shoulders in rage, landing in the now-cleared space in front of him.

Dark matter, purified matter, he didn't care anymore as he stiffened his muscles and infused them with any raw power he could get a hold of. The enormous chieftain slavered from its mouth as it roared towards him.

"I was born in this fucking town you reptile!" Jaeger roared back at it.

He swung his blade so hard into its side that the sheets of metal armour it wore crumpled. The chieftain folded sideways as its body was flung into its crowded warriors.

Jaeger howled with anger as he felt Pebbles' pain. Behind him, several scimitars bit deep into the skygoat's flanks. Jaeger had barely released half of the power he had been holding and twirled back towards his companion.

Lifting his right arm, he flung forks of white lightning at the dozens of scaleskins that had swarmed around Pebbles. The skygoat thundered towards him, not even breaking stride as Jaeger leapt onto its back and continued to bowl through the frenzied scaleskins all around them.

With a great hind-legged leap, Pebbles launched them both back into the air again. In that same moment, Jaeger felt an avalanche of DarkLand energy and power rolling up towards them both from below. He immediately realised that the driving power behind the unusually brave scaleskins was the same power he had encountered last year in Grantanmar. He shielded himself and Pebbles with purified magic as the attack washed over them while they gained altitude.

Jaeger clenched his power and held on as he looked back over his shoulder. He had found their attacker. Jaeger wheeled Pebbles around and descended. The contemptuous demon watched them almost arrogantly as they hurtled back down towards it. Behind it, the defenders of West-Yield stood frozen; both fearful of approaching the demon, but also mesmerized by Jaeger and his mythical skygoat as they confronted the enemy.

As he landed and their swords clashed, Jaeger could feel the metallic compounds in his weapon pulsating with silver energy. It was if the blade itself could feel the close proximity to that which it was made to kill. The demon also seemed to sense this purpose radiating from his blade. The demon-slaying rune combinations that were engraved along its length now glowed with potency. The contemptuous sneer on its face turned to a look of panic.

This was something the demon was unaccustomed to, and its fighting took on a degree of desperation. Jaeger sensed the vulnerability with a sudden slash across its sword arm. The demon released its sword as a flow of black blood gushed forth from its wounded forearm. Jaeger pressed harder.

With nothing reliable to protect itself with anymore, he sheared through the demon's raised arm from atop Pebbles' back. The demon screeched and fled out of the reach of Jaeger's weapon, but the damage was done.

The scaleskins appeared lost without the command of the demon, and now seemed all too aware of the titanic beast and its rider wreaking carnage in their midst. Many of them now shied away from Pebbles as he bucked and butted at them. Jaeger directed Pebbles back towards the fleeing demon-shaman, as it made its way closer to the wagons blockading West-Yield.

Pebbles ran the demon down before it reached them, and with a little amplification from Jaeger's magic; Pebbles' horns pounded the evil creature into the ground, leaving a demon imprint in the cracked cobblestones beneath it.

Jaeger swung down from his mount again, determined to drive his enchanted blade through the demon until he was certain it had no life left in it. Pebbles now created a fearsome barrier between the scaleskin forces and the wagons barring the entrance to West-Yield. The enemy held back uncertainly.

The town's defenders didn't appear to be much more organized than their attackers right now, but the few archers who were still alive, had found new vantage points and were pouring arrows into their ranks. The scaleskins hesitated at first, before Jaeger drove his sword deep into the demon's chest. This was the last straw. With their leader dead and their confidence shattered they broke, fleeing back away from the town.

Jaeger thought he heard someone call his name as he leapt back onto Pebbles again. He was still so berserk with rage that he could think of nothing other than hunting down every scaleskin in the region and killing them before they escaped. They flew ahead of the retreating forces, landing again now. This time they stood between their enemies and the forest, preventing their escape.

Jaeger arced sheets of white lightning again and again, out towards the routing enemies as they scattered and tried to avoid him to reach the tree-line. It occurred to him that whilst honing his clerical abilities with the monks, his powers as a mage must have increased considerably. His strength was not unlimited however, and the rage that had initially fueled him was finally beginning to simmer.

The spell-casting needed to stop, he had never put his body through a fraction of what he had harnessed today and he realised the pain and exhaustion he had caused himself. Leaping back into the sky together, Jaeger placed his hand affectionately on Pebbles, checking to see if there had been any wounds that he had missed in the heat of battle. There were many and he quickly poured his clerical healing into all of them, feeling guilty that he had been oblivious to his companion's pain.

Jaeger finally began to calm himself as they both glided quietly back down into West-Yield. The day had been won, but the western entrance of his home town was a ruin. He was unsure how many of his old neighbours had been killed, the battle appeared to have only just begun when he arrived. Jaeger just hoped that his urgency in returning when he did had been enough. He now desperately wanted to see his family.

Jaeger studied Tevin intently as they sat down to their first family dinner since he had left for the peaks. Tevin seemed like a different person somehow, but then Jaeger was in no position to judge. All of his family seemed different to him as he looked around the table. It was taking a little time to bring the warmth back out of them, and he wondered if his behavior during the battle had somehow changed the way they viewed him.

He had slept almost all day and despite repeatedly healing the pain and exhaustion in his muscles, some of the deeper effects of harnessing excessive magic seemed to be a little too profound to heal.

"So that skygoat is yours?" Bellan started. His little sister had grown a lot recently.

"Pebbles," Jaeger smiled at her. "I guess you

could say that, we are very close. He saved me when I first found the Thin Air Peaks."

"So, you did find them?" Tevin added almost accusingly.

"I did, yes," Jaeger replied.

"And here I was beginning to think you were just looking for new and more elaborate excuses to be anywhere but home," his father added a little more meanly.

"I found the peaks because I had to. You have no idea what I saw last year. Well, maybe you do now. But I found the peaks, and Pebbles, and I was able to save West-Yield because of it."

"It was lucky coincidence that you were here to help," Tevin retorted.

"It wasn't!" Jaeger insisted adamantly. "That's the point, I knew I had to be back here to help urgently. It's similar to how I knew I had to reach the Thin Air Peaks. I learned that when I was with the Monks."

"By visiting the monks, you learned that you needed to come home?" Tevin scoffed.

"No, I learned that I can sense things that are going to happen. It's an ability that makes me a seer of some sort."

"So, you can see into the future?" Bellan interrupted excitedly.

"It's not quite how it's described in the stories Bellan. But I've always had some sense of things that are about to happen. I could feel right before a sword was swung at my head, I could feel when something was wrong somewhere, like in West-Yield. I was racing to get home and I knew I didn't have much time to make it."

"That's all very exciting to hear Jaeger, but you seem to be missing the point," Tevin continued to press. Jaeger had never seen him like this before.

"What do you want me to say, dad? That I'm not the perfect son? I agree. I could have stayed on this farm with you instead of chasing adventure at the first opportunity I got. I'm not the perfect boyfriend either. I could have happily stayed with Aema in Conorbatia and studied magic together with her until the end of the world came to our doorstep. But you know what? We would all be dead now if I wasn't such a shitty son who found dwarves, and runes, and monks, and magic and Pebbles, instead of staying at home."

Tevin had been simmering towards Jaeger ever since he had ended the battle in front of his old town. The lack of logic and unfairness of everything seemed to have finally become too much to bear.

"I hope that's enough to make up for everything, because I also hope that one day soon, I can return to West-Yield again in peace with you guys. I hope that what I have done is enough for Aema to forgive me too, because when I do come back here one day, I want to bring her with me." Tevin's prodding seemed to be the trigger for Jaeger unloading months of internal conflict and self-loathing.

Everybody at the table sat in silence. Bellan looked at her older brother a little sympathetically. She had always looked up to Jaeger without getting involved in any judgement.

"So, you have a girlfriend?" Tevin finally responded. Jaeger could have laughed.

"Yes I do. Or I did anyway, her name is Aema. I think I mentioned her briefly before I left earlier this year."

"You might have, Jaeger. I didn't pick up that she was your girlfriend. I'm sorry for making you feel like you have done something wrong, you haven't. For some reason recently I truly felt that we had lost you for good, it was a difficult likelihood for me to accept. Then after what I saw out there, before you arrived." Tevin shuddered looking out the windows. "It scared me more than anything has ever scared me before. I thought I was about to lose everything."

"It was a demon," Jaeger said, "I saw one last year. They are everywhere, they have coordinated attacks on the dwarfs, and they have been leading the scaleskins to wipe out The Plateau."

"I see," Tevin muttered. Jaeger looked around at his family. Mendel seemed to have nothing but sympathy in her eyes as she looked back at him. Jaeger might have changed drastically this year, but so had they. They all seemed to have become a little harder, a little less carefree, and a little bit haunted.

For the next couple of days Jaeger tried to enjoy the time that he had back in West-Yield. He wanted to help with the town rebuild, but that would take weeks, going into months. Instead, his clerical healing abilities were a miracle to the town in the immediate aftermath of the devastating assault.

Unfortunately, some of the defenders crushed on the walls had died instantly, but Jaeger had been able to save anyone who still had a pulse at the end of the battle. The minimal loss of lives was better than anybody could have possibly hoped for, while Lennard and Margie were left speechless when they saw the work that Jaeger had spared them from.

"You will send me out of business if you stay here Jaeger," Margie marveled.

"I wouldn't worry about that Margie. I don't have long before I have to return to Conorbatia."

Jaeger could still remember the level of awe he had held Margie in, when she had worked all night saving townspeople from the last attack on West-Yield. That all seemed like a lifetime ago now.

"Oh, I wasn't worried, I have just about done my time in healing and would happily mix a little concoction here and there in retirement. If there were more people out there that could do what you do, The Plateau would be a different nation entirely overnight."

"There is actually an entire mountain full of them in the Thin Air Peaks," Jaeger mused a little bitterly. "Unfortunately, they didn't seem to have much interest in changing The Plateau overnight."

"Well at least we have you," Margie smiled, and Jaeger felt comforted by the genuine warmth it carried. The woman still felt like a more skilled healer than the clerics Jaeger had learned from in the peaks.

Bellan got on with Pebbles famously. The young caprinae was still quite youthful and had never been around such playful human company before. The monks of the Thin Air Peaks were a caring and considerate community, but they were all a little too mundane for Pebbles to have ever interacted with them like Bellan.

The two of them swooped overhead as Jaeger took the route to Grummason's by foot. He remembered the difference between the turnoff to his home and Faline's, which he had unwittingly missed one day. That too, had seemed like a lifetime ago now, and while Jaeger had still tried to maintain his friendship with her in Conorbatia, he also saw Faline very differently to how he used to as a young, infatuated teenager.

"Are you looking forward to building those walls again?" Jaeger asked lightly when he saw Grummason.

"Not particularly," his oldest friend admitted. "Not after seeing how easily that shaman pulled them down."

"That was a demon," Jaeger corrected.

"Aye, demon. Looked a bit like a scaleskin shaman at first, not so much once it started waving its arms around. Not so much when it came closer."

"It's a confusing situation," Jaeger admitted. "I'm not sure if they are able to move around freely, but so far I have only heard of them possessing scaleskin shamans, or roachkin warlocks. In a sense they still are the shamans or warlocks, but they are demons at the same time. That's partly why they are so hard to see properly."

"You seem to have become an expert since I last saw you. You certainly didn't have much trouble killing our one," Grummason praised Jaeger almost fiercely.

"The blade I killed it with is a dwarven runesword." Jaeger drew his sword from its hilt and handed it to his friend.

Grummason studied the runes intently, holding the sword almost reverently. Jaeger again realised the connection that all expatriate dwarves craved with their homeland. Jaeger felt the sudden urge to offer to fly

Grummason there immediately.

"You should let Karnsmith see this before you leave," Grummason murmured eventually.

"I still have the sword he made me in my pack," Jaeger changed the subject. "You don't think he would be offended if I showed I was using another sword now?"

"Not for a sword like this," Grummason assured him. "He will appreciate seeing it, I know I do."

"We will visit Aridhold together someday Grummason. The subways are open to The Plateau again for the first time in centuries. You will get to see your homeland in your lifetime, and I am looking forward to being there with you when you do."

"You've changed, Jaeger," his friend noted. "You're still the same Jaeger, but you have changed a lot since you left West-Yield."

"For the better I hope?" Jaeger laughed.

"For the better," Grummason nodded as he handed back the runesword.

They both visited the mason home again, greeting Jaeger's old employers and friends, before the pair hiked down to the local river with Bellan and Pebbles. It almost felt like they were kids again to Jaeger. All the memories of building ropes and bridges, and looking for adventures and challenges with his old friend, came flooding back as he toured his old stomping ground.

There was also a fear and sadness in West-Yield that he wasn't used to. Jaeger guessed it was only natural after seeing a demon outside their remote town just days earlier. Like the rest of The Plateau, the stakes were rising, and the forces that were at play had probably started to make the town defenders feel a little more futile and a little less prepared. When it was time to leave, Jaeger felt like his home town had been a welcome breath of nostalgia, but West-Yield had also been dragged into The Plateau's greater problems now. Something he wished he could have spared his childhood home from.

21 THE EMPEROR'S RECKONING

Marrick led the silent procession towards the southern entrance to Conorbatia under the cold drizzle of night. The rain wasn't pouring, but it had not stopped either. The puddles of mud had made coach travel difficult until they finally reached the cobbled roads just outside the city.

Emperor Hildebrante had been hearing constant reports for months, detailing the ambitions of Donagarn and his mercenaries. Like the constant nagging of a tick bite; Marrick's Emperor had become increasingly frustrated at the reports of civil disruption, while he had greater worries to deal with.

The final straw had been when that messenger arrived, informing them that Conorbatia was no longer the emperor's city. Emperor Hildebrante had not finished his tour, but departed from the frontline with a hundred soldiers immediately.

The capital city of The Plateau was now openly under the control of Donagarn and the mercenaries of

Silo. Darroch had been unequivocally clear to Marrick; the emperor's safety was Marrick's only responsibility, nothing else was to take precedence. As he rode up towards the barred southern gate to the city, Marrick was hailed from the watchtower.

"Who goes there?" came the challenge. The emperor's royal banner was clearly visible from the leading carriage. Marrick shook his head with disappointment.

"We carry the emperor's banner sir! who trained you?" He knew the small detachment of soldiers left in Conorbatia were not the elite guard, but this was embarrassing.

The gates opened immediately to Marrick's relief. At least the embarrassment stopped there, he thought. He was wrong. Behind the gates was a company of fifty men, not a single uniform was to be seen among them.

"How do we know it's the emperor carrying his banner?" the scarred leader of the company asked confidently.

It made no sense, if they were really so paranoid about who they let in, then it was unprofessional to have opened the gates. "How do we know that the scaleskins haven't taken his banners and ridden north from the frontline? From what I hear they're doing pretty well down there?"

"Do I look like a scaleskin you idiot?" Marrick swore, he had lost patience when he pointed out the banner.

"It's fine lieutenant," came the emperor's voice. Hildebrante stepped down from his coach and walked towards the mercenaries. "I am your Emperor. Now stand aside, we will discuss why you are guarding an imperial gate with your employer." Scarface didn't appear intimidated and remained in the way.

"I told you to move," Hildebrante repeated.

His voice lowered threateningly, and his hand moved to his sword. His soldiers had now formed a disciplined line behind their Emperor, as his personal bodyguard stepped in alongside him to their left. Marrick remained poised like a coiled spring on his Emperor's right. The disorganized crowd before them almost looked comical opposite the disciplined ranks of their Emperor.

"Your Emperor just gave you an order," Marrick warned them, his hand now also on the hilt of his sword.

"Fuck the Emperor," Scarface spat.

Hildebrante's sword moved through his chest so quickly that scarface didn't even have time to flinch. He did scream however, just before the sword pierced his heart.

Marrick leapt forward slicing through the closest mercenaries behind scarface. They had reacted slowly to their leader's death, but a few blades swung his way eventually, as Marrick and the Emperor's men hacked their way through their own people. Within a minute, every last mercenary lay dead before the open entrance to the city's southern gate.

"Who trained you?" Marrick asked again incredulously to the dead bodies littering the cobblestones.

"Sergeant, clear these bodies from my roads immediately," Hildebrante ordered one of his men. "I want these streets clean, and men in uniforms guarding the gates again by the time I reach the palace. I need to have a word with someone there."

***

Aema and Nasgro had conscripted their friends to form a guerrilla unit since Nasgro's little sister had arrived. She had appeared outside his dorm late on the same night that they had rescued Berran. Professor Worley had listened intently and told the students to leave the situation in his hands. However, from what Aema could see, the professors had their hands tied. They had a duty of care to the student's families now.

Aema at least had the peace of mind in knowing that her family lived far to the north next to the halfling province. Nasgro on the other hand was furious. It had only been a couple of days, but he was desperate to locate and rescue his parents. Tonight, they all planned to slip into the streets of Conorbatia and find out what they could on Donagarn's estate.

If they came across trouble, they knew they had no choice but to fight and kill any mercenaries that could identify them. They all knew the risks, and had discussed the likelihood that some prisoners might be made an example of if mercenaries went missing. Despite this, they concluded that it was the only remaining course of action left to take.

Julia disappeared into the streets ahead. Nasgro had insisted that they would all be better off having his little sister with them and he seemed to be right. Throughout the night she had intermittently returned to them and warned them of patrols up ahead.

As they approached the town square, she now reported that an entire convoy of soldiers had marched down the main road and directly into the palace. It had been an unexpected development, and Aema was unsure if it was exciting or concerning.

"If there are soldiers in the city again, we need to know if they are fighting, or if they have made some sort of truce with the mercenaries. We can't go any further until we find out." Aema insisted.

"Of course we can," Nasgro whispered. "Whether they are here to help or not, it doesn't stop us from getting onto the estate without crossing paths with them."

"Okay, you're right Nasgro. But before we continue, what do you think they're doing here?"

"I'm not sure. But it is night time, so I think a truce is unlikely," Nasgro reasoned.

"Do you want to try to approach them? Or would you prefer to continue on tonight with our current mission then?"

"I'd rather go on with our mission, if by some chance there was a truce then we will have immediately identified ourselves once we talk to them."

"I don't think that's likely" Odette interrupted. "These are the soldiers of our Emperor, they might be our only allies in this city right now, and they might also need our help."

Nasgro seemed a little surprised at his girlfriend's response, and more than a little bit patriotic. "You're right babe, if our Emperor needs us then we must help him."

Aema rolled her eyes.

***

Jaeger soared happily over The Plateau's capital

city. He looked down at the few lights he could see below him, reaching out from windows and street corners. He had never realised that human civilisation could look so beautiful from above. When he finally saw Aema again, this would be one of the first things he was going to show her.

Pebbles banked sharply as Jaeger picked out the college grounds towards the eastern edge of the city. He could barely believe he was finally going to see Aema again after leaving her late last year.

When he landed on the college grounds, the campus was dark and silent. He walked quietly alongside Pebbles across the lawns outside the student accommodation, taking in the familiar scenery by the bluish light of the moon.

"Stay here for me for a little bit buddy. I need to see someone urgently, but we will figure out somewhere nice for you to stay here as soon as I have spoken to her," Jaeger assured his companion.

Pebbles snorted impatiently, the night was cold and drizzly. Nowhere near as cold as the Thin Air Peaks, but there was a miserable soggy wetness to this winter weather back on The Plateau.

"I won't be long," Jaeger promised.

Without lingering any longer, Jaeger raced up to the dorms towards the room that Aema had been in last year. He had left before the second year started, but knew that students rarely changed rooms over the course of their time at Clouds College. The corridors were dead silent as he made his way to Aema's room, and Jaeger realised that it must be very close to midnight by now.

He realised it would be quite uncomfortable if

he got the wrong room, but not the end of the world. It was certainly not enough to refrain from knocking. Jaeger raised his hand to the door and paused for a moment, nervous at how Aema would react and what he should say. He also realised that while Pebbles was a lovable companion, an entire day of sitting on his back in cold wet weather had rubbed quite a powerful smell off onto Jaeger. Dismissing all of these thoughts he knocked.

Several moments of utter silence went by before Jaeger realised nobody was coming to answer the door. Cringing a little at the noise, Jaeger rapped again harder on the door.

That should do it. If he knocked any louder, he would be waking up all of the students in the rooms next door. Again, time went by without any response, and this time Jaeger tested the door tentatively. It was locked, and one way or another he knew somebody should have answered by now.

"Aema," Jaeger called up against the door quietly. "Aema," he tried again just a fraction louder, after getting no response.

"Shut! Up!" a girl's voice called back from one of the adjacent rooms.

Jaeger tested the door slowly but forcefully again. It was definitely locked. He was becoming a little concerned now, he hadn't seen Aema in half a year and had no idea why her own room could be locked and go unanswered at this time of night. Waiting anxiously outside for a few more long minutes, Jaeger contemplated his options. Eventually concern gave out and he placed his hand back to the door against the lock.

Inhaling deeply, he drew all the DarkLand

221

matter nearby into him, purifying it through his lungs and body. It burned a little, and he quickly channeled it into the lock, heating the small parts he could now sense with the purified matter that extended out from him. As he tried to melt through the metal, the wood around it caught fire. Jaeger quickly readjusted his approach, burning through an entire fist of wood that was supporting the lock.

Once the lock hung there loosely, he pulled the metal clear from its connection to the wall. The door swung inwards as he harnessed a frosty ball of ice to douse the embers. He cringed at the damage he had caused. He had been back at the college for less than an hour and had already vandalized a bedroom. Explaining this would be unpleasant, but for now he just needed to find Aema and see that she was okay.

He lit the room with a hovering globe of flame. There was nobody in here. Quickly appraising the contents, Jaeger confirmed that it was definitely Aema's. She had always been a bit messy behind closed doors and he recognized her dresses strewn across the floor. Wherever she was, her room had still been used recently.

Now Jaeger realised that he would need to find her before she came back to discover the ruins of her door. As he stepped back into the corridor, he considered leaving a note to reassure her, but his selfish preferences took precedence. If Aema was going to find out he was back, it would be when she saw him, not by finding some strange note after all these months.

Jaeger quickly tried the rooms of Lisle and Dinara. He was a little less confident in the location of these two but at least confirmed that nobody was answering the dorms that he tried. After being told to shut-up again in these places, Jaeger started to gain some confidence that Aema may be out somewhere with her friends.

He wasn't even certain what day it was, but figured the next plan of attack would be to find one of the guys and wake them up. Anybody he could start asking questions would do at this stage.

Jaeger came outside to find a slightly unimpressed Pebbles waiting for him. Without bothering to jump onto Pebbles back, Jaeger strolled with Pebbles back through the grounds of his old campus. He had learned an immense amount this year, and after the battle of West-Yield, Jaeger had realised that he now wielded incredible power, more than any of the other mages at the college.

Despite all this, he felt he had unfinished business with his studies, and hoped that he would be accepted back to finish them at some stage. It was still important to him, if the war in the south could ever be won.

Back in the boy's dormitories, Jaeger passed his old room nostalgically. He knocked on Berran's old room first which was nearby. No answer, along with the familiar instructions to shut-up coming from the surrounding rooms. Something was definitely going on. With little confidence that he would get answers, Jaeger confirmed that Nasgro and Ellis were also not in their rooms.

By the time he was finished, Jaeger felt incredibly impatient but exhausted. It was now the early hours of the morning and he had been awake since very early the day before. He had also spent most of those waking hours flying, and he was sure that Pebbles would probably have appreciated finding somewhere to settle down and rest when they had finally reached their destination. Without finding any of his friends, Jaeger had no such place for either of them.

Looking at Pebbles he sighed and mounted the skygoat once again. They soared low over the campus, scanning the tavern and other possible hangouts for any sign of his friends. Everything was dead quiet at Clouds College, when Jaeger made up his mind that he would not find them on campus. The last location he could think of, was the little creek that was a favourite hangout for Aema and him last year.

"Sorry for the long night buddy," he apologized to Pebbles. "We're just gonna have to keep looking again when the sun is up."

He led Pebbles to the stream and they both drank deeply. With little else left to do, the pair of them curled up on the lawns and closed their eyes. Sleep took both easily. The wet ground was unpleasant, but Jaeger had become comfortable resisting the cold through his time meditating in the peaks.

The sun was still below the horizon when Jaeger woke suddenly. He was immediately overcome with a gut-wrenching sense of dread and nudged Pebbles to wake up also. Harnessing and purifying the matter around him, Jaeger assessed Pebbles for strain and soreness, washing what he could out of the skygoat's powerful limbs.

As soon as he was done, he leapt onto Pebbles back. Without knowing exactly where he was going, he urged Pebbles into flight. They gained a little altitude and then moved back towards Conorbatia. Somewhere out there in this city he was going to find Aema and his friends.

***

"Sir, there is a group of students from the college outside to see you," one of the city soldiers informed the emperor.

Marrick had been relieved to find that at least the emperor's palace had not been overrun when they reached it. They had found every soldier in the city had retreated back to this location on the night that Silo had struck.

Apparently reports had erupted all over the city that night of attacks on homes, while numerous small patrols of the emperor's soldiers were suddenly ambushed and murdered. It had been an utter disaster. By the time the steward had any idea of what was going on, the only surviving soldiers had escaped and made their own way back to the palace.

A concentrated force of the emperor's men had easily pushed back one attack from Silo on the palace that night. After that, a calm had settled over Conorbatia square. Donagarn's mercenaries appeared satisfied that the city was theirs and left the small bastion of soldiers to their precious palace, opposite his heavily fortified estate.

Marrick escorted the small group of students through the palace to their Emperor. Despite early reports from the steward that the college was siding with the emperor, he could not feel comfortable that they were allowing anybody capable of an assassination near his primary responsibility.

"So, you left the campus tonight to hunt mercenaries?" Marrick clarified with the scrawny curly haired young student who seemed to be in charge.

"We were doing reconnaissance," the student explained.

"And you are at the Palace now because you say you crossed paths with our convoy tonight by coincidence?"

"My little sister saw your convoy entering the palace. When she told us about it, we decided that we would come to you first before we went any closer to Donagarn's estate."

"I'm sorry mate, but why would your little sister have seen us enter the palace at this time of night?" Marrick insisted.

"Because she was with us!" the young student insisted. "Three nights ago, Donagarn's mercenaries broke into my parent's home and kidnapped them. Julia escaped and told us. She sneaks and hides and climbs things all day, she got away and we brought her with us tonight because she is better at scouting than any of us are." The little girl beside the young mage looked up at her older brother excitedly at the sudden cluster of compliments.

Marrick sighed, the student's story made a bit more sense now and he was just glad that the little girl seemed to have missed the seriousness of what she had been through.

"Just through here," he escorted the group through two enormous gilded doors into the great hall of the palace.

At the end of the great hall, Emperor Hildebrante stood at the bottom of the steps to the throne with a handful of soldiers. They formed up and Marrick nodded to the soldiers lining the halls on either side. Some loosely nocked arrows to their bows without aiming.

Marrick knew that mages could easily deflect missiles and realised that if anything here was to go wrong, he would need to react lightning-fast to eliminate the students, being the only soldier close enough to them. He looked at the blonde girl beside the curly haired student, and wondered if she had any idea how dangerous any sudden movements would be right now.

"Gentlemen," the emperor greeted the young student. "And ladies," he also observed looking at the entire group before him.

"Your highness," curly replied reverently. "My name is Nasgro, my friends and I here have been on the streets of your city tonight. We were opposing Silo's mercenaries when we saw your convoy re-enter the palace."

"Well, I'm sorry you have had to oppose anything in my absence, Nasgro," Emperor Hildebrante replied with sincerity. "What can I do for you?"

"Nothing your highness, we just wanted to see if there was anything we could do to help when we realised you were back."

"I see," Hildebrante considered thoughtfully, "and you are from Clouds College I understand?"

"Yes your highness."

"Well then before I make any more moves, I will need to summon professor Worley from the college. We will need his help before we go back into the city to arrest Donagarn."

"We can speak to the professor," Nasgro offered. "We can speak to him tonight before the sun rises. Be careful going out abroad in the daylight my Emperor, Silo has thousands of mercenaries now and they will swarm to you when they find out you are back in the city."

"Thank you Nasgro, please just call me Hildebrante. I will speak to my steward tonight to ensure a full debrief on the situation in my city. In the meantime, Marrick here will take a small detachment of soldiers and escort you back to the college to speak to Worley."

"Yes Hildebra-"

"Marrick!?" the blonde girl gasped before she could realise that she had just interrupted a conversation with her Emperor. Everybody paused and looked at her.

"That's me," Marrick confirmed. The young girl looked mortified.

"Did you travel with Jaeger? He used to tell me about his friend Marrick from Darroch's army all the time."

"I did indeed," Marrick smiled, even Hildebrante appeared to relax pleasantly after she had spoken. "I take it you were... close... to him when he was studying at the college?"

"Yes," she blushed. "He was very close to all of us, but I was his. He was my-" she stuttered.

"You and Jaeger sound like you were an item" Emperor Hildebrante added helpfully.

"Yes," Aema agreed, she looked like she had gone from embarrassed to the verge of tears suddenly.

"It is very nice to meet you and your friends, Aema," the emperor said warmly. "I'm sure you and

Marrick will have lots of fond memories to share while he escorts you back to your college."

Aema smiled back at her Emperor gratefully, tears silently trickling down her cheeks as she nodded.

"Emperor!" a soldier called from the end of the hall. "There are thousands of mercenaries filling Conorbatia square outside. We will not be able to leave freely from the Palace."

***

The sun was just breaching the horizon below Jaeger, as he soared with Pebbles over the centre of Conorbatia. With the light streaming up into the sky behind him, Jaeger searched the city ahead of him for what he was racing towards.

He knew that there was somewhere down there that he desperately needed to be, and his thoughts were squarely centered around Aema as he searched. By Conorbatia square in front of the Palace, he could see hundreds of torches flickering in the twilight below. Pebbles' powerful wings stopped beating and spread to their full span, before the skygoat swooped down from the skies towards the scene below.

As they came near, the crowd appeared to be quite agitated and every person Jaeger could see was carrying a weapon. Their attention was directed at the Palace gates that they surrounded. None of them had moved to breach the gates yet, but from what Jaeger could tell, it looked like the population of Conorbatia was holding their own palace under siege.

A few moments later, the attention of the crowd shifted solely to the enormous winged beast that was descending towards them. Jaeger had been pleasantly reminded when he returned to The Plateau, that people were usually quite surprised to see one of the fabled aves-caprinae alive and carrying a human.

Unsure of the situation, they landed forcefully on the palace side of the gates. Jaeger dismounted and walked towards the crowd.

"What's happening here?" he enquired to anybody who would answer.

"We're here for the footmen and their Emperor!" one of the men at the front spat. "Who are you?"

"I'm Jaeger son of Tevin, and I am a loyal subject of Emperor Hildebrante. What do you want with him?"

"Son, you and that skygoat must have been living under a rock," the man scoffed. "We want your Emperor so we can be done with him, this city belongs to Silo."

Jaeger nearly fell back with shock at the statement, drawing his sword in outrage. He had just spent half a year trying to find help for these people. When he had left, his Emperor was riding to war to defend them too. Now he had returned to find demons terrorizing his home town on the western borders of The Plateau, and somehow amongst all of that Silo had started a bloody revolution!

Before he could do or say any more, soldiers ran out across the courtyard from the Palace towards him.

"Stand down sir!" one of them yelled, hefting his spear nervously at Pebbles. The crowd went wild at the terrified soldiers for coming out from the cover of the palace and into view.

"I'm stood down!" Jaeger insisted, holding his sword to the ground in his left hand with his right hand in the air. "Please relax, and don't point your weapons at my companion here."

The soldier looked back between Pebbles and Jaeger several times before he spoke again. "Companion? That's a bloody skygoat!" This brought a lot of laughter and jeers from the angry mob beyond the gates. The soldier was clearly processing a lot right now.

"Yes he is. His name is Pebbles and he is my companion. My name is Jaeger, I am a friend, and if Darroch or Emperor Hildebrante are in the palace I would very much like to speak to them."

"Darroch is in the south. You can come with me and I'll see if the… palace wants to speak to you," the same soldier added hesitantly.

The soldiers led Jaeger and Pebbles away from the palace fence-line to the jeering and abuse of the crowd. They made no move to scale the spiked fences yet, but there was no doubting their hostility and intentions. Above the cacophony of the masses behind him, Jaeger distinctly heard a familiar voice call his name from high up in the distance.

***

Aema sat with her friends in the guest wing of the palace. She had only spoken briefly with Marrick after their revelation, before they had been led to this temporary place of accommodation to rest. There had been no way to escape back to Clouds College without violence. Outside in the dark, the torches of Silo's mercenaries dotted Conorbatia Square like thousands of angry little fireflies.

They all stayed in the one room together, sprawled across the bed and floor waiting. As Aema opened her eyes drowsily, she noted that it was still quite dark outside, and that some commotion out there had woken her up. Afraid that the Palace was under attack, she raced to the window to see.

On the ground below, she could see the number of mercenaries had increased significantly, although they still waited beyond the Palace gates. There was a man and some enormous goat crossing the courtyard with a handful of soldiers leading him. She was several stories up and quite a distance from them, but Aema's heart began to race when she recognized the gait of the man as well as his outline. She couldn't quite believe it, but from here it looked like it was him.

"Jaeger!" she yelled as loud as she possibly could. The man's head lifted immediately to the upper stories of the palace. She could have cried with relief.

"Jaeger!" she waved from her window. He could see her now. "Guys, its Jaeger!" she called back to the others in the room. She had already woken them and they raced over to the window.

When she looked back, Jaeger was shoving one of the soldiers to the ground. He raced towards the enormous goat, leaping onto its back, and then something incredible happened. Two enormous wings exploded from the goat's sides, as more soldiers ran in towards the pair. Their spears bounced back off the air metres away from Jaeger and his skygoat, as they both took to the sky.

***

Jaeger surged high towards the window that was three stories above the courtyard below. He could make out Aema's face now even if he hadn't recognized her voice. She waved frantically and was joined by Nasgro, Odette, Berran, Lisle, Dinara and Ellis, all squeezing their heads out of the large window to the guest accommodation of the palace.

It felt like almost a lifetime ago when Jaeger himself had been a welcome guest in these rooms. He had no idea why his friends were here of all places, but right now he didn't care.

Aema yanked back through her friends from the window and pulled the double-doors to the balcony open. Pebbles wheeled back from the window and then banked sideways, straightening out just as they cleared the balcony railing and landing inside the doors. Aema leapt aside from the mighty beast as it landed, while Jaeger dived from Pebbles' back into her arms.

"I looked for you in your room!" Jaeger exclaimed. His face was muffled by her hair in the tight embrace, her arms were wrapped tightly around his neck. "I got back late in the night and have been looking for you everywhere!"

Aema sobbed into his chest as he spoke and the others poured into view when he looked up.

"What's happened?" he asked the chorus of voices coming his way.

"Do you want the long version or the short version?" Nasgro asked.

"I have no idea," Jaeger admitted.

"It will have to be the short version I think," Nasgro decided.

"Maybe just for now," Jaeger agreed, he noted that the others seemed quite comfortable deferring to Nasgro now to do the talking. Obviously a lot had changed.

"Well, it started very close to the time that you left. Since Emperor Hildebrante marched south, Donagarn pretty much started an arms-race here in the city. He just began to hire more and more mercenaries until they outnumbered the soldiers in Conorbatia. Shortly afterwards, other business owners started hiring mercenaries too. I'm not sure if it was to protect themselves from Silo, or just following his lead, but most of them did it too late. It was all too little too late."

"So that mob outside are all just mercenaries?" Jaeger narrowed his eyes suspiciously.

"Absolutely, Donagarn used his thugs to intimidate all of the other stores and farms to sell out. With the exception of one man named Justin, he virtually owns everything in Conorbatia right now."

"How did the people here allow that?" Jaeger asked incredulously.

"They had no choice. He has been kidnapping anybody who opposes him. Last night we were out to find where he is keeping them before we saw the emperor return to the city, that's when we came here."

"Emperor Hildebrante is here!?"

"He only just arrived. Silo have been terrorizing this city for months now, my family were kidnapped a few nights ago when it all happened."

"Oh no," Jaeger felt the blood drain from his face looking at his friend. Nasgro appeared to be maintaining control of himself, but who knew what was going on inside his head.

"Yeah," Nasgro replied. "That kicked off after they trespassed on the college. The professors banned Silo's mercenaries from coming here, but Kostian brought them to the tavern and they abducted Berran, because…" Nasgro looked at Aema suddenly, realizing where his story was leading.

"Jates has been asking me to join him for a drink all year," Aema explained almost apologetically. Jaeger let that sink in, it wasn't a nice feeling but there wasn't much he could say.

"Jates?" he repeated, looking at Nasgro to see how he felt about it.

"Hey don't look at me, you all know I can't stand him." Nasgro held his hands up.

"Aema has had it terrible this year after you left!" Lisle jumped in defensively. "I've seen her struggle. Nobody likes Jates but I was glad to see her get out at least!"

Between Nasgro and now the quiet Lisle speaking out, Jaeger was struggling to process the changes that had happened since he left. It was enough to worry about just socially, let alone the events outside their window.

"I get it," Jaeger said placatingly.

"Anyway," Nasgro continued. "There was an argument at The Pilgrim's Oasis a few nights ago when Aema went there to meet Jates. From what I understand, Kostian hit Aema and then his thugs bashed Berran and took him hostage."

"They what!?" Jaeger roared. He looked up at Berran and then Aema, it felt like his heart was going to stop when he saw the tears in her eyes. For the first time, he noticed the colour surrounding her left eye. "I'm going to kill him!"

"I think we all would like to, but just wait till the end." Nasgro assured. "Everything blew up after that, we went straight to professor Worley who went straight to Donagarn's estate with us. He threatened Donagarn who backed down and released Berran, then Worley expelled Kostian on the spot and put his girlfriend Faline in her place for complaining." Jaeger simply shook his head at this. Deep down he had known for a while what she was like.

"Anyway, the last of it is that later that night, Donagarn sent his mercenaries on a rampage through Conorbatia. They snatched families from their homes across the city, anybody associated with the college."

"Nasgro, I'm so sorry," Jaeger shook his head sadly. "It looks like more than I can possibly imagine has happened while I was gone." He kept his arm around Aema and squeezed her shoulders tightly.

"Which brings us to you now!" Nasgro noted. Just then a heavy knock was heard at the door. The door was unlocked and opened.

Marrick stood there with a detachment of soldiers.

"That's him sir!" one of the soldiers from outside pointed.

"Relax," Marrick laughed, running forward to embrace his old friend. "I heard you came back with a skygoat," he chuckled.

"This is Pebbles," Jaeger introduced him to Marrick as well as the rest of his friends for the first time. Pebbles snorted with outrage at being ignored for so long. "Pebbles, this is my very good friend Marrick, and my," he paused looking at Aema who was smiling warmly at him through tears. He wasn't sure if he was allowed to use 'girlfriend' again just yet. "Aema" he smiled. "And Nasgro, and Berran, and Lisle, and Odette and Dinara, and Ellis," he pointed his way through his friends.

"I'm sorry to speed this up Jaeger," Marrick interrupted, "but we have a situation right now." Below the balcony they all could see the crowds had now parted to allow a wagon loaded with a tree trunk to roll through. Soldiers were pouring into the courtyard below to guard the palace entrance, as the battering ram reached the gates.

Jaeger stood before the entrance to the palace as Donagarn led his army quietly through the shattered gates. Despite Marrick's insistence, the emperor refused to remain hidden, and stood before nearly three hundred loyal soldiers as they waited. Pebbles bellowed at the oncoming mob as Jaeger clenched up with hatred at the sight of Kostian. Jaeger watched as his very personal enemy approached the palace beside his father.

"Donagarn!" the emperor called out ominously. "You have committed treason against your nation, whatever happens with your men today, I sentence you to death."

Donagarn chuckled mirthlessly. "I am here to assume my title as Emperor, by competency. There will be no treason once you are gone. I only hope that we can complete this transition peacefully without losing any more good soldiers," he smirked at the ranks of uniformed men behind the emperor.

Jaeger looked around. However scared these men had been when he arrived, their eyes burned with the same hatred for this man and his small army. Not a single one of them would lay their weapons down in the presence of their Emperor. Kostian eyed Jaeger off with a hatred that almost matched his. All around him Jaeger felt his friends harnessing DarkLand matter to themselves.

"Father," Kostian interrupted, pointing at the students.

"Ah yes," Donagarn noticed. "You will also tell your friends from the college to stand down before this goes any further. I am holding their families, and my men have strict instructions to ride directly to the farm where they are being kept the moment they see spells interfering here today. So, you see my curly haired friend," Donagarn singled out Nasgro, "if my son so much as feels a shiver down his spine from your harnessing, your mother will be dead within the hour," Donagarn smirked.

"What do you mean my mother?" Nasgro asked. His face had gone pale.

"Well, my men reported that she was the only one we were able to take alive," Donagarn confirmed. "Your father murdered one of my employees when we came to your home, and that little sister of yours was nowhere to be found."

Nasgro looked utterly at a loss for words or action. Odette grabbed him, wrapping his arm around her shoulder before he could stagger and fall. Jaeger had never seen anything so painful as watching his friend right now.

"As I said," Emperor Hildebrante responded icily. "You will be sentenced to death for your treason. I also promise that we will bring justice to the men who were involved in your father's murder, Nasgro." There may have been thousands of mercenaries standing in front of the emperor and his small force, but he spoke with absolute certainty.

"You leave me with no choice Hildebrante," Donagarn responded with false remorse. He called past the emperor to the men behind him. "Soldiers of The Plateau, you do not need to die for this weak man. Any man who takes a knee while we do what is necessary, can serve me with a clear conscience when I am Emperor."

Emperor Hildebrante didn't even look back to see if the message had any effect. As Donagarn raised his hand Jaeger stepped forward, he could immediately feel Kostian harnessing DarkLand matter the moment he took a step. Jaeger drew his sword and walked forward towards the tyrant. Donagarn melted back behind his guards as they stepped past him with weapons drawn.

"You can't save him now," Jaeger snarled at the mercenaries. Somewhere in this army were the men who had helped Kostian assault Aema and abduct Berran.

Kostian struck without warning, attempting to paralyze Jaeger with a flood of DarkLand matter. Jaeger could feel the attempt repel back from the field of protection he held a metre from his body, as he breathed in deeply. He looked across at the disgraced student with contempt. With a mixture of surprise and desperation, Kostian hurled an enormous ball of fire at Jaeger's defences. Again, the attempt stopped dead a metre from Jaeger's body.

"The students are using magic!" Donagarn called. Several of his mercenaries pushed their way back through the crowd while others signaled to riders at the back of their army.

"Why don't you try that again?" Jaeger growled, his eyes fixed on Kostian. Jaeger continued to push forward, now pulsating with power.

Without a word, two mercenaries leapt at him, swinging their blades primitively at his head. Jaeger didn't even bother to block, and their swords bounced back off his field of power. With a sharp lunge he ran one of them through. The rest fell back as he continued to walk towards Kostian. Kostian desperately began hurling more and more attacks at Jaeger as he approached.

Jaeger could feel himself harnessing DarkLand matter through his palms at the same time that he continued to inhale and process purified matter to maintain his defences. He knew exactly what he was planning to do. Pausing directly in front of Kostian, Jaeger lowered his sword and sheathed it. He then looked into Kostian's eyes as he turned his palms outwards to the young man he had hated from the moment they met.

Kostian's eyes bulged as his body stiffened and he began to realise what was happening to him. Jaeger continued to flood Kostian's muscles with DarkLand matter, paralyzing him the same way he had seen Kostian practice on scaleskin prisoners in Grantanmar. The same way Charnel had paralyzed Jaeger on their last night in that evil place so that Kostian could torture him too.

He held Kostian upright for a few moments, giving him a chance to appreciate his situation, and then unleashed a punch infused with all the supernatural power he could hold. His fist cracked Kostian in the same eye that he had struck Aema. Kostian was hurled backwards several metres, cartwheeling from the point of impact. His body was limp where it came to rest.

"Kill him!" Donagarn shrieked as he ran towards Jaeger.

Only a handful of mercenaries charged with him, Jaeger slashed at them without paying attention to their weapons which continued to bounce off the field of power he maintained around him. As Donagarn charged in blindly, Jaeger leapt forward catching his sword arm at the wrist with his right hand. Sheathing his sword and grabbing Donagarn's shirt with his left hand, Jaeger yanked with all his power, flinging the treasonous tyrant forwards to fall at the feet of their Emperor.

"Drop your weapons now!" Jaeger roared at the army before him. Nasgro had already lost control, throwing fireballs deep into their ranks where the messengers had left. The emperor's soldiers all stood in perfect unison with the points of their weapons facing their enemies.

"Drop them!" Jaeger yelled again, arcing a sheet of lightning through dozens of the thugs crowded before him. This was the last straw, weapons clattered to the ground across the courtyard as the soldiers of the emperor advanced. Many mercenaries fled back towards the broken gates, starting a mass panic.

"Thank you Jaeger," Emperor Hildebrante said simply, before looking down with the point of his sword pressed against Donagarn's chest. "Take this man into custody," he instructed his men. Marrick stepped forward with several men, rolling Donagarn over and tying his hands behind his back.

"I have to get to that farm, emperor," Jaeger apologized, before waving Nasgro to join him. His friend was a mess of rage and grief. "Come with me Nasgro. Aema, please come with me too. We can follow their riders to the farm and rescue anybody who is being held there."

The pair both followed Jaeger over to Pebbles, who seemed very much aware that all three of them intended to ride away from this place on his back. With a little awkward placing, they all managed to climb on, and Jaeger supported Pebbles' powerful wings with an exertion of power to lift them from the ground. As they gained height over the masses evacuating Conorbatia Square, they were able to easily pick out the riders further down the roads leaving the city.

22 THE EMPEROR'S JUSTICE

Jaeger looked out across Conorbatia Square. Once again, he was an honored guest in the palace of his Emperor. He had not yet managed to arrange a dorm back at Clouds College, but Emperor Hildebrante had insisted that he would always have a room at the palace whenever he was back in the city and needed one.

"Are you okay?" Aema asked, rising from their bed and joining him at the window.

The sun had only just risen and the city was still shadowed by the palace and other tall buildings, as they stared back towards the western entrance to Conorbatia. So much had happened and there had been so little time to collect all the pieces that had been missing in the day after Donagarn's arrest. Jaeger was just glad that he had been able to thoroughly bathe and sleep comfortably back with Aema again. He would just have to enjoy one step at a time until the dust settled.

"I should be asking *you* that question, Aema. I don't know half of what has happened while I was gone,

243

but I wish I had never left you."

"A lot has happened, but you came back and we are all okay. I think in the longer run we will actually all be better off because you left when you did. You did things yesterday I could barely understand. And you made it look so easy," Aema added in amazement.

"I don't think Nasgro is okay," Jaeger disagreed.

"No your right, but that didn't happen because you left. I don't understand why you have always been so intent to blame yourself for anything you can. It's really unhealthy."

"I don't know either," Jaeger agreed. "I think that I have felt so much guilt over being away from you all year, that maybe I am looking for something I can find to prove I did the wrong thing."

"You're different to the people here Jaeger. I don't know if it's a West-Yield thing, or a Jaeger thing, but I have never met anybody who chooses to hold themselves responsible for so many things that aren't their responsibility."

"Maybe the people in Conorbatia don't feel the need to hold themselves responsible for enough," Jaeger countered.

"The people in Conorbatia *definitely* don't take enough responsibility beyond of their own private ambitions," Aema agreed. "But I still think you go too far the other way."

"Probably," Jaeger agreed. He held her chin looking at the fading colours of bruising around her eye. There was very little he could say about it, or anything else for that matter. He simply gave his girlfriend a kiss and decided to be grateful that she was still here.

"Why don't we go find our friends today. There

is a lot we all need to catch up on and I guess it will be easier to tell my stories to everybody at once," he smiled.

"Sounds good to me," Aema agreed with another kiss.

Aema and Jaeger strolled through the streets towards Clouds College beside Pebbles casually. Pebbles had enjoyed a comfortable night in the emperor's private stables, and had received a great deal of grooming in the process. The three of them were enjoying the pleasant stroll, as Jaeger and Aema sipped the hot coffees they had taken with them from the palace kitchen. The morning was frosty and the streets leading east were busy. Jaeger smiled at the stares of the residents and merchants as they passed them by.

"Pebbles is going to attract a lot of attention in this city," Aema observed. "Most people believed that the stories about the aves-caprinae were just fables. *I* thought they were just fables until yesterday!"

"Hear that buddy? Nobody believes in you," Jaeger patted Pebbles affectionately. Pebbles sidestepped playfully and butted Jaeger, spilling his coffee. "First clean clothes I've worn in weeks!" Jaeger complained, rubbing the liquid as it soaked into the front of his warm tunic.

It felt good to be back on college grounds as they crossed onto the campus. The stares of the students were just as surprised as the residents of Conorbatia, but there were less people about at this time of morning here. As they made their way towards the student accommodation, Jaeger was reminded to confess about destroying Aema's door. She hadn't been back since then, but understood the panic Jaeger had felt when he returned and couldn't find anybody.

It took until nearly the afternoon to gather everyone together. They all settled around in a group by the creek that had always been so special to Aema and Jaeger. The only ones not there were Nasgro and Odette. It had been devastating to witness Nasgro's reunion with just his mother. They rescued her and all the other families from one of Donagarn's acquired farms. He was now on a temporary break from the college and was staying with his mother and his little sister at home while they grieved.

"I can't believe Nasgro was running things for most of this year," Jaeger exclaimed, lacking a little enthusiasm as he thought of the loss his friend had suffered.

"He's smart," Berran agreed, "really smart. Aema kind of instigated a lot of the resistance to Silo, but when Nasgro bought in you could just tell he knew exactly how far we could push things and how to go about it."

"He paid a horrible price for what we did," Aema added remorsefully.

"Donagarn had this planned for months Aema," Lisle interjected. "He knew that he would never control the college until he was Emperor, so he was always going to try to find a way to hold the college ransom and keep them out of the fight."

"She's right," Berran agreed.

"You and Berran paid a price too don't forget." Lisle continued. "I know it's a lot easier to accept casualties on the southern frontline, but there is always going to be irreparable loss in war, and what Donagarn did was war. You were just one of the only people fighting."

"I like that Lisle, you are absolutely right," Jaeger agreed.

"And what about you?" Berran added with a little more enthusiasm. "We all want to know what you've been doing. You can't expect to disappear for half a year, and then come back with some crazy new powers and a skygoat-"

"-Pebbles," Jaeger corrected.

"Sorry, Pebbles. You can't come back with Pebbles and all these new powers and then expect that Aema is the only one you have to explain it to. We want first-hand information!" he demanded lightheartedly.

"Don't worry, I'll tell you anything you want to know," Jaeger promised.

"Okay then, did you tell Aema about your quest last night?" Berran asked.

"Just a little"

"Then what were you two doing?"

"None of your business" Jaeger pinched his friend.

"Not off to a good start answering all of our questions then are you?" Berran laughed.

"About my *quest*," Jaeger clarified. "I'll tell you guys anything you want to know about my 'quest', as long as somebody else is asking. Berran isn't allowed to ask questions anymore."

They all sat around, enthralled by Jaeger's adventures. From the nomads in the desert, to the unique vegetation atop the Thin Air Peaks. Most of the questions were directed at the monks' unique method of manipulating purified magic and the fact that Pebbles and entire herds of skygoats were living up there. Pebbles was showered with attention and seemed to very much enjoy the company of young humans on The Plateau. In very little time, Jaeger had ended up promising rides over the city for all of them, with Pebbles' consent of course.

The most interesting piece of information was the confirmation that Worley had also spent a significant period of time living amongst the monks of the peaks. It seemed to be a big breakthrough to hear Jaeger speak so freely about something that Worley had never officially acknowledged. Jaeger had to explain the mentality of the monks of the peaks to make sense of this, as well as the differences between how both of them had left the peaks.

By the end of the day, Jaeger and Aema were finally returning together through the streets of Conorbatia back to the palace. Pebbles strolled alongside them pleasantly. They were all enjoying the casual pace they were able to move at, without needing to take to the skies to get back.

Nobody wanted to leave Nasgro alone for too long. It was important even though he remained with his family, that he knew they were there for him. Instead, they agreed that Jaeger and Aema could fly to his home early in the morning tomorrow and offer for all of his friends to join him on their way to Conorbatia Square. Tomorrow the city would witness the emperor's justice.

Nearly the entire city gathered into Conorbatia Square in the morning. Their numbers filled the square and trailed back along the streets leading in from the markets. Farmers, business owners, families who had been freed, everybody had been affected in some way by the terror that Donagarn had brought to their streets. Some were now curious if they would get their stores and land returned to them, others were just here to see justice served.

At the top of the steps to the palace, Marrick stood beside his Emperor. Having witnessed Nasgro's pain and loss first-hand, Emperor Hildebrante had invited his family to stand present at the top of the steps, as a symbol for all in the crowd who had suffered.

Jaeger stood with Aema alongside Nasgro, his family, and the rest of his friends. There was something sickeningly unpleasant about an event of this nature. Jaeger knew that it would provide himself and his friends no pleasure, but he hoped that it would at least offer closure.

Emperor Hildebrante stood before his massed people with his sword unsheathed, point down resting on the flagstones. Clasped in irons and cowled with a hood over his head, Donagarn was brought before him. The masses stirred angrily at the sight of the man who had oppressed, robbed and murdered the population of Conorbatia. A silence fell over them as their Emperor raised his sword for their attention.

"People of Conorbatia," he boomed. Worley stood beside Marrick to the right of the emperor, supporting the projection of Hildebrante's voice. "I will keep this ugly affair simple. As your Emperor I failed all of you. It has been my priority to defend you from the enemies beyond our borders, and in doing so I failed to protect you from a great enemy within." He turned to Donagarn, removing the hood from his head.

"For the high crimes of treason and mass murder, I sentence you to death."

Donagarn resisted the soldiers as they pushed him towards the chopping block. Public executions had not been a thing in The Plateau for decades, so there were no restraints to hold him in position, as he thrashed in defiance against his sentence. After a few moments, Hildebrante raised a placating hand to his soldiers and they stepped back, releasing the prisoner.

Donagarn pulled back to his knees and looked up at his Emperor, a smirk just edging onto the corner of his lips, before Hildebrante beheaded him where he knelt. It was unorthodox and unexpected, but Jaeger felt a mixture of relief and revulsion. The circus that had been Donagarn and his years manipulating this city was over. Hildebrante turned to his people again. His face betrayed no emotion and he stood the picture of the emperor he truly was in that moment.

"Farms, stores, businesses; all that was unlawfully obtained from you will be returned," he began. "More-over, the Silo estate and all lands and businesses that it owned before this year will be seized by the crown." A murmur went through the masses at this. "These assets will be managed by my steward, where all restitution will be paid from, to those who suffered at the hands of this criminal. Please understand that this will take time, so I suggest for now you return to your farms and businesses as if you never lost them, and prepare any claim you have on restitution to the palace when you feel you are ready."

The masses before him became a hive of noise and small conversation. Emperor Hildebrante looked out across his people and then back at Worley, the professor gave him a reassuring nod that his voice would still be loud enough to be heard.

"As your Emperor, I will return to our nation's frontline again soon. Any mercenaries who served Silo during their brief disruption to this city, will accompany me as enlisted men. Those who committed crimes during the disruption will remain in Conorbatia to await trial. Again, this will take some time, however if you have any crimes to report please do so in the coming weeks. When I depart again, I hope to leave you far safer than I did the last time."

The emperor turned to Jaeger and Nasgro, acknowledging them both personally along with Nasgro's family, before he left the steps in front of his people. Jaeger wasn't sure if they had expected more when they gathered here this morning, but the emperor had said all that he had felt compelled to say.

After they had left Conorbatia Square together, Jaeger and Aema walked Nasgro and his family home. It turned out to be a gloomy day right up until that evening, however Jaeger was at least happy that he would finally have some time to catch up with his old friend Marrick tomorrow. They had spoken briefly at the top of the steps to the palace and made plans to free time up the following day. Jaeger's return to The Plateau had required more information to be processed than he had ever imagined was possible, but he was glad that Marrick was finally next on this list.

At breakfast, Aema said she would return to the college to get back to her studies and repair an unfortunate incident involving the door to her room. She left Jaeger and Marrick politely to finish their meal in the common hall and went on her way. Marrick was amused to hear about that story and many more from Jaeger's trips, to the Thin Air Peaks, Aridhold, and West-Yield.

Marrick had spent the entire year to-date in the south with Darroch and Hildebrante. He had been preparing and defending Darroch's newly organised southern front. Marrick said that he had witnessed great progress along the forts in their preparation for war. Things had been going better than anybody had expected for the first few months and Emperor Hildebrante's tour had been perfectly timed.

The emperor had become as much a man of war as he was a statesman during his time in the south. Despite the events in the city the last time he had left, Marrick said that Hildebrante was confident that his advisors and staff could implement all the declarations he had made today.

It would take a long time to get to the bottom of the investigations and trials for all the mercenaries who committed murder and other crimes during Silo's coup. Even within the first few days since the fall of Donagarn and Silo, stories were beginning to emerge of blackmail and intimidation, even among the mercenaries serving Donagarn. This seemed to be verified by the tactics he had used to force owners to sell their businesses, however it did not exonerate the mercenaries of all wrongdoing.

It was to be a long process, identifying the crimes committed by thugs during Silo's brief reign over the city. Any mercenaries accused of serious crimes along with their treason would remain in the city to be lawfully trialed. If guilty they would be adequately sentenced, if innocent, they would be safe to return their debt on The Plateau's frontline.

Hildebrante had meant what he said about returning quickly too. Marrick explained that towards the end of his tour of the south, alarming reports had suddenly begun to flood in from the forts. Emperor Hildebrante's return to Conorbatia had not been conveniently timed, and with order restored, he had much greater concerns to return to. His steward would be charged with leading the investigations and trials against all those accused. These trials would be forever remembered in The Plateau's history as *The Silo Coup Trials*.

23 THE PLATEAU IN FLAMES

"Professor we need to get you down off these walls," Erilain shouted at Harbold.

Harbold raised his hand to concede. He knew when he was defeated, he just needed Erilain to give him one more minute before he tried to stand. Fatigue was not a suitable word to describe what he felt anymore. After the expenditure of energy harnessing the sheer mass of DarkLand matter that had been channeled through his body, Harbold was thoroughly spent.

It had been a ruse, all of it. The scaleskin attacks had been restrained up until this point, their shamans had been bait. Even demons were pawns in this attack. After defeating the first demon-shaman, another had appeared. Soldiers and battle-mages alike had died in the process of killing both, but these two had only been a feint by the enemy.

As soon as Harbold and every remaining battle-mage in the city were done spending their last energy defeating the second demon-shaman, over a dozen more appeared at once. Colonel Hurn had charged bravely to his death in a suicide mission, just so that Harbold had a chance of killing it, and it had all been for nothing. The colonel of Derby was dead, and there were now just two mages left in the city, both of them spent.

"We have to leave professor!" Erilain insisted. "There is an entire disturbance of demons out there tearing down the walls to the city."

"Did you just, use my collective noun for demons?" Harbold gasped between breaths.

"Yes, I did sir," Erilain smiled. "Did you think I would forget all of your lectures the moment I left Clouds to serve down here?"

"Well, I think you may be the first person to use that term from personal experience," Harbold noted.

"Nobody is going to know if we don't get out of here!" she reminded him.

"No, good point" Harbold agreed, finally forcing himself to rise from the battlement he was slumped against.

Soldiers were holding their ground honorably across the length of the remaining walls of Derby that were intact. Harbold watched as regiments formed up to defend each of the breaches. The pride of The Plateau was facing mayhem with discipline, but the city was now leaderless.

"Captain!" Harbold called to the leader of the nearest regiment. "This city needs to be evacuated."

"Can't evacuate it if I abandon this breach!" the captain called back.

"Can I borrow one of your men to send a

message to Lieutenant Hadvar?"

"Lieutenant's dead sir," the captain replied simply.

"Who is in charge of the city?" Harbold demanded.

"As far as I know there's nothing but captains and companies left alive in Derby, you are the highest-ranking man left in the city." The captain didn't say it pointedly, but Harbold realised that if any lives were going to make it out the northern entrance from Derby, he would have to be the one to organize them.

"Thank you, captain, in that case I will need to borrow several messengers from your company."

All along the frontline, walls were being systematically dismantled to rubble. Harbold had called all of the companies defending breaches to remain fifty paces back from the walls, after an entire regiment was crushed by the crumbling masonry. He had also called all of the archers down from the walls. The frontline was now just a mixture of tall mountains of rubble and breaches, defended across open fields. Archers flanked wide on either side of the regiments, positioned strategically to pin-cushion the enemy troops charging through the breaches to engage their spearmen.

Meanwhile behind the destruction, the city was evacuating. The defence of the breaches was going quite successfully for now. With spearmen fifty paces back and archers on either side of them, the flood of scaleskins were being shot dead in rows for as long as the soldiers could hold the line. Harbold watched with satisfaction from atop the horse he had been provided, as an entire volley shot directly into the sides of the oncoming defenders entering the fields of the city.

He knew that it was only a matter of time. Soon the demon-shamans outside would be done with their demolition of the city walls. Once they entered the city, arrows and spears would be useless. The brave soldiers defending the breaches would all die then, and Harbold would be smart not to pit his powers against them. It would be pointless with just two exhausted mages left in Derby, and he knew that the demon-shamans were now waiting to root out any last surviving mages.

"Don't even think about it," he cautioned Erilain as she began harnessing.

"It's okay professor, I have recovered a little and can give a bit more."

"No!" he shouted now. "Let it go immediately!" Erilain froze and slowly unclenched her harnessing as instructed.

"What is the problem?" she asked finally, after letting all of the matter go.

"They're searching for us. Don't you see? the first two demons were bait to lure every battle-mage in the city to the walls. They could raze the rest of Derby in minute if they wanted to. Those demon-shamans are still waiting out there because they want to see if any more battle-mages try to help defend the city."

"They're here for us?" Erilain looked terrified.

"They don't care about our soldiers. They have tens of thousands of scaleskins at their command. They just want to exterminate any battle-mages that they can, before they move past Derby and deeper into The Plateau."

"Deeper into The Plateau?" Erilain's face had gone pale.

"Look around Erilain, this isn't Grantanmar. Darroch was prepared for that fortress to fall. There is no contingency plan that could have prepared us to fight an entire disturbance of demons" he smiled at her encouragingly.

"So, they are going to hunt us down across The Plateau until there is nothing left?" Erilain looked about ready to give in.

"I never said that. Once we have evacuated as many men as possible from Derby, we need to head north to evacuate all of the nearby towns. I honestly don't know how we will stop them then, but we don't have to have answers to everything right away. Damage reduction today, solutions tomorrow."

A messenger rode out across the fields from the city towards the two battle-mages. Harbold felt a slight weight of relief lift from his shoulders as he recognized the messenger. This had been the last one that he had sent to scour the eastern and western wings of the city. The fact that he was alive meant that the enemy forces had not encircled the men defending the breaches.

"Sir, the last evacuees have passed through the northern gates, there are two regiments waiting there as you instructed."

"Good news at last," Harbold replied. "Call the archers back from all of the breaches too, and make note of the names of all the captains who remain behind. The least history can do is remember the sacrifice of their regiments."

***

Darroch stood alongside his colonel in the

watchtower of Sorrento. The heat was stifling hot and the humidity was as bad as it had ever been in the jungles to the south.

"More water please soldier," Darroch called down, without taking his eyes off The Plateau's edge beyond the walls.

"Yes general, I'll make sure you have enough up there," a soldier called back to him from the ground.

"Can you see them coming?" Colonel Aggans asked, watching his commander intently. "No. But they're out there. I'd imagine we will find out soon enough when that sun goes down, and *they'll* know when the entire slope before us catches fire" he added with a grin.

Nothing seemed to get the better of Darroch, not even this silent, humid, tension that had been building for the last two days. Or maybe he was just better at hiding it than everybody else.

The water arrived and the sun continued to drift lower in the west. Darroch called for his reserve battle-mages to be roused from off-duty. He seemed to know as well as anybody that the tension could no longer become any greater without something having to give. They were joined by several battle-mages in the watchtower, as dozens more were distributed along the battlements to the south. Sorrento was better supplied, with more soldiers and magic users than anywhere else along the southern frontline by double.

The skies turned a brilliant mix of crimson and orange, as the changing of the watch along the walls concluded. As the last of the day-watch completed their handover and began their march back towards their barracks, a fireball suddenly appeared from below the line of the slopes beyond the walls. The fireball had no curvature in its trajectory as it streaked across the skies. It passed above the walls like a dark purple comet, standing out distinctly against the stunning background of the sunset.

As the defenders along the walls watched the fireball gradually burn out in the distant skies, the roar of thousands of scaleskins filled the evening. Along the length of the slopes the horde appeared. Without pause, dozens of red fireballs returned fire from the walls, as the assembled battle-mages of Sorrento responded. Wherever the fireballs struck, scaleskins fell dead in large clusters.

Even more effective, was the fuel this ignited. Just one hundred yards from the walls, and one hundred yards in along the flats from the edge of The Plateau, a wall of fire lit up the twilight. The burning wall killed hundreds of scaleskins immediately, cutting off thousands more who had already passed the trap. Arrows showered overhead from behind the walls of Sorrento, raining down amongst the attackers. But they did not stop their charge.

With their numbers rapidly thinning, the scaleskins charged towards the wall without fear. Darroch measured the bodies littered across the killing fields against the numbers still charging forward relentlessly. He estimated that a handful of ladders may reach the walls once the halfling sharpshooters were done with them, but with the wall of fire cutting the attackers off from the rest of their army, they would be futile.

As predicted, several ladders were raised against the city walls. There must have only been a few dozen scaleskins left as they climbed, and within a few more minutes the defenders along the walls had speared every last one trying to enter the city. The closest the enemy had come in months, had not cost Sorrento a single life so far, as the flames burned along the horizon behind them.

Darroch saw clearly from his watchtower as a section of flames a hundred yards wide extinguished suddenly. A wall of black mist rose up over the edge of the slope, smothering the fires and shrouding the fields from sight.

Out of the mist another fireball emerged, this time the size of a large wagon. The purple fireball trailed darkness in its wake as it flew directly towards the watchtower. Waves of static and bright light rose up to intercept the fireball as it reached the walls, passing over them and on towards the watchtower.

The fireball had almost entirely been dispelled when it struck the watchtower, penetrating the round walls below Darroch's position.

"Evacuate the tower!" Darroch called, as he saw arcs of lightning and fireballs erupting from across the walls back into the mist in retaliation.

There was a metal pole driven directly through the centre of the watchtower for quick escape, and Darroch glided down it smoothly to the ground. He raced across the lawns to the nearest battlement with colonel Aggans, climbing the stairs just in time to see the demon-shaman below.

As the mist dissipated under the barrage from Sorrento's battle-mages, a terrifying figure emerged at the head of thousands more scaleskins. The horde held still in a perfect line, as the demon-shaman stepped forward and raised its arms above its head.

The soulless shadow that stood above the shaman became taller, and what could have been two enormous arms also rose towards the sky from within the shadow. From that single dual-shape, fireballs and lightning exploded forwards in a dozen directions. The lightning arced forwards into the walls so fast that no counter-spells could be cast to stop them in time.

Here and there, a handful of unlucky soldiers were killed from atop the battlements, and the strong dwarf-made masonry was scorched wherever the lightning struck. The fireballs were met with more resistance, as again static and matter leapt out from the walls to intercept the demon-shaman's sorcery. What came next was something Darroch would never forget. Months of training and education had fortified the entire southern frontline of The Plateau, and Sorrento was better trained and better resourced than any other fortress.

Every form of magical projectile that Darroch had ever seen or heard of, hurtled out from the walls now, all centered on the evil figure that had just assaulted them. The first handful fell short into an abyss of darkness, perhaps ten yards short of the demon-shaman. After this, the main barrage arrived, which was when the attacks broke through. The area around the creature disappeared from clear view, as lightning, fireballs, and clouds of energy invisible to the naked eye detonated on its position.

For more than a minute, both sides of the battle watched the awesome display, before the smoke and energy cleared. The mist across the horde of scaleskins had completely cleared, and a crater now stood where the demon-shaman had been. After a few more moments the battle-mages along the walls opened fire on the enemy forces.

The scaleskins appeared to be disoriented and afraid, and it didn't take long for the neat ranks to break into a rout, back towards the slope that descended from the edge of The Plateau. Across the field below, a rider called up to Darroch and colonel Aggans. They both descended sharply to meet him. The rider sat astride another mounted messenger, who appeared both ragged and breathless now that they had reached the outer walls.

"Sir, this messenger just arrived from Derby in the east. The fortress has fallen."

Darroch looked at the man as they both dismounted. The messenger carried no letter to hand to him.

"Commander," the messenger saluted. "Professor Harbold dispatched me after taking command of the city. He said to tell you they killed two demons before an entire disturbance of them attacked the city simultaneously. That is what they're called when a group of demons are together in one place." The messenger explained.

"I'm familiar with the professor's teachings," Darroch said with just the slightest amusement. "How many did he estimate in this disturbance?"

"He said maybe twenty. He said to tell you that they targeted the battle-mages first by drawing them out with the first two demons, before they destroyed every wall along the city's frontline. They will be roaming freely across The Plateau by now."

"We will move to intercept them." Darroch

assured him. "Colonel, I will be mobilizing half of our forces and battle-mages to depart tonight. You will monitor this attack tonight in that time to see if they are planning to do anything similar here, however once the army is ready, I will be leaving with it."

Colonel Aggans nodded and walked with Darroch back across the lawn to the horses stabled by the watchtower. After climbing onto his warhorse, Darroch turned back to colonel Aggans. "Colonel, the capital of the south is now yours. Good luck."

***

Harbold rode hard now towards Cork. This was now the third town he had reached since the fall of Derby. He had been forced to abandon the first two with no more than a handful of hours sleeping between them, and held very little hope that Cork would be any different as he looked sideways at Erilain. She too was strained with exhaustion and looked easily ten years older than she had two days ago. They rode at the head of a company of horsemen nearly one hundred strong.

The bulk of the army evacuated from Derby, had marched day and night directly north. They had been regularly harassed by the enemy, but had fortunately managed to stay ahead of the demons. Harbold had doubled back south twice to check on this army. Both times they had been engaged by much smaller forces of enemies hunting them as they retreated. It had been easy to fight them off, but allowed no rest and no breathing room, as they tried to break clear of danger with as many lives as possible. The enemy appeared to be everywhere at once.

Harbold gathered himself as he was hailed down by the captain of the guard in Cork.

"Derby has fallen and the enemy marches north," Harbold announced as his small force pulled up at the gates.

"Damn you, that's bad news sir!" the captain replied. "You don't mince much with words do you?"

"There is no time and no point," Harbold replied. "I need your entire town evacuating north within two hours. I also need them to leave any horses and wagons that are not absolutely essential behind. The army that is marching behind us needs every one that they can get."

"This is a town, not a fortress sir. A lot of those wagons and horses are privately owned. And what would you consider 'absolutely essential' anyway?" The captain asked.

"Essential is anybody too old to walk on foot. Privately owned or not, the town population will be safe moving north on foot as long as the army of Derby remains behind them, and that army needs all the resources it can get. Understood?"

"Understood," the captain nodded bleakly. "Do you have any other requests?"

Harbold considered this briefly. "Food, any food and supplies that can be prepared would go a long way when the army arrives in this town. If they can arrive in Cork to empty lodgings and food to eat, they may be allowed to rest for a few hours with a full stomach. The enemy forces will hit soon after that and force them to retreat further north."

***

It was late morning as Darroch looked out over the eastern province of The Plateau. Smoke could be seen rising in the distance from various points as far as the eye could see. He had deliberately maneuvered his forces at the tallest hill he could find, when the scouts began to report signs of destruction ahead in the lands they were entering. Surveying the devastation, there were no signs of enemy forces moving within sight. The landscape bowled conveniently from the point they were looking out from.

"Halt the army here and setup position," he instructed his lieutenants. "I want scouting parties searching in every direction within a one-hundred-and-eighty-degree radius from this lookout. If they see the enemy moving from any of these directions, they are to report back at camp. If they find a tall position like this one deeper into the lands ahead, tell them to report back. We will have to creep our way forward from here onwards, but I want the enemy forces to be aware of our presence. With a little luck we can draw them into a fight without spreading ourselves too thin."

Officers dispatched from Darroch's position immediately on various duties from his directive. Within an hour a command tent had been established at the top of the hill and defensive barricades had been driven into the ground below. Dozens of mounted companies had been dispatched in multiple directions from the hilltop, with strict instructions on how to engage any enemy forces they encountered.

As his lieutenants continued to oversee the setup, Darroch settled back down and waited to see what news returned. By evening the first patrols began to return, each patrol captain reporting directly to the command tent.

"Just more towns burning as we rode north of our eastern position sir," the first returned captain explained. "We circled every town we came by and they were abandoned after the enemy razed them. Good news is none of the northern towns had dead bodies. Either our forces got there first and warned them, or the demons are mopping up after themselves."

"We've come across nothing of the sort fortunately, so I will assume the former," Darroch replied. The sun had not yet set as two more captains dismounted and entered. "Gentlemen, what did you find?" Darroch greeted them as they joined him.

"Burned and abandoned towns for a hundred miles south east" the first one reported. "No contact with the enemy."

"Much of the same sir," the second captain added when Darroch turned to him. "Except that we did make contact with a large contingent of wolf-riders. They could have been acting as a vanguard for the invasion to catch stragglers."

"What makes you say that?" Darroch asked.

"We fled north when they caught us by surprise for a short while, came across an abandoned town they hadn't put to the torch yet."

"What was your initial direction?" Darroch probed.

"Directly east sir, initially. We rode back west-south-west after deviating north to escape the vanguard. By the time we lost them, they knew we were returning to the west, just as instructed," the captain added.

The returning captains all had similar reports as

they trickled back to the camp after dark. It was not until late in the evening that more interesting information arrived. Sometime shortly after Darroch had retired to his tent, he was roused back to the command centre with news that the last captain unaccounted for, had returned. As Darroch reached the entrance to the command tent, he was greeted by over two-dozen haggard soldiers with their horses pegged outside.

"Come in, all of you," he invited, knowing without doubt that he had found survivors from Derby.

***

Harbold was pleasantly surprised that he had been allowed a full night's sleep, before he was woken by sightings of the enemy. The retreating army from Derby had arrived hours behind Harbold's small force. Here the exhausted infantry had also managed a few hours in the comfortable lodging of the abandoned town.

The wounded had been immediately fed and then placed in carts and wagons to continue north of the town. The rest had been allowed a meal and some sleep. They now jogged along on foot beside Harbold and his small company of horsemen, leading them further north.

The main army of scaleskins had continued to roll onwards over everything in their path, but they were at least not as fast as the small war-bands of wolf riders. It was the mounted slags with their small crude bows that were causing most of the difficulty. They were not strong enough to defeat the large army retreating from derby, but they allowed it no rest and hunted the open plains of The Plateau relentlessly for easy victims.

Harbold looked at Erilain and then the mounted company he had with him. Erilain looked far more capable after the brief rest they had managed during the night, the cavalry also appeared more up to the task today. There were only fifty of them now, as Harbold had sent half of them ahead with the wagons overnight to escort the wounded. Looking out across the ranks of infantry marching north, he wasn't so sure that a few hours of sleep was enough.

Approximately three thousand men on foot, force-marched through injury and exhaustion, with the mild hope that they would reach the next town without being overtaken. There, if they were lucky, they would get a brief sleep and then begin the journey all over again. It would take many more days like this before they were far enough north for relief forces to intercept them.

Unfortunately, there was nothing but small towns between the south eastern frontline and Conorbatia, and without mobilizing the entire college of magic; Harbold struggled to fathom how they would stop the army that had destroyed derby at all.

As the morning began to wind into the afternoon, the first enemy patrols were spotted. The exhausted army knew the drill now and the central units of infantry continued marching without paying the reports any attention. Archers took up the rear and flanked both sides of the army, to return fire with longer range when the wolf riders began sneaking closer with their short bows.

Unfortunately, the main thing the army lacked was cavalry. They had lost the majority of their mounted soldiers along with colonel Hurn when he had bravely charged the enemy shamans. Harbold had been forced to dispatch even more north to send word to The Plateau and escort wounded soldiers ahead of the main army. The rest were basically now on patrol in every direction to warn the surrounding towns and ensure that enemy forces could not surprise the army as it retreated.

The wolf riders knew this as they gathered on both sides of the army. They hung back out of range of the archers, taunting the small contingent of cavalry riding with Harbold. For more than an hour, more and more wolf riders accumulated on either side, as the infantry tried to ignore the enemy while marching further north. As the numbers of wolf riders continued to grow, a small company of ten horsemen charged into view from the north, leading twice as many unmanned horses with them.

"Sir we evacuated the town of Everton ahead this morning, they left food, horses and wagons behind as instructed. However, we were forced to abandon the town an hour ago when the wolf riders arrived. They circled the town while more arrived before attacking. We were lucky to make a break back south to tell you."

Harbold looked ahead noting a small plume of smoke dispersing far in the distance. "Filthy reptiles!" he swore. "How many of them?"

"More than a hundred when we left sir"

"That does it, I'll deal with this. Cavalry!" he called, looking for a few moments at the hundreds of wolf riders now stalking the army beyond bow range.

Harbold urged his horse forward into a canter. He was joined by Erilain and the small company of remaining mounted soldiers he had with him. They rode swiftly now, already a hundred yards ahead of the army when he saw the wolf riders respond.

Like an angry swarm, they were drawn to the horsemen riding away from the protection of the main force. Within a few more minutes Harbold saw the wolf riders close into the gap he had put between his company and the army behind them, while more raced to overtake and surround him.

Only a small opening in the ring of enemies remained ahead, as the horsemen increased their pace. They were faster than the wolves at full speed, however Harbold could see them quickly squeezing in on either side. He reigned in sharply. Trying to outrun them would be pointless when the raiders came within range with their short bows in a few more moments.

"You take the left side," he called to Erilain as he led his horse clear of the company on the right.

The wolf riders charged into range, whooping and jeering with arrows nocked, as Harbold harnessed the matter around him inwards. The first shot landed metres away from where he was sitting, and Harbold watched the second as it arced towards him, finding its mark. With a slight shove, Harbold halted the arrow mid-flight a few metres from his body, before releasing a fork of lightning back towards the enemy.

A dozen wolves and their riders fell dead fifty yards from Harbold, and the rest scattered. They wanted nothing to do with this uneven exchange of missiles. On the left side of the company Erilain was discharging dozens of miniature fireballs, the wolf riders were agile but the projectiles were small enough and directed in clusters, managing to hit a handful of enemies. Arrows began to fall among the riders behind Harbold from the north and south and several of his soldiers went down.

He had misjudged the situation in his anger and they did not have enough mages to protect all of them.

"Draw in close!" he instructed the riders, pulling back towards them and creating a smaller circumference to protect with magic.

They did as instructed and he now managed to create a shield large enough to shelter all of the men around him. As more arrows fell up against the shield he held, Harbold unleashed another arc of lightning back towards the attackers who had crept in close from the north. Maintaining his shield while attacking was an exhausting exercise, and Harbold knew he would not be able to do this for long. He looked back at the army now half a mile behind them. Archers were jogging ahead to support him. If he could hold out until they were within range, his company might not pay the ultimate price for his brash decision.

Harbold continued to maintain the shield across his entire small force and returned fire to the north and the east. Erilain continued to find targets to the west of their formation as more and more wolf riders were drawn away from the main army towards them. The enemy seemed to have become fixated on the cavalry since Harbold had begun using magic, and the raiders were now dying consistently just to get near him.

Suddenly the wolf riders broke into a charge from all directions, hoping to ride through the mages and their small bodyguard of cavalry at whatever cost necessary. The cost was great. As they rode in, Erilain was able to hit dozens with her spray of tiny fireballs now. Harbold dropped his shield for a moment to unleash a wave of detonations at the oncoming charge. Pockets of raw DarkLand matter sped forward from his position in high velocity bubbles, detonating suddenly as the raiders ran through them.

The impact was devastating, dozens of raiders fell dead with many more stumbling over their bodies in the carnage. Arrows found their targets among the clustered cavalry behind him without Harbold's shield. He heard the sudden screams of his men as they slumped or fell from their horses. Suddenly a roaring cheer went up from the army behind them. Harbold didn't have time to look back to see what the excitement was all about. He recovered his shield and unleashed with everything he had.

"Charge the raiders to the south!" he ordered the few mounted soldiers he had left. Over half of them had died because he had led them away from the army.

The cavalry formed up and charged. Spears held high, they picked out their targets. A few more arrows picked off the men before over a score of them struck the wolf riders at full speed. Wolves were impaled on thrown spears and goblins were beheaded by the quickly drawn swords of The Plateau's knights. Several more went down, but more emerged from the other side of the small skirmish. A quick glance showed Harbold why the army had been cheering.

Thousands of mounted soldiers had appeared from the west, and were now charging across the plains at full speed towards the raiders. Harbold and Erilain cantered behind the men who had broken through the enemy lines, maintaining their shields behind them with the last of their energy. Within another minute they had ridden well within range of the army, and expertly measured arrows now sailed overhead into the raiders still chasing them.

Their pursuit became a rout as the mounted knights broke across the enemy lines like a tidal wave from the west. Behind him, Harbold heard the war-cries of the relief force as they rode down wolf riders who had been hunting him just moments earlier. The raiders had overextended themselves with their clear orders to eliminate The Plateau's mages, and would now be unable to escape. The riders of The Plateau would outrun and kill every last one of them before they got away.

24 HARBOLD'S HYPOTHESIS

Jaeger soared high over Conorbatia with Aema's arms wrapped tightly around his waist. Their pleasant day by the creek together had made Pebbles become restless. Shortly after the young skygoat had made his boredom quite clear to them, they had agreed to go for a flight together over the city. Pebbles now had the strength and size to accommodate two riders on his back quite easily, and was using this strength to test the limits of Aema's comfort in the skies.

He banked sharply without warning as she pointed out the street they had met with Justin to Jaeger. Her hands returned sharply to Jaeger's waist and he could feel her harnessing small amounts of DarkLand matter through her clenched hands. He wasn't sure how she thought magic would be able to help her up here.

"Just roll with his movements," Jaeger called back over his shoulder. "The more you resist him the less you are going to feel secure on his back."

"I'm trying!" she called back in annoyance,

squeezing Jaeger's waist tighter and tilting off balance as Pebbles straightened out again. Jaeger laughed. Of all the problems in their lives, this was by far the most pleasant.

Conorbatia had mostly returned to normality and Clouds College had continued to keep its students busy. The professors hadn't managed to figure out what to do with Jaeger yet. He desperately wanted to be a part of the studies he had turned his back on last year, but there were a couple of details that needed to be figured out.

Firstly, no student could pick up a year of study halfway through. Last year he had only missed a few weeks when he began his additional tuition. Secondly, Jaeger's powers at harnessing magic were greater than most of the master mages now, albeit in completely different ways to what they taught.

Only Worley could properly understand where Jaeger was at, having spent a period of time in the peaks with the monks that he still refused to say much about. However even Worley had entirely concluded his studies at Clouds College before this, and he appeared to be unsure if it would be counterproductive for Jaeger to continue.

The one thing they agreed on, was that it would be impossible for students to learn anything about purified magic in an environment where there was none. Unfortunately, there was no way of reverse-engineering that process.

Pebbles now carried the pair south beyond the entrance to the city. This was a trick that he usually adopted to extend playtime when he sensed that Jaeger would soon ask to return home. The further Pebbles pushed beyond the edge of Conorbatia, the longer it would take them to return. As the city gate faded into the distance behind them, Jaeger noticed a lone rider racing along the emperor's paths as if all the DarkLand hordes were chasing him.

He nudged Pebbles lower for a closer look. The rider was ragged and his horse looked exhausted, but he still urged it forward relentlessly. As they passed overhead in the opposite direction, the rider looked up with a haunted and fearful look on his face. Jaeger remembered that the lack of familiarity with skygoats on The Plateau, could possibly be an intimidating sight for some, especially if they were already on edge.

"Was he a messenger?" Aema asked.

"I'm not sure, whatever message he has for the emperor it doesn't look good." Jaeger responded.

He nudged Pebbles again, this time to gain altitude. Pebbles responded excitedly, the powerful beats of his wings pulling them further and further into the sky. Jaeger wanted to push further south to see if anything was chasing the rider, while Pebbles seemed aware that playtime had clearly been extended.

The speed they could travel at was twice that of a fast horse, and the land below rolled away beneath them without any signs of danger or pursuit. After nearly an hour, they spotted a cluster of horsemen patrolling the area warily. Jaeger found the behaviour disturbing, and said as much.

"They look like they are expecting to find enemies the way they are moving," he explained to Aema.

"I don't really know how patrols are supposed to act," Aema admitted. "But they do look very nervous from here. Why don't we just ask them?"

"Yep, good idea," Jaeger agreed.

Pebbles descended gracefully again, gliding back to the earth like a kite, with his enormous wings fixed at full extension. They were spotted very quickly and deliberately landed fifty yards away to avoid causing any alarm. Jaeger knew that anything new could create tension when approaching men who were on high alert.

The patrol formed up expertly as they landed, and then cantered across the open fields towards him once he had come to a halt. Jaeger inhaled deeply and prepared to shield Pebbles and Aema if necessary. He held his hand up in a gesture of peace as they approached.

"Where do you come from?" the patrol captain called to them as they pulled up.

"We are from Conorbatia," Jaeger confirmed. "I grew up in West-Yield but we both are from Clouds College now."

"When did skygoats become normal in Conorbatia?" the captain asked, relaxing his guard.

"They're not really, but it's a long story."

"I bet it is. I didn't think the stories of the mythical aves-caprinae were real. But then I didn't particularly give too much thought to demons either until recently," the captain admitted.

"What has happened on the frontline?" Jaeger asked ominously.

"The frontline? The frontline has fallen in the east days ago. The entire Plateau is in flames." The haunted look returned to the captain's face.

"Which fortress fell? What do you mean the entire Plateau?" Jaeger demanded.

"Derby, we were defending Derby when the demons returned. They managed to kill the first one but then they kept coming. There was no holding it, our enemies are too powerful now. It's not a fair fight."

"What did commander Darroch say? How far have they spread beyond Derby?"

"Messengers left for the commander in Sorrento through the night while we defended the city. But we didn't have time to wait for a response. The city fell, and they have been burning towns in every direction ever since. They have their own patrols of wolf riders moving faster than the army could retreat. They're organized, they have been hunting us down as quickly as we could get away, and they're destroying the towns across The Plateau faster than we can reach them to prepare them."

"They will die," Jaeger snarled, nudging Pebbles to take flight again.

"You can't fight these demons," the captain warned.

"I've killed their demons before," Jaeger assured the captain.

"Jaeger no!" Aema interrupted. "We're not racing south like this. And you're not taking me back just to head south alone! We need to tell Emperor Hildebrante first and then travel south with an army, and mages."

"Listen to her mate," the captain agreed. "You look like there is a lot I don't know about you, but this is going to take an army of men and mages if anything is going to stop them."

"Thank you," Aema acknowledged the captain with exasperation. Her tone carried months of frustration and stress at Jaeger's impulsiveness. "Is there anything we can do to help you before we return to Conorbatia?"

"Nothing I can think of, that skygoat would definitely come in handy rounding up all the refugees to the south. But only if young Jaeger here can keep himself from picking fights with any demons," the captain added with amusement.

"Thanks," Jaeger responded dryly.

"Anytime," the captain replied. Jaeger couldn't hold back his smile, he suddenly felt like he was talking to an older version of Marrick.

"If that's all, we will get back to the palace immediately."

"Good luck," the captain nodded. "Hopefully we won't be too far behind you. Actually, ask the emperor to send some relief patrols please. We have been at it for days now, barely slept."

"Done," Jaeger promised. He nudged Pebbles back into flight as the patrol watched them in awe. Hopefully the sight of the mighty skygoat had been a pleasant distraction for them after all the unpleasant discoveries they had made recently.

Jaeger took his seat at the great table of the emperor's military council. An enormous detailed map of The Plateau fit perfectly from corner to corner of the rectangular table that seated over a dozen men. To his left sat professor Worley. Opposite him Emperor Hildebrante and Marrick stood, leaning deeply across the map from its southern orientation. Professor Sharelle was also there, along with Professor Harbold who had arrived late the night before.

Harbold had been fighting and protecting the retreat from Derby for days, before finally riding hard towards the capital. He looked beyond any description of worn out, but there was also a fierceness in his eyes that showed he was not ready to stop just yet. Jaeger made a mental note to offer his powers to heal Harbold's fatigue and injuries after the council.

Around them were several other high-ranking military officials, along with Hildebrante's steward Morrison. Jaeger had been clearly welcome and expected among these men, after his impressive display during Donagarn's attempted coup. Darroch was the only one missing.

"How many of these towns should I mark destroyed or fallen?" Hildebrante asked Harbold and the several officers who had returned from the field.

"Draw a large square from here," Harbold reached across the table pointing halfway south from Conorbatia to the frontline. "To here. To here." He pointed again at various corners. "They moved very quickly once they were clear of Derby, the only lines of containment you can expect to hold for a little while, is commander Darroch along this longitudinal line to the west. His forces took up several positions along the central Plateau when he realised how far they had spread."

"And you trust that he can hold those lines after what you saw?" Hildebrante questioned Harbold.

"I don't trust anything against what I saw, but if we are going to put our faith in any judgement, it will have to be in Darroch. He has a lot of resources prepared at his disposal and he is a genius in spreading them creatively, even when he is losing."

"Okay good," Hildebrante thanked Harbold. Drawing cotton lines across pins that had been placed along the map where he had been shown.

"Clouds College will suspend classes and can mobilise south with your army" Worley promised. "I can add dozens of master mages and professors to the forces you move south with."

"Again good," Hildebrante passed notes to Morrison. "I need to know when we may receive relief forces from the dwarves," he asked.

"King Borgisliege has assured us that the first regiments will arrive right behind their messenger. I would say they will be in Conorbatia by the end of the week. A message also arrived just now from High King Fëadarliege, he has assured us that all of the dwarf strongholds can now be sealed and put into hibernation if necessary.

"Apparently, they have been working on it all year. If they have to, they can completely seal off and abandon any stronghold to redistribute their forces where necessary. They believe they can then return to the stronghold to reopen them any time they want, and can guarantee that they will be untarnished when they do."

"Thank you," Hildebrante acknowledged. "Sounds like a secret that we could use along the frontline. How do you propose we spread the army when we push south Marrick?"

Marrick stood again over the table, holding several pins and figurines. "We do not have a large force in reserve here anymore, even if we wait until the end of the week for the dwarves of Aridhold to arrive. The bulk of the army is with Darroch holding this imaginary western border.

"If we push south, we will want to hold a single main force along the roads to the south. We can hope to retake all the destroyed towns along this route, and then run patrols wide to report where the enemy's forces are moving. With a little luck we can defeat them in the open fields all the way back to Derby."

"And if we reach Derby?" Hildebrante pressed.

"I would expect a siege," Marrick said plainly. "If the might of Clouds College is enough to defeat the demons they have running loose across The Plateau, we will be able to merge with Darroch's forces for a siege."

"You're being too optimistic," Harbold interrupted. "The enemy's armies aren't just led by demons anymore. They are populated by them. They tested us at the fortress. The first demon-possessed shaman drew out our mages before we killed it. The second one again was almost more than we could handle, but it was there to bring all of our battle-mages into one place. Once we were spent, several more of them appeared together. There is a small army of demons out there, taking shape in the bodies of scaleskin shamans to travel freely north."

"Why do they need to possess shamans to come north?" Jaeger asked. Professor Harbold had gained his post-graduate rank studying demonology, and held more knowledge than anybody on The Plateau regarding their nature.

"Because they can't exist beyond The DarkLand portal in this world alone. I believe that somehow they have managed to lure scaleskins and roachkin to come to them in the south, cross into the DarkLands through the Portal, and return as hosts for them to invade our continent."

Expressions of surprise and awe rippled across the council at this revelation. Jaeger looked aside to Worley who had shown no reaction.

"That is not everything," Harbold continued. "I do not believe the number of demons we are seeing could be possible without leadership."

"What kind of leadership do those bastards need!?" Marrick demanded. "Every one of them seems happy enough pulling the strings behind entire armies of scaleskins and their shamans."

"There is a small army of demons on The Plateau, and probably more to the south. They're working together consistently towards a common cause Marrick. The only reason I can think of for that is that they have leadership, the leadership of a demon prince."

"You believe that one of the six demon princes is now at large on The Plateau?"

"I didn't say he was on The Plateau yet," Harbold corrected. "But I believe that one may be on the continent, yes."

"And who would *he* be possessing?" Marrick demanded in exasperation. "Some scaleskin shaman-prince?"

"It is entirely possible that the demon princes can sustain themselves on this plane without a host. Although this should greatly weaken them."

"Oh great, I was beginning to think you only had bad news to predict." Marrick said sarcastically.

"Well, all of this is just predictions and conjecture," Harbold assured him. "But if you're craving good predictions then look at it this way; I believe that The DarkLand portal itself is a very inefficient and energy-intensive creation.

"How the elves learned there were six princes on the other side of it, I don't know, but it is widely accepted that the portal is a violation of all the physics and natural forces that exist in this world. The strength of all six princes combined is possibly the only thing maintaining it. If one of them has decided to go rogue and pass through it, then we could possibly close the portal forever by killing him."

"That's actually very good news," Marrick noted. "We just have to defeat his army of demons first before we get to him."

"Either way I'd like a shot at him," the professor admitted.

Everybody around the table looked emboldened by Harbold's fierce statement. Suddenly a knock was heard beyond the doors to the war council. A rigid soldier entered and paced professionally to the table to his Emperor.

"Sir, hundreds of men have just… landed, in the city. On the backs of more… skygoats," he explained looking past Emperor Hildebrante at Jaeger.

25 A MUSTER OF MANY RACES

Salmor approached the palace filled with a mixture of fascination and intent. He had never seen Conorbatia. Even when he had been born on The Plateau, he had not ventured far from his home town until the day he left for the peaks. The sight of the emperor's palace and the mansions along the road that led to it, made it clear that despite its challenges, the civilisation of man had been thriving.

There was an energy in this city that Jaeger and even his former protégé Worley could probably not pick up on. It was an undercurrent of corruption and self-interest, that left a sour taste in Salmor's mouth as he waited with the monks who had journeyed with him.

He reminded himself of his last proper conversation with Jaeger, about how he had realised that it was not his place to judge and look down on others. He was here to do something more than serve his own needs too, but that didn't make the taste in his mouth any easier to swallow.

He was led through into the palace, while the other monks waited outside. Once word returned from inside, many men at arms had offered to provide food and care for the herd of aves-caprinae that had borne the monks to the city.

The emperor's soldiers led him to the throne room, where the emperor now waited for him. Salmor took in the rich throne where the emperor sat, as he approached the foot of the steps below. The man before him looked confident and fit to sit on the lavish throne.

"Welcome to my city," he was greeted. "I am Emperor Hildebrante. We were at a war council when you arrived, and it appears that two of the men at the council have already met you if I am right in guessing that your name is Salmor?"

"That is the name I am known by, yes," Salmor replied humbly. "I can only assume that the two souls you have on your war council go by the names Worley and Jaeger if they know me."

"You are correct Salmor. We have never had contact or visitors from the monks of the Thin Air Peaks. Many on The Plateau even believe your society to be nothing more than a myth. How can I be of assistance to you after you have come so far?"

"If you already know two souls who know me from the peaks, then you have had contact with our society," Salmor corrected. "But the monks and I have not traveled this far on the generous backs of the mighty aves-caprinae to receive your assistance Emperor Hildebrante. We have come to offer your people ours."

"Thank you," Emperor Hildebrante said plainly. "Are the monks and caprinae here to join us in our war against the demons within our borders?"

"We will protect the souls of this nation from the evil they face," Salmor clarified.

"Then I would ask you to join me in our council," Hildebrante offered. "There we can both determine how you can offer this protection."

Salmor was again led further into the palace to the war council alongside the human Emperor. Within the council room, he saw his old protégé Worley and the young man Jaeger. Worley remained very much the same soul who had humbly departed the Thin Air Peaks, after he had finally decided his time there was complete. Jaeger on the other hand, appeared to have become even more troubled and warlike since he had left.

The young man had always had lot of good in him, but a lot of aggression too. His face lit up with excitement at the sight of Salmor joining them here in this war council. Jaeger was now burdened with an aura of violence behind his happiness at seeing that the monks had come to their aid.

Salmor realised that this young man had killed one of the demons he had spoken of since his return home. He seated himself around the large table, noting the map above it was marked by various figures and symbols of destroyed cities.

"So, what would you ask of us now that we offer our aid?" Salmor asked, noting the symbols of war distastefully.

"You must forgive my ignorance, but what exactly can you do?" the emperor asked candidly. "The powers of the monks in the mountains are legendary, but also unclear to me as they have only been legend until now."

"We are healers and preservers by nature," Salmor began. "Our lives consist of a very close relationship with the environment we share around us in the peaks. We use the pure matter around us to grow trees that can not only protect and shelter our homes, but also protect themselves from the harsh wild forces of nature high above the world. We can heal and restore the creatures that live peacefully in the peaks with us." Salmor could have gone on, but noted a degree of impatience he was becoming a little more used to since Jaeger's arrival in the peaks.

"My army and its mages will be going to war in the coming days," Hildebrante explained. "We have lost several towns to the south and thousands of my people are currently displaced by the armies of demons and scaleskins that now hunt freely across our lands. From what I understand, your monks could do a lot to provide healing and assistance to those refugees if we can find them."

"I apologise for speaking on behalf of Salmor," Jaeger interjected. "But the monks would be capable of providing powerful protection for soldiers in the line of battle. Both physically and magically. The monks can heal troops even while they are being struck by enemy weapons, and ward off powerful magical attacks.

"The powers of these monks are slightly different to what I have learned because of my training at Clouds College, but their ability to dispel and ward off enemy magic-users would be equal to or greater than any mages from the college."

Jaeger looked up at young Worley while he spoke, who nodded his agreeance. Salmor noted great similarities but subtle differences between the two.

"Is this correct? And if so, would your people be willing to provide this assistance?" the emperor asked politely.

"I can only speak for what I would be prepared to offer myself," Salmor answered shrewdly. "I will do what I must to help your people, even if it is not the path that I would happily choose for myself." He looked meaningfully at Jaeger as he said this.

"We will speak to the other monks who have come this far, and ask if they will do the same then," Emperor Hildebrante concluded respectfully.

***

Borgisliege fiddled absently with his enormous battle-axe. His master runesmith continued to inform him that the stronghold was now completely sealed off from the outside world, with the one exception being their access to the platforms beneath the stronghold.

Word had been received from The Plateau, that Emperor Hildebrante would be marching south to reclaim the large swathes of his nation that had been lost. After this, the army of The Plateau intended to continue marching beyond their borders. Their ambassador claimed that they intended to make war with a demon prince.

The actions of the human Emperor were far too bold for Borgisliege, or even the entire dwarven union, to simply send regiments as a token show of support. Shortly after the message was received, High King Fëadarliege had declared that Runehold; the capital of their people, would be sealed off and temporarily abandoned. The High King intended to escort his people to the safety of Brackenhold, before leading his entire army to war.

After reviewing the information he had received from Emperor Hildebrante's war council, it was a war that the High King hoped may end the evil influence of the DarkLand Portal permanently. Borgis felt a mixture of irritation and rage building inside him. One other stronghold would be allowed to join the dwarven armies marching to The Plateau, while the other strongholds would have to remain active to protect the displaced populations left behind.

Naturally, the close links between Aridhold and The Plateau had allowed him first opportunity to volunteer, and he had taken it. Now he sat silently, brooding over the details of roachkin potentially infesting every tunnel and unsealed cavern that they had purged over the last year. Once they left, his people would have to reside in Coronahold temporarily. Here they would have to remain, while his army fought abroad alongside his High King and the human Emperor on The Plateau.

The only assurance he had, was that the runesmiths of the stronghold believed that even a mighty demon-warlock would not be able to break in and breach the abandoned city while they were gone. If they somehow did, many of the wards that had been placed over the city had made it uninhabitable until carefully removed. Any creature that entered before this would die a slow and painful death.

"I will admit that what you say is as good as I can expect runemaster Federsmith. Thank you for all the work you and your apprentices have completed for

Aridhold."

"Ach, welcome king. I am aching to get at this demon prince as much as you are," Federsmith replied.

Borgis wasn't so sure about how soon he wanted to meet the demon prince. He could barely imagine what powers they would be up against after his brief encounter with the demon-warlock beneath his city months earlier.

Whatever this alleged demon prince was capable of, it would be far beyond anything his people had ever fought. Come to think of it, Borgis realised that he was looking forward to the encounter as much as Federsmith.

"Well, if all that's left is to leave now, then we had better be about it." Borgisliege rose from his throne at length.

He left the throne room behind, escorted by his royal guard alongside his runemaster. The streets below were lined with ranks upon ranks of soldiers. Aridhold had called in all the garrisons from their desert outposts, and ten thousand dwarves now stood motionless before him.

At his signal, the massive army began the slow organized march through Aridhold's only remaining unsealed exit. Additional wind-up carts had been assembled in the great northern subway below, and soon the entire army would emerge into the lands north of The Plateau. From there they would all march south to join the human Emperor's Great War.

It took nearly half an hour for the streets to finally empty. Borgis watched on with fascination, as the runesmith's of Aridhold placed careful wards across the streets and buildings once they were clear. As he stepped through the great doors to the underway, they were closed behind him before more careful wards were placed. If they ever did return to this stronghold, Borgisliege hoped that at least a few of these runesmiths would survive to reopen it for them.

***

The elven king could sense that everywhere in the world around him, things had been quietly in motion before coming to a brief standstill. Just like the eerie calm that came before those famous cyclones that were known to sweep his islands every few years. For many months now, his people had been forced to watch countless evils drift past their islands from The DarkLand Portal.

He had recalled his ships and pegasus riders, with strict orders not to stray too far from the shores of their people and the safety of numbers for their own protection. As such, a number of the larger gaps between his islands had now become a thoroughfare for the demon prince and his forces.

Allendrion's mages and elder advisors had been telling him for months that something had to be done. That things would only get worse if he allowed the reach of his realm to shrink, while the enemies around it grew. But nothing short of assembling his armies and sailing out to attack the DarkLand Portal itself sprang to mind, and that would be suicide.

He had continually declined their plans and watched the world around him fall apart while he did so. Something told him that it had never been the time to strike, that at some point not too far ahead, an opportune moment would present itself where he could realistically challenge his enemies on an even playing field.

He sensed that this opportune moment had finally arrived. He had marshaled the bulk of his forces to assemble in the valley below the lookout of his roost. From the throne he had saddled to the back of his dragon, Allendrion watched as the elves mustered below him, many of them riding the magical creatures of the islands.

One hundred thousand trained warriors would be prepared by the end of the day. Allendrion snorted at his own hesitation in waiting this long to marshal such a mighty force.

His great-dragon roared anxiously at what may have been a tremor. Allendrion surveyed his people far below as the masses paused. Another more distinctive tremor shook the mountaintop, shivering the marble foundations of his dragon roost.

Below him several unicorn riders were stampeding the edge of the valley as even more Pegasus riders took to the air. The trees above the southern side of the valley appeared to be moving, when Allendrion recognized the beginnings of a great landslide.

He could only watch in horror as thousands of his assembled warriors were buried alive beneath the moving wall of trees, mud and debris. With several powerful beating strokes, he urged his dragon into the skies and towards the victims below.

He would burn the trees to ash and petrify the soaking mud solid, before he saw these lands kill more of his own people. He would wrench every elf he could get to and carry them clear of this natural disaster. As he swooped deeper into the valley, several Pegasus riders moved to intercept him.

"Wait my king!" one of them wailed as he moved to ignore them.

"Wait!? What could possibly be more important than preventing this natural disaster right now?"

"This disaster is not natural my king, it is the demons. They have appeared on the shores across the mountains, the demon prince is with them."

This ends The Monk's Apprentice, Book 2 of the DarkLand Portal series.

Allendrion, Borgisliege and Hildebrante, all return in Book 3 The Demon Prince,

as do the adventures of Aema & Jaeger.

The DarkLand Portal Series

The DarkLand Portal Series is a fantasy epic that explores the desperate situation of mankind and the other estranged civilised races of Thylacine. Their survival exists among hostile territories dominated by scaleskins, roachkin and now demons too. To make matters worse, schemes and greed fester in Conorbatia - the largest and most sheltered city on The Plateau - where the need for unity is greatest.

The Hero of Aridhold

The DarkLand Portal Series Book I

"Every time you decide to play the hero, somebody has to suffer for it"

Jaeger hadn't hesitated to join Commander Darroch's mission when his small force passed through West-Yield. His decision however, was motivated by a multitude of reasons; Some were noble, while others simply stemmed from a desire to escape the direction his life was taking.

He never knew the far-reaching implications that his decision would have, or that it would one day land him at the legendary Clouds College of Magic.

The Monk's Apprentice

The DarkLand Portal Series Book II

"At some point we need to stop expecting our Emperor to make everything fair and nice, and do something ourselves. The thing I liked about Jaeger is that he always seemed to get that."

Aema had been left picking up the pieces in Conorbatia after Jaeger's sudden departure. Amongst coming to terms with the sudden loss, she seemed to have a knack for thrusting herself right into the middle of the events and corruption that is slowly taking over the city.

Meanwhile, the emperor continues to prepare his people for war in the South, ignorant to the cancer gnawing at the centre of his empire back home.

The question of whether Jaeger is alive, what he is doing, and how he can possibly think that he is helping, seems to have eluded everyone. As the hero of Aridhold slowly becomes more of a memory than a person.

The Demon Prince

The DarkLand Portal Series Book III

The Demon Prince is the third and final installment in The DarkLand Portal fantasy epic that explores the desperate situation of mankind and the other estranged civilised races of Thylacine. Their survival exists among hostile territories dominated by scaleskins, roachkin and now demons too. To make matters worse, schemes and greed fester in Conorbatia - the largest and most sheltered city on The Plateau - where the need for unity is greatest.